Joe
Jones

Also by Anne Lamott

Hard Laughter

Rosie

All New People

Operating Instructions

Bird By Bird

Crooked Little Heart

Traveling Mercies

Blue Shoe

Joe Jones

A novel

ANNE LAMOTT

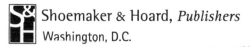 Shoemaker & Hoard, *Publishers*
Washington, D.C.

First published by North Point Press in 1985

LIBRARY OF CONGRESS CATALOGING-IN-PUBLICATION DATA
Lamott, Anne.
    Joe Jones : a novel / Anne Lamott.
      p. cm.
    ISBN 1-59376-003-5 (acid-free paper)
    I. Title.
PS3562.A4645 J64 2003
813'.54—dc21   2003013463

Cover design by Rory Phoenix. Text design by Amy Evans McClure
Printed in the United States of America on acid-free paper

 Shoemaker & Hoard
A Division of Avalon Publishing Group Incorporated
Distributed by Publishers Group West
Printed in the United States of America

10 9 8 7 6 5 4 3 2

THE AUTHOR wishes to acknowledge the following people, who have loved and supported me out of all sense of proportion: Elizabeth McKee and Abigail Thomas; my mothers, Nikki, Dudu, and Mary Hall; my aunts and uncles and cousins; my writer friends, John Kaye, Bill Ryan, Warren Wallace, Michael Fessier, Sylvie Pasche, Ted Hoagland, Alice Adams, and Evan Connell, who has had to put up with so much; the men who helped me understand Joe Jones; Johno, Leroy, Larry Barnett; the Rev. William Rankin, and Phyllis of the Lakeville Marina; Francis Stewart's sister Charlotte, who gave me the street vendor calls; and special gratitude for the vision and integrity and faith of Bill Turnbull and Jack Shoemaker of North Point Press.

Thanks also to Nancy Palmer-Jones, again and again, and Trish Hoard.

The lines quoted on p. 270 are from "Ascension" by Philip Levine from *One for the Rose* (Atheneum). Reprinted by permission; ©1981 Philip Levine. Originally in *The New Yorker.*

The epigraph, "Musée des Beaux Arts" (p. vii), by W.H. Auden, is from his *Collected Shorter Poems 1924–1957,* copyright ©1940, 1968 by W.H. Auden, published by Random House, Inc., New York, and reprinted by permission.

This one is dedicated to Pat Gomez and Joanne Greenbaum.

It is also dedicated to the wisdom and words and love of Don Sherwood, Ben Chamberlain, and Ken Lamott.

It is for my brothers, John and Steve, and my friend Jack Erdmann, Ruth Costello, and my espoused sisters, Mary, Pam, Lynn, Megan, and Abby, and for the Schleigers.

It is for my darling brilliant friend Jane Vandenburgh, —Joie!—who lightly, deftly edited this book for me, in February, 2003. And it is for her husband, my dear friend Jack Shoemaker, who originally published *Joe Jones* at North Point Press in 1985, and who has loved it, and me, ever since.

About suffering they were never wrong,
The Old Masters: how well they understood
Its human position; how it takes place
While someone else is eating or opening a window or just walking
    dully along;
How, when the aged are reverently, passionately waiting
for the miraculous birth, there always must be
Children who did not specially want it to happen, skating
On a pond at the edge of the wood:
They never forgot
That even the dreadful martyrdom must run its course
Anyhow in a corner, some untidy spot
Where the dogs go on with their doggy life and the torturer's horse
Scratches its innocent behind on a tree.

In Brueghel's Icarus, for instance: how everything turns away
Quite leisurely from the disaster; the ploughman may
Have heard the splash, the forsaken cry,
But for him it was not an important failure; the sun shone
As it had to on the white legs disappearing into the green
Water; and the expensive delicate ship that must have seen
Something amazing, a boy falling out of the sky,
Had somewhere to get to and sailed calmly on.

W. H. Auden
"Musée des Beaux Arts"

Joe
Jones

ONE

THE WINTER RAINS ARE OVER. In new green meadows orange poppies bloom. Purple and white lupine grows everywhere. Sails filling with sea breeze, boats slice through the bay. An egret leaps off a lonely black piling. Sea lions bark, gulls cry, the herring are back. Mud hens and mallards paddle around, and old Japanese people fish from the shore with ice chests beside them on the sand.

A woman sings softly as she walks along the water, shanties and old cowboy songs. She is wearing a necklace whose gold letters spell APRIL, although that is not her name, and is dressed in what she will tell her customers is a tribute to Spring: green culottes, blue T-shirt, pink sneakers, white socks.

She ambles along, sexy and sweet, near forty, somewhere on the cusp between curvaceous and fat. Her lips are full and thin out into dimples. Her skin is finely crinkled around peaceful brown eyes. She bleaches her short hair pale blonde, but other than this she resembles the torch singer Helen Morgan. A wreath of plastic grapes would not look out of place on her head.

Jessie's Cafe is a restaurant from another era, the sort of broken-down waterfront dive one might expect to find in Steinbeck or Saroyan. The main room is empty when Louise steps inside, but she hears water running and the clatter of dishes coming from the back room.

"Willie?"

She walks to the back room, where a fair, slight man in his early twenties stands over an aluminum sink full of soapsuds and dishes.

"Hey, Lou."

"Kisses?" She closes her eyes and puckers up. He kisses her. She opens her eyes and surveys the mess. Dishes are stacked on every available surface, and both garbage cans are full. She exhales noisily. "Looks like Pompeii after the big event."

"Coffee's made."

"Good."

"Grill's on."

"Great."

She leans in the doorway, watching him work. He scowls.

"Don't stare at me."

"Cut your hair again, didn't you." It is not a question.

He shrugs. "Maybe."

"Maybe? You're starting to look like a molting deer."

He turns and gives her the finger.

"No kidding, ducks."

He whisks a dirty potato masher through the soapsuds, pretending to ignore her.

"Willie, no lie—you look like some old deer that the others in the herd are trying to nudge gently out towards the highway."

"Oh, go away."

"You burnt, baby, huh?"

"Get *out* of here."

"Up all night?"

"No."

"Willie, my love, you'd lie if the truth would work."

"Lou?" plaintively.

"Willie?" she whines. "Why do you do that shit?"

"What shit?"

"Dexedrine. Hearts."

"It's none of your business what I do after work."

"Yes, it is. I'm your best friend."

"So why don't you get off my case."

"Because my love for you is not *blind* and *sloppy*. It is harsh, and strong."

He rolls his eyes. He has heard this line so many times before. It was from one of Virginia Woolf's journals.

"Let me get my work done."

She laughs at him. "It's not like you're doing brain surgery."

He smiles through a scowl.

"I'm not saying it's my business that you hang out with a bunch of possibly AIDS-riddled screaming nellie faggots."

"You're homophobic."

"No, I am *not* homophobic. Maybe I have certain aesthetic problems with the, how you say, graphics of what you guys do."

"Why don't you just try not to think about it."

A Handi Wipe falls from the shelf above the sink, off to his left, and he startles, as if a guillotine blade has just dropped. "See?"

"Well, don't be a hypocrite, man. You used to do it."

"I used to do a lot of shit I don't do anymore."

"So . . ."

"I used to cry when different foods on my plate touched each other. But I don't anymore. It's kid's stuff, man."

"What."

"Speed."

"Well, it's cheaper than coke."

"Yeah, so's Drano."

"Lou—"

"Willie? Read my lips. In about two hours, you're gonna hit the wall. Won't be nothin' left of you but buttons and hair. Who's gonna serve the food I cook? Who's going to help me clean up?"

"I, I—"

"You're gonna woofle around all day, mewling and puking. And then you're going to go into your algae browser mode."

"Lou—"

"I want you to straighten up and fly right."

"Get out of here."

"I couldn't take it if something happened to you."

"Luuuuuu...Get out of here."

"You drive me out of my mind, Louise."

"Kisses."

He laughs at her quietly, bends forward to kiss her.

"Thank you. How we doing on mayo?"

"Check it out, man."

She walks behind him to the far end of the narrow room, to the burlap bags of potatoes and onions, the bins of beans and flour and sugar, the plastic gallon containers of mayonnaise and mustard and relish. There is plenty of everything.

The main room is in reasonably good shape. Louise wipes down the bar, arranges place settings at the counter and tables, pushes in chairs, grooms the vases of blue daisies. She goes behind the bar to put on Willie's favorite tape, Frank Sinatra's *Greatest Hits*, and turns the volume on loud. She can almost smell Willie smiling in the back room. She salts the grill behind the counter, checks the stove's oil well, studies the two packed refrigerators as if looking for something to wear, reaches for parsley, scallions, and celery. She takes them to the cutting board, where she begins mincing, threshing, dicing. She puts the heat on under pots of beans and soup on the burners, and turns the grill up a tad. She stirs leftover hotcake batter, adjusts the temperature of the deep-fat fryer, and is doing this all at once, like lateral juggling.

Cutting, stirring, tasting soups, tamale pie from yesterday, through it all she's chanting silently, over and under Sinatra, *the power of God is in me, the grace of God surrounds me, the power of God is in me.* She can wrap herself in this protection the way a parrot fish spins a transparent sleeping bag around itself at night on the ocean's cold floor. Chanting quiets her crazy mind, and now, shelling peas, she does it to keep from hag-riding her breakup with Joe, three months before.

Left to its own devices, her mind is a fat hummingbird flitting through leafy trees of anxiety, apology, sorrow, excuses, and dreams of grandeur, dreams of humiliation. Sometimes she watches it run off, and it makes her laugh and shake her head. It's like a video game. Bright fast blips of worry and anger come at her, and, after fending them off, she's attacked by the huge lumbering Czechoslovakian blobs of tiredness and broken-spiritedness which break into small, faster missiles of regret when she fires at them. *What a half-baked species we are,* she thinks, and does what she can to make her insides more habitable.

"Willie?" she calls.

"Yeah?"

"Come here."

"No, I'm busy. I'll be there in a minute."

"Now, right now, right this second. Immédiatement. Ee-mmmeee-ja-mah."

"Lou," he whines from the back room, "I'm going to come out there, and you're just gonna make me give you kisses...."

She continues the lateral juggling. Willie shuffles in.

"I'm not givin' you kisses."

"Come here!"

He walks over to her at the grill.

"Dolly, will you see if there's an opened can of tomato paste in the fridge? I've got my hands full."

"Just open a new one, Lou."

"Come on."

"No, Lou, what if it's been there a coupla days? It's gonna look like something cultured in a petri dish."

"Please, darling?"

Willie walks wistfully to one of the refrigerators, opens it, looks inside, shakes his head. "*Algae* browser," he says, abstractedly. "What a lovely, soupy existence."

One year ago, nearly to the day, at Willie's behest, Louise broke the news to his grandmother Jessie that Willie was gay. Louise and Jessie were sitting on the porch of the cafe with cups of jasmine tea. Louise waited for Jessie to arrange herself in the director's chair, and for the peeping, clucking, and cooing to subside, before giving her the news. Jessie did not respond immediately—her hearing aid rang. She looked up and around, then back at Louise's face.

After a moment, with deeply concerned indignation, she said, "I thought he just had good posture."

Willie is an angel with butter-colored hair. Willie, an orphan, steps high over bugs, lives with—takes care of—his grandmother, but now for the last six months there's been speed in his life. Shit, thinks Louise from the pinnacle of her wise old years, too soon old, too late smart. "Listen to your *broc*coli," she shouts at him. It is an old Mel Brooks routine: Listen to your broccoli and your broccoli will tell you how to eat it. Listen to your broccoli, she urges Willie. "But I *do*, Louise," he pleads.

"Then why don't you ever turn it down when it's offered?"

"Because I'm weak."

They both smiled at the truth when he said that. He isn't weak, Louise knows. Innocence has a lot of power. When he's on, his sweetness can light up the room. His presence is somehow reassuring, like wrapping oneself in a towel still warm from the dryer. He knows it, and used to mince up to the initially homophobic Joe Jones with a mug of coffee and twitter, "Cream and *two* sugars?" batting his long blond lashes. But on days after nights on speed, he moves around the restaurant like a gopher who has left his hole and is being stalked by a cat.

"Willie?"

"NO MORE KISSES."

"No more kisses. Will you go see if the mail's come?"

"I'm trying to get the pans scoured. Why ya always have to be Miss Takeover Broad?"

"Please."

Grumbling, he leaves the back room and shuffles out the door. He returns with a pile of letters, mostly bills, she guesses.

"Letter from Joe," he says, holding out an envelope. Her eyes grow wide as she stares at it.

"I can't stay here much longer," it begins. "I know you don't want me right now, but this place sucks. I could take it if you were here. Honest, Lou. Hawaii seems almost evil to me.

"It's probably good to remember that Hawaii for a couple of hundred years experienced the same measure of white domination that India, Africa, South America, and other places did: geographically a goodly distance from 'Home' for the whiteys that made all the rules and did all the raping of women, resources, and manpower. So, during his time of power, whitey behaved toward the native population in ways he could never get away with at home. This always seems to have long-lasting effects on the native population, like turning a huge percentage of them into shitheels, thieves, craven liars, and people you wouldn't want to meet on the beach. It also does quite a trip on the local whitey population, turning many of *them* into shitheels, liars, thieves (on a grand scale), and deeply neurotic guilt-ridden despots. The only reason you'd want to meet *them* on the beach is because they *own* the beach. So my plan is this—Everybody go home. It should all be done on a racial basis. All the whiteys should live in whiteyland, and all the natives should live in nativeland, and those who are the result of mixing the races could either commit suicide or join the merchant marine. I have to go now. In tomorrow's letter I will tell you my plans for the merchant marine.

"I miss you. I'm sorry and I want to come home, Joe Jones."

Not Joe, not JJ—Joe Jones.

Louise puts the letter down on the candy counter, licks her lips, and stares off into space as if suddenly following a flicker of a partially remembered dream.

At noon, Willie and Louise stand side by side at the cutting board assembling baklava. Willie paints paper-thin sheets of filo dough with melted butter and lays the bands on top of the nutmeat mixture Louise spreads in the pan.

"Honey."

"Little flower."

"Lou. I mean, drizzle the honey on top."

"Oh."

Willie, in charge of desserts, as always, lowers more buttery sheets into the pan. Louise is staring off into space.

"Scalpel."

"Huh?"

"Lou! Come on. Pay attention."

Louise looks into the pan, shakes her head to clear it, and spreads another layer of nutmeat.

They both look out the window as an old Plymouth screeches into the parking lot. "There's Grandma." The car comes to an abrupt halt twenty feet shy of the row of trees where white lines indicate parking spaces. The car bucks forward for several feet and stops again. Jessie's wizened face is fierce with concentration—you can almost see that her knuckles are white on the wheel. The car bursts forward again, stopping a foot in front of the eucalyptuses. "God!" Willie yells, "I can't take it." Jessie backs the car up a bit. Willie shakes his head. A moment later the car shoots forward and comes to rest against a tree.

"Ouch!" Willie cries. "Boomp! It makes my *nose* hurt."

After another moment, Jessie scuttles out of the car as if it is about to burst into flame. She stands several feet away, gaping at it. Then she dusts off her hands and stands sizing up the world— the bay, the trees, and, finally, her cafe, where Willie and Louise stand waving at the window.

She is thin, stooped and gorgeous at seventy-nine. She drapes a green beaded cardigan over her antler-like shoulders and draws herself up to her full five-foot-three.

Her walk is like an egret in muddy water up to its knees, strutting, jutting.

Willie and Louise turn and smile at each other and wait to hear her footsteps on the wooden steps of the porch.

"She shouldn't be driving, Willie."

"I don't want to deal with it today."

Louise nods. In a moment they hear her footsteps and what sounds like an excited dove clearing her throat. Throwing open the front door, she steps inside and stands, poised expectantly.

"Jessie, my love."

"Grannnnndma."

"Willie, Louisa, oh!" Jessie clasps her hands in joy.

Her voice has a lovely silvery rustle to it, like birdseed going up a vacuum cleaner.

"I missed you," Louise cries, having not seen her since last night. "You must have a seat imm—eee-ja-*mow*, and I'll bring you a lovely cup of tea."

Jessie sits down at her table, one by the window.

"Did you remember to buy me a paper?"

"Have I ever forgotten?"

"What's that?"

"Have I ever forgotten?"

Louise washes honey and nutmeat off her hands and brings Jessie a cup of tea and the morning's *Chronicle*. Louise bends down and kisses Jessie's neck a dozen times.

"You're my love, Lou," the old woman says. "You're my love, and Willie."

Jessie has owned the cafe for seven years now, Louise's been the cook for six.

"I lived," Jessie said once, "on a farm near New Orleans, back when the vendors sold food on the street. Just after dawn you'd hear horse-hooves and cart wheels, and the vendors would cry as loud as they could, 'Yellllllllow ba*na*nas, *la*dy, dime a *do*zen.' 'Strawwwwwwwwwwwwwwberries, strawbries.' And this most mournful man of all, oh, *love*, so sad, he'd cry, 'IIIIIIIIII've got algator pirs.' Alligator pears, don't you see? Avocados."

Jessie's Cafe begins to fill up with favorite regulars, strangers, and extras sent over by central casting. Louise greets them all from the grill, berates and cajoles and insults them while she shakes a corn dog in the deep-fat fryer, ladles out soup or cassoulet, flips burgers, and rubs rosemary between her fingers that she then massages into lamb chops.

"Thanks a lot, Lou."

"Hey, thank *you*. Take it easy—Keep 'em in the boat."

"Yeah, okay, see ya later."

"Club 'em if you have to, okay? But keep 'em in the boat."

"Hi, Jessie. Gee, you look so pretty today."

"Hi, Dana! Hi, Sam. Hi Booney."

Jessie beams at the new arrivals, Sam and Dana Waters, classically mellow California couple with their two-year-old son in a stroller, which they carry up the stairs of the porch, the baby prince in his litter.

"Hello, Gristdancers," Louise calls from the grill. Joe nicknamed them four years ago, when they first started coming in. They had both been reading books by Ram Dass—Sam was reading *Grist for the Mill* and Dana was reading *The Only Dance There Is*.

Sam is a fine painter, a Marin County local colorist—landscapes and seascapes. Dana quit her job as a graphic designer when Boone was born. Louise loves them, like she used to love the fellow members of her high school basketball team—camaraderie within a prescribed arena.

"Hi, Willie," they say as Willie comes in from the back.

"Hi." Willie smiles. He bends down to look into Boone's serious face. The child looks like a large howler monkey, his hairline beginning only an inch above his forehead, his lower face and jaw canted forward so it occurs to you you could almost fit a muzzle on him. Boone studies Willie as if a message is appearing on Willie's face.

"You gotta get Boone a bigger stroller," says Louise. "He's too big for that one. It makes him look like an outpatient."

Serving these people fills her account. Thinking of Joe drains her just as living with him used to. But no matter how much she cooks and serves, chants and prays, his presence in her head is a sickness that gives her fever dreams: Happy and bad memories agonize her. She so vividly remembers his devotion to everyone at Jessies's, his eagerness to please, how sweet and funny and bashful he could be, how much Willie loved to tease him.

Joe took Jessie out on a date the year before, dinner and a movie on her birthday, and while driving her home he smashed

into a deer that jumped out in front of the car. He was distraught
when he told Louise about it in bed that night. The next morning at the cafe, Willie came over and punched him in the arm,
shaking his head with admiration. "Heard you bagged a *buck*,"
he enthused. Joe smiled sheepishly.

*Don't think about that now. Think about his self-centeredness.
Think about his unfaithfulness. No, don't think of him at all.* But it
is as if there is a picture of Louise's skeleton, and over it is a transparency showing her muscular system, and over that there's a
transparency of her organs, and over that is a transparency of her
cardiovascular system, and over that is a transparency of Joe
Jones. It is dark gray with regret, depression, anger, and what the
poet Lermontov called the bitter record of the heart. *God*, she
prays, *take away the obsession, take away the hate. Let what I have
here now be enough.*

Yearning, said another poet, is blindness.

Jessie's best friend Georgia Malone arrives at three by taxi. An
empress dowager, Isak Dinesen in an aqua double-knit pantsuit,
she shuffles in wearing surgical paper slippers and a white beaded
turban.

"Why, Georgia!" Jessie cries, with delight.

"Pffffttttttt."

"Sit down! Yoo-hoo, Louise, Georgia's here."

"Hi, Georgia." When Louise turns around from the grill, Georgia has sat down next to Jessie and is glaring out the window.
Louise studies them. Jessie, a one-woman aviary, runs through
her repertoire of bird-sounds, coos, clucks, peeps, cheeps, and
occasional whistles of inhalation. Georgia periodically makes the
only sound anyone in the cafe has ever heard her make, an abrupt
spluttery raspberry. Joe called it Georgia's fark. Sometimes hours
pass between the two old women in their seats by the window
and the only noises are the birdsong and the Bronx cheer, unless,

like elephants, they communicate by tummy rumbles, too low to be heard by other human ears. It is one of the goddamnedest things Louise has ever witnessed, this particular best-friendship. When Jessie chatters, Georgia glowers—when Jessie reads, Georgia appears snubbed.

Today Jessie chatters. "Did you watch TV last night? Not much on, was there, Louise? What did I watch last night? Did I tell you?"

"I don't know, Jessie."

"Willie?" Willie sticks his head out from the back room. "Did I tell you what I watched last night?" Willie shakes his head. "Oh, for Pete's sake, I wanted to tell Georgia. Yes, now wait, I remember; it was that nice, thin young man from New York. Singing. What's his name, Louise?"

"Who?"

"That nice, thin young man from New York."

Louise asks, "What does he do?"

"He sings. And he plays the banjo."

Louise thinks for a moment, asks, incredulously, "Pete Seeger?" Jessie nods.

"Pfft."

"Jessie," Louise tells her, "he's no longer young, and he never lived in New York City."

"I've been thinking, Georgia," Jessie continues. "We ought to go to the zoo. Joe took me there last year. They have a new white tiger there, a boy. Maybe some day next week—"

"Pfft." Georgia is glaring.

"It was just an idea, Georgia. You don't have to get sore."

Louise is still at the grill, chanting, chanting to keep Joe at bay, *the grace of God surrounds me.* Her craving for him can be, and is now, a lag as jangling as the craving that hits when the last line of cocaine has been snorted. It's like a mosquito bite, late at night, on the fingertip.

Joe Jones is such a mix. Self-centered and giving, devoted,

unfaithful, sad and funny, needy, tough, arrogant, and shy. Stricken by fears of death, given to flights of whimsy. So loyal and committed to all of them, and then he'd go and sleep with someone who meant nothing to him, destroying his life in the process —his home, with Louise, and the one real family he's ever had, the people at Jessie's cafe.

He was out of a job when they first met. The high school at which he coached basketball had been closed down because of state budget cuts. Joe was broke, and so, for her thirty-eighth birthday, he gave her a beautifully wrapped library book. It was a collection of photographs by Imogen Cunningham of people over ninety. One was a gnarled old woman wearing a bookie's visor. There was a quote at the top of the page. "When we were young," she said, "we were all puritans and all we talked about was whether it was right or it was wrong. And then I married a man from Sardinia."

"I'll take it back for you in a month," Joe said.

It became her favorite book in the world. Jessie and Georgia went through it almost every day. By the end of the month Joe had landed a job as a security guard, guarding things no one would want to steal.

Please, God, she prays, *send me someone else to love.*

"Pfft."

Louise smiles at the grill. *Okay, I get it,* she says silently. She brings the two old women a lovely pot of tea and a plate of Willie's lemon cookies, hot from the oven. Georgia beams mischievously, almost evilly, at the cookies, as if she is getting away with something.

Remember what Jessie said last year, Louise: You have no new ideas on how to make it work. You have tried everything with Joe. You have been trying so hard to make a silk purse out of a sow's ear—maybe you two should just be friends. But you can't save yourself, Louise. Because we are addicted to our allergies, and you are allergic to Joe. But stop trying to be your own savior. Give it up to God. Let God be your savior. It gets you off the hook, and it puts God on the hook, where He belongs.

Louise looks over at Jessie's frail, stooped back. Thank You for Jessie, she prays, thank You for Willie, for people to serve. I'm doing the best I can. It's just that—I've been sick, You know? Do You remember that old joke, where the lion is dangling the mouse by the tail, swinging it back and forth before his eyes and sneering? He says to the mouse, "You are the weakest, most pitiful creature I've ever seen in my entire life," and the mouse says, "I've been *sick*."

She sits down on the porch with a cup of tea and reads Joe's letter again. It doesn't really sound like him at all. There is a reason for this, which Louise will never know.

While Joe was lunching with his mother at the yacht club, a funny old guy wearing black socks with sandals, Bermuda shorts, and a porkpie hat sat down at their table and started to talk, and this is what he said: It's probably good to remember that Hawaii for a couple hundred years experienced the same measure of white domination that India, Africa, South America, and other places did...."

Joe Jones is not well educated, but his memory serves him well.

TWO

J OE HAS BEEN LYING DOWN in his mother's lanai all day, in the mood Louise calls the "His Dog Loved Him, But She Died." He stares out at the tropical foliage and listens to the rustle of the palm fronds, to gekkos, and birds, but over these sounds he keeps hearing the honking of the sea lions in the waters near Jessie's Cafe.

He bites down hard on his wrist. Louise calls this his "Doing an Existence Check." He stares off into space thinking of her peaceful eyes. He looks as wistfully noble as the man in the Windsong commercials, who can't seem to forget you because Windsong *stays on his mind*.

His mother's favorite photographs cover the walls. Joe at five years old, astride a knock-kneed horse. His sister Mary thirty years ago as Betsy Ross for Halloween. His parents on their wedding day. Mary's first communion. Mary at ten with her cello, Joe with the trumpet he played in the basement every afternoon for several months, blowing it as if to awaken souls for the Resurrection.

His mother is at the club, working on her tan, working off her lunch. She will be home at four. The girls are coming for bridge at eight. "Louise and I just needed some time apart," he told her, when he called to see if he could come stay for a while. His mother was delighted. Joe's mother loves having him around, especially when she can show him off to her friends.

He gets up, goes into the kitchen for a beer, and studies a reflection of himself in a spatula.

Back in the lanai, he lies down, yawns, begins to doze. What he misses so badly right now about Louise is her skin against his, her big golden Scandinavian warmth, her big bottom bulldozing him off the bed as she sleeps. He has to push her away to keep himself from falling out of bed. It's like pushing on the neck of a huge loving dog, a hard warm muscle that's needing to be stroked.

Joe Jones puts on his baseball cap and walks down the road to the beach and stops beside a steaming tar cart. It looks like you could stick a fork into the steaming cylinder and pull out a hot dog. *Did you eat tar, Louise?* he thinks. *I practically lived on the stuff, me and Stevie Gronewald.* He bends to pick up a shard of gleaming hardened black tar, closes his eyes, and inhales its black pitchy scent.

Did you eat tar, Louise? he thinks as he looks around.

The world was like this delicatessen, he thinks, and we were like goats eating everything. Sour grass, nasturtiums, crabapples, plums—half a dozen different kinds of plums—some on the ground of the neighbors' yards, some still in the trees. Bushels and bushels of blackberries, too, in fields and gullies, wherever, beside the road. We'd eat them hard and green or red, we'd eat them purple black.

He is jumpy on the beach, especially when he lies down and tries to keep his eyes closed. He sighs and sits up. In his head is what hell must be like, the consuming longing for someone who no longer wants you. He wonders if she misses him yet. It's been three months. She said not so long before that lying with him in bed was like Huxley's description of God, having that rich round oceanic feeling in your stomach.

They lay in bed and laughed and talked, they lay in bed and read. She was reading a book on LBJ right before they broke up. She read him a passage where Lyndon Johnson is in Australia or New Zealand—Joe Jones can't remember which—and gets on a plane called the *Wabash Cannonball.* This is during WW II. And for no particular reason LBJ gets off for a while, and when he gets back on, someone has taken his seat. The plane is packed. Being a good-natured man, he says, "No, y'all go on." Johnson gets off and waits for another. The *Wabash Cannonball* is shot down by a Japanese bomber, killing all on board.

She says it's enough proof for her there's a God, but then, almost everything for Louise is a proof of God: The way the outdoors looks, and that out of the primeval ooze arose Mozart, Matisse, and Willie. She and her God drive him crazy sometimes. So he reminds her that one boy in the Jonestown compound was at a dentist appointment in Guyana when the 914 others drank the Kool-Aid. This boy's mother, father, and five siblings die. But he lives, he resurfaces in L.A. five years later, where he shoots up a schoolyard, killing a girl, wounding eleven children. So where does Louise's God fit into this?

All she can say is that God was there in the aftermath, in the caring and shared grief of the people who took care of the survivors.

"But what if Willie gets AIDS?"

"If Willie gets AIDS, God will see him and us through."

Then the next day he hears her in the back room, begging Willie not to sleep with Haitians.

"I don't even *know* any Haitians," Willie said.

Willie will never forgive him, he knows. Louise may, but Willie won't.

Willie was like a baby brother, he'd climb onto his lap as light sometimes, light as a feather. Right before he and Louise broke up, Louise brought a VCR in to hook up to the television at the restaurant, so that Jessie and Georgia could see *From Mao to Mozart*. Louise had already seen it several times. Willie watched it sitting in Joe's lap. Jessie cried when it was over. "Doesn't it make you proud to be a human being?" Louise asked Joe at the end. "Or at least, it makes you go around for a few days not being so ashamed, which is about the best we can hope for these days."

"She is such a mushhead," Willie said to Joe.

The last thing Willie said to him was, "Joe? You're a rotten shit-fuck slut, and I hope you rot in hell."

Joe watches his mother make dinner. She is making a huge canned-salmon salad, with low-cal mayonnaise. He believes his mother has cared more about her weight all these years than she ever cared about either of her children, and he thinks she's passed this burden of self-centeredness on to him. He told Louise he thinks his mother loves him most when he's making her friends laugh. He isn't sure he likes her very much. Louise says it's okay not to like your mother. She didn't like either of her parents, both of whom are dead. Once she went to see a priest while they were still alive and cried because she had so much guilt about it. The priest said he didn't like his mother either. Louise asked if that was allowed. The priest said, I love her, I honor her, I just don't like her.

So how do you act around her? Louise asked.

Kind, he replied. And very, very polite.

Joe cringes at the kitchen table. He feels like he's about to cry. Then he sighs instead and goes to stand by his mother while she dices celery for the salad.

They have wine with dinner. He has to do all the talking. The way his mother puts her fork down between each tiny bite to rest it as she chews begins to make his neck hurt. Why won't she god-damn *eat!*

She is staring sadly at her plate, probably thinking about Mary.

"I wish you could meet Jessie, Mom. She's such a character. She's wise, she's batty. She treats me like a grandson, and some-times like a lover."

"How old is she getting to be?"

"Eighty at the end of summer."

"Still getting about?"

"She's still driving. But she's afraid to ride her bike anymore, afraid, you know, of breaking her hip."

His mother, fork resting, stares unhappily at her plate.

"You thinking about Mary, Mom?"

She shrugs. "I guess."

"We can always hire someone to kidnap her. Deprogram her in some motel."

"We could, but won't." She sighs. "Your father would turn in his grave."

"Try not to dwell on it, Mom."

"Then tell me something cheerful."

Joe thinks for a minute.

"Did I tell you about the time I took Jessie to the city to shop?" His mother shakes her head.

"She wanted a new couch, and we spent all day going from store to store, and she didn't see anything she liked at all until finally we find a beautiful brown linen couch at Macy's. It's got six pillows in different colors, you know, to demonstrate the other available colors and fabrics? And Jessie just loves it, I can tell, she's peeping and cooing, sitting on it, sort of bouncing up and down, but then she gets up and stares at it for the longest time, shakes her head, sighs, and says she wants to leave.

"So I say, 'What was the matter with that one?' And she says, in this very fussy voice she gets sometimes, 'I *hated* the orange pillow, and I wasn't *crazy* about the green.'"

His mother smiles.

"Was that cheerful enough?"

"Sounds like the two of you have a mutual admiration society," she says coldly.

He really can't stand her, he decides, but he does enjoy her friend, Alice, who arrives early for bridge.

Alice is big and fat and red and dresses like Don Ho. She adores Joe, who makes her a piña colada and brings it to her and sits with her on the couch in the lanai while his mother cleans the kitchen.

"She seems sad tonight."

"She's always sad about Mary."

"Well, of course. Who wouldn't be." Alice has beautiful teeth and paints a bigger set of lips around her mouth than the ones she has been given. She smokes long brown Shermans and laughs a lot.

"When did Mary join?"

"I don't know—eight, nine years ago by now."

"What was she like?"

"As a child?"

Alice nods.

"Meaner'n catshit."

Alice roars.

"Honest to God, Alice. See, we slept in the same room until she was eleven, when Mom had a room added on. So night after night we'd lie in our beds in the dark, and she'd just *crucify me, man*. Like, for instance, when I was four, I got bit by a bee on the hand, and my hand just fuckin' exploded. It was like nearly the size of a football. And it hurt like hell. So, needless to say, after that I'm a little bit edgy when I see a bee.

"So there we are, lying in the dark, she's in her bed, I'm in mine, and I'd just want to hear her voice, I'd want to hear *my* voice, in the dark. I sometimes wasn't all that sure I was really there.

"So I'd go, 'Mare?'

"And she'd go, 'Shut up.'

"And I'd say, 'But—'

"'Joey?' she'd say, 'if you don't shut up I'm sending for The Bees.'"

"'No! Not the Beeeeees!'

"'The *Beeeeees!*' she says. She's almost growling. 'I ruuuule the Beeeees. I controooool the Bees!'

"'Mare—'

"'Bizzzzzzzzzzzzzzz.'

"'NO, NO!'

"'Hey, you two, knock it off in there.'

"So she whispers, with her leering, buzzing voice, 'Bizzzz-zzzzzz.'

"And this one time, we were watching this movie on the TV in the basement on a Saturday night, about this mad scientist who cuts up this woman, right? Great movie, this scientist cuts up a woman, then connects parts of her to an animal. It's like heavy-duty shit, man, I'm like seven at the time and it's Emma."

"Emma?" Alice asks.

"I forgot to say, the cut-up one's named Emma.

"So that night we're getting ready for bed, I'm putting on pajamas and Mary's in the can, brushing her teeth, washing her face. Then she comes into the bedroom, totally freaked.

"'What's the matter?'

"'Emma's head is in the toilet,' she tells me.

"'No!'

"'Yes! Bleeding. *Bobbing* up and down—'

"'Joey? Have you brushed your teeth?'

"'No, but, Mommy, listen—'

"'Come on, honey, snap to it.'

"'MOMMY! THERE'S A WOMAN'S HEAD IN THE TOILET.'

"'Don't be ridiculous, what are you talking about?'

"'It's EMMA'S HEAD, IN THE TOILET. *BOBBING* UP AND DOWN.'

"'Where on earth did you get such an idea—'

"And Mary's leering at me in this way, it's like, I snitch and, you know, she's sending for *The Bees.*"

Alice laughs so hard her face turns purple.

"Now, okay, let's see. Mary gets her own room when she's eleven, I'm nine. And when she's twelve, she makes a fortune babysitting. I mean, it's too hideous to think of, what she does to those poor babies, especially the boy babies, I mean, *God.*

"Anyway. She gets all this money together, present money too, you know, birthdays, Christmas, and, man, she's tighter than *bark.* She saves every penny, and she's totally into ownership and privacy, so she buys a used television set. Can't stand sharing *anything*—you know, like it burns her out when we're watching TV in the basement, 'cause, you know, my little eyes and ears are sucking up half what's coming out in images and sounds? So her hit is somehow *diluted?* So. Okay, she has her own TV and I'm not allowed in her room, so if I want to watch I have to go downstairs and watch it alone. No, *not alone* because, you see, she has me convinced that the water heater in the closet is really a robot, and there's the small issue of the head in the toilet, plus Beeeeees at any time. On Sunday nights my dad watches *Bonanza* with me, but usually it's just me and the robot.

"But, you see, on Friday nights, *Twilight Zone* is on. There's no way I can watch it alone. So I say, 'Mare? Can I watch the *Twilight Zone* with you?' She says no. I beg. She still says no. So I go to Mom or Dad and make them make Mary let me watch it with her. And you know what she does? She marks off four one-foot linoleum squares of her floor with masking tape, and I am allowed to sit within this two-foot square, clutching my knees to my chest. You with me, Alice?"

"Dear God."

"But that's not all. I am only allowed to speak at commercials, but first I have to announce that I wish to speak, by saying, 'Cheep?' I swear to you, Alice. And then she could say, 'Okay, go ahead,' or, without even looking at me, she could say, 'Uncheep,' and I'd have to wait for the next commercial to petition her again. She's like the parole board and I'm sitting there, clutching my knees to my chest—because if even the toe of my sneaker goes over the tape, she slugs me—going, 'Cheep?'"

Joe's mother walks into the room, frowning.

"Honestly, Joe. I think you made half of that up."

"Swear to God, Mom."

"Alice? I wouldn't believe a word he's said."

"Now, don't be a party pooper, Ann."

"It's just that I don't like to see my daughter misrepresented."

"Mom, the Mary you knew and the Mary I knew were two completely different people."

"The Mary I knew used to watch you sleep, afraid you'd stop breathing."

This stops Joe cold. "Really?"

"Yes. One time when you had the flu she stayed up half the night by your bed watching you, because she was afraid you'd vomit in your sleep and choke to death."

Joe stares off into space.

"And another thing, Joe. On your ninth birthday, I sent you outside to play while I baked your birthday cake, and Mary came in crying, just moved and heartbroken, because she'd seen you in the garden, bending down to whisper to our cat, 'It's my ninth birthday.'"

Joe smiles. This is exactly the kind of story he can't wait to tell Louise.

He stares at a pay phone in the nightclub where he goes to hide while his mother's girls play bridge. Joe could call Louise, pretend to be drunk, sound like he's on the verge of tears, and somehow shoehorn in the birthday story. Lou's heart would melt.

Instead of calling Louise, he gets drunk, alone, at the bar, then has two cups of coffee before driving home. The caffeine keeps him awake until dawn.

He lies in bed tossing and turning all night, overheating badly, suffering through one bout of Heart Awareness after another. He is afraid he is going to die. He is afraid because his father, Edwin, died so young, at fifty-one. Joe Jones is only thirty-five but he's afraid that his heart will give out too. If Louise were with him, she would hold him, comfort him, and make him laugh at himself. She thinks his fear of death is funny.

"Do you know what Hitchcock wanted written on his tombstone?" she asked him one time. "'This is what we DO to bad little boys.'"

He tried so hard to be good, but he always ended up feeling defeated. Now those early defeats make good stories, but at the time his soul felt like a snail who is having salt poured on it.

His all-time worst memory is *Farmer in the Dell*—it was Willie's favorite Joe Jones' story. Humanist educators had apparently banned the game by the time Willie came along; Willie'd never even heard of it.

"Willie, it was like, let's kill this little boy's *soul*. This is kindergarten, right? And the teacher would say, 'Hey! Let's go outside, children, and play *Farmer in the Dell*,' and my heart would just fucking *sink*.

"We'd all trudge outside, all these innocent little kids, and the teacher makes you form a ring, holding hands. And one kid is picked to be the farmer, and so he stands inside the ring, and all the kids start singing, 'The farmer in the dell, the farmer in the dell, hi-ho the derry-o, the farmer in the dell.'

"Then, the farmer takes the wife, the farmer takes the wife, hi-ho the derry-o, *so* forth. And the kid who's the farmer chooses a little girl to be his wife, and she goes into the ring, and everyone starts singing, 'The wife takes the dog, the wife takes the dog,'—you get it—she picks someone to be the dog, and all the kids who are left in the ring now are getting all clammy and sick.

"And the dog takes the cat, and then the cat takes the rat, and it's okay to be the rat, I mean, actually it's fuckin' salvation to be the rat because, *the rat takes the cheese.* See some poor fucker gets picked to be the *cheese,* and it's the worst moment of your life because they're all singing, 'The *cheese* stands alone, the *cheese* stands alone...' Everyone, the farmer, the wife, the dog, the entire fucking kindergarten, starts this terrible chanting—it's like the Inquisition—hands over their heads, they're *leering* at the cheese, singing, 'The *cheese* stands alone, the *cheese* stands alone, hi-ho the derry-o, the cheese stands *alone.*'"

Willie laughs so hard that he starts to choke.

"So *fuckin' sick,*" says Joe Jones. "The other kids, the ones who weren't the cheese, were like *Lord of the Flies*—'Piggy, Piggy, Piggy....'

"God," he continues, "you'd just stand there, it would not *fucking* end and it'd be *so* bad, you'd start getting like this *film* in your mouth..."

Willie howls with laughter, can't talk.

Joe Jones smiles, he says, "I'm not kidding, man. You remember that last asshole who shot up everyone at McDonald's? He was probably this incredibly sensitive little boy who was picked to be the *cheese* one too many times."

Joe wakes up sick and exhausted. He feels like crying. He feels that he is going to snap if he doesn't get to talk to Louise. Thinking of Willie's hating him makes him queasy. "You're a rotten shitfuck slut, and I hope you rot in hell," Willie said.

Joe nods. *I know*, he thinks, *that's exactly what I am.*

His mother has left him a note in the kitchen. She will be at the club until four. There is bacon in the oven, coffee on the stove. He feels somewhat less rocky after he's eaten, but it's a "Life is Hard Then You Die" kind of day. He reads the paper, waters his mother's garden, considers and discards the idea of going for a swim in the ocean, and spends most of the day cradling his head in his hands. At three he lies down on the chaise in the lanai and watches *Name That Tune.*

"Joe?" Willie would say, out of the blue. "I can name that tune in five notes."

"I can name that tune in *four* notes."

"Come on, Joe, remember? You gotta say my name first."

"Okay. Willie? I can name that tune in *four* notes."

"Joe? *I* can name that tune in three notes."

"Willie? *Name that tune.*"

Joe Jones goes for a walk on the beach alone at sunset. Rotting in hell in paradise, blinking back tears as he walks, desperately missing Louise, deserted, desperately missing his father.

His gravest childhood fear was that his father would leave.

"I won't leave you. You're my boy and I love you."

"You promise you won't leave?"

"I promise."

Edwin moved out when Joe was nine and a half, returned, rather nonchalantly, when he was eleven. They fished together, played catch, went to ball games at Candlestick Park, roughed it, in love, and they watched "Bonanza" on Sunday nights. Edwin was most himself with Joe, Joe thought. He could be with his boy without being pressured—didn't have to be the big camper, didn't have to amuse or listen, could just *be*, think, look, could just do his life, with Joe's warm body beside him.

And he was a teacher. Like Louise, Joe's dad was the person in the boat beside the long-distance swimmer, urging him on, "Pull, *pull*," offering broth, little by little, through the channel swim of growing up.

"Joe?" he told him when Joe was eleven, "you quit too easily. You quit the trumpet, you quit your paper route. You got to *stick with* it to get results. Honest, believe me. You always want maximum glory for minimum effort."

Joe hung his head in disappointment and frustration.

"There's an old story about a teenage boy and his best friend, who are kidding around with the first boy's little brother," Edwin said.

"'Watch this,' he whispers to his friend. 'Alfie doesn't know anything about money. He falls for this same trick every time. Hey, Alfie! Come over here a minute.'

"Alfie eagerly trots over. His brother has a nickel and a dime in his hand and holds them out to Alfie. 'Take whichever one you want.' Alfie takes the nickel and runs off.

"His brother snickers. 'See? He does it every time.'

"Later the friend feels sorry for Alfie, takes him aside, and explains: 'See, even though the nickel is bigger, the dime is twice as valuable.'

"'*I know that*,' says Alfie. 'But I take the dime and the game's over.'"

Joe Jones thought this over.

"So," his father said, "start settling for the nickel."

Christmas the year of his father's return looked exactly right, "Norman Rockwell Meets the Bouviers," no holds barred. His mother made breakfast of scrambled eggs and sausage, and there was a pitcher of fresh-squeezed orange juice. Danish pastries baking filled the house with yeasty, buttery, almond smells. Joe's stocking alone was a windfall: chocolates, pencils with his name embossed in gold, a wallet like his father's, tangerines, baseball cards, two E.C. comics—a "Tales from the Crypt" and a "Vault of Horror"—a coin wrapper of dimes.

Joe Jones is lying on a towel on the beach talking to her in his head. Lou, he tells her, it was all so fuckin' perfect, carols on the stereo, a big red bow on Skipper. And from Santa Claus—from *Santa Claus*, Lou!—it says so on the card—a black ten-speed bike. Okay?

But, Lou, he's saying, there was something *so* profoundly wrong with the picture and I didn't yet know what it was.

Later that day, we were waiting for the aunts and uncles and cousins to come. My grandma and grandpa were coming at three. And at one or so, my best friend comes over. Now this guy's name is Stevie, and he is a *nerd*, man, he is a wimp skinhead *nerd*. He's one of those kids who, the next year, in seventh grade, will be a member of the wimp skinhead nerd clique who've learned to write in italics over the summer. Who spent their summers writing in italic and reading J.R.R. Tolkien. Get the picture? My best friend, Stevie Gronewald.

So Steve shows up on his bike, and his dad's given him a pellet gun for Christmas. Gonna make a *man* out of him, right, gonna turn this wimp skinhead weirdo nerd into, what's that guy's name who got up on the tower in Texas and—right, Charles Whitman. Anyway.

So my folks are in their bedroom with the door closed when he shows up. Mary's in her room, stacking and restacking chocolate doubloons, all but cackling; she's a perverted evil miser out of Dickens. So Stevie and I go out to the empty lot next to our house and start shooting away with the pellet gun, taking turns, shooting at cans and birds. We can't hit anything, but we're aiming at stuff, and it's sort of perversely bringing me into the *Now*. And then, out of the blue, I get an idea. I think, What would it be like to shoot at the windshield of my father's car?

It was like a light bulb going off above my head. It seemed like a good idea at the time—this is what I'm calling my autobiography, Louise: *It Seemed Like a Good Idea at the Time.*

So we take the gun and I start shooting at the windshield, and it made this enormously satisfying cracking, this spider-webbing of glass. I mean, it was fucking *sexual*. So then, almost blithely, with calm self-assurance—like it's a job well done—I shoot out all the other windows, too. And then, and *only* then, do I realize I'm in trouble.

Stevie hides the gun in the bushes—we tear into the house and tell my dad that Stevie and I rode up on our bikes right when these two hoodlums with a pellet gun were riding away on a motorcycle—we saw them shoot out his car windows. And my dad is like *so* bummed, but, since he can't drive the car, he asks me and Stevie to cruise around on our bikes and look for the hoods. So we get on our bikes and ride all around the neighborhood, sweating, man, we're amped out of our minds on adrenalin, and after a few minutes, we are firmly convinced that we *are* looking for hoodlums, and we're righteously pissed at what they did to my dad's car.

Stevie goes home. I pedal back to my house, and I say I couldn't find them and my dad says he's calling the sheriff and I crack. I break down, and cry, confess.

And, you know, my father was more heartbroken than anything else? Why had I? *How could I do this?* It had been such a beautiful Christmas. I just sobbed. I couldn't explain.

Did I have a mean streak?

Once he told Louise he thought he might have a mean streak, and she said we all have that crippling self-absorption, we all have chains of fear and greed that make us do destructive things.

"I don't think my daddy did," he said.

"Sure he did, darling."

Joe Jones doesn't believe it. He could give dozens of examples of what a fine, loyal man Edwin Jones was. For instance, he took

his wife to church every Sunday, after he came back. He didn't
believe in God, but he stood by her side every Sunday, Mr. and
Mrs. Jones, because he knew how much he had humiliated her
by his leaving.

Mary hadn't come to the service when their father died six
years ago. She was already lost to Jesus. She said he hadn't *really*
died, that no one ever *really* dies. It was just that they couldn't
see him yet, because he was in Hell.

At Edwin's funeral, the congregation sang his favorite song,
the song he most often sang in the shower: *Shall we gather at the
river, where bright angel feet have trod, with its crystal tide forever,
flowing by the throne of God.*

Joe wore his father's black pin-striped suit, and wept. He was
twenty-nine.

Now on Sunday mornings Joe and his mother sleep in. Then they
go to the club for brunch with the girls. Joe endures it—they sit
outside at a table in the shade and sip frothy drinks. When Ann
Jones and her son approach, one of the girls inevitably cries out
with astonishment, "Didn't you get *tall*, Joe!" as if he's grown
since last Sunday.

THREE

All right. Here are my plans for the Merchant Marine. Those in the Hawaiian population of mixed marriages would make for an enormous Merchant Marine, and it would cost next to nothing to send anything anywhere. Trade would be stimulated, and everybody would get rich quick, and nobody would dare to start WW III because they'd be bombing their customers. I would be the Supreme Head of the MM and control everything and start a new religion that would teach that only through a spanking clean set of orifices can God be found. (This would also eliminate tooth decay and ear wax.) "Clean up!" would blare from loudspeakers twice a day. Love to Jessie, Willie, you, love, love, Joe Jones.

"I THINK I'M GONNA kill myself Friday," Willie says scowling when Louise goes into the back room to get a pastry brush.
"How come?"
"I'm *so* tired of doing dishes."

Fay Musberger drudges into the cafe a few minutes after Louise flips the "Closed" sign over to "Open." Nearly fifty now, she's been coming in for years with resigned testiness, as if she is here for her barium enema, rather than tea and toast.

Louise smiles pleasantly from the grill while Fay sinks into a chair. Before putting the book that she holds onto the table, she takes a napkin from the dispenser and wipes off the space in front of her.

"What was there, googe on the table or something?"

"I just?" Fay shrugs.

"You got to watch that sort of thing, baby, and I'll tell you why. It starts out with wiping off tables that are already clean." Louise is advancing with a mug of tea. "And pretty soon, every time you pat a dog, you gotta go wash your hands. Next thing you know, you're like Howard Hughes, having to cover your toast with a fresh Kleenex between every bite."

Louise places the tea in front of Fay. "Really," she says, "two pieces of toast, we're talking—I don't know, I'm guessing here— twenty, twenty-five pieces of Kleenex." She smiles. Fay seems annoyed when she looks up, as if Louise is the tenth person to interrupt her meal for an autograph. "What are you reading, Fay?"

"H.G. Wells."

"Which one?"

"*A Short History of the World*."

"Never read it. Is it good?"

Fay breathes out a small sarcastic laugh. "Would I be wasting my time on it if—"

"Hey, look. You don't have to get *sore*."

Fay's smile says: Are you done?

"So, how early does it start?"

Fay waits. "Slime," Fay says finally.

Louise goes into the back room, where Willie is washing dishes. "How you doing, love?"

He clips out the answer, flat and nasal. "Slime," he says. Lou laughs, they both shake their heads. *Thank You, God*, she prays, walking back to the grill, *thank You for not making me have to be*

Fay. She begins assembling the ingredients for tamale pie, Jessie's favorite dish.

It's sort of pleasant in my head a lot of the time, she thinks, as she folds two cups of cornmeal into the beef, olives, corn, salsa, and eggs. More and more inhabitable, she thinks, with every passing year.

"Do you like yourself?" Willie asked wistfully not too long before. Louise mulled it over for a moment and said, "I wouldn't go that far. But I get along with myself pretty well these days."

Thank You, also, she prays, *for not making me be Joe.* So hard inside that head of his, like a crowded off-night at the old Fillmore West, the show you're watching, the band on the stage, the ceiling on fire with light shows and strobe lights, oily lights on one wall, slides on another, dilapidated movies on the third, and stoned naked fat people pushing and stepping over you.

Someday Joe is going to have to face the fact that he is capable of betraying the most basic trust of the people he cares most about, that he always has and always will worry more about the inconvenience he'll experience, than about the hurt he's caused. She hid her knowledge of this from Joe but carried it around in her pocket, hidden and slightly repulsive, like a used bloody Band-Aid wadded in a cotton handkercheif, until finally, finally, she grew tired of having it and threw it away.

Really, she thinks to herself, you ought to be in love with someone you wouldn't mind being.

It is a slow day at Jessie's Cafe. Jessie and Georgia sit at their table, Jessie with a picture book called *People of the Willow*, Georgia staring glumly out to sea, formulating her plans for world peace.

Cocoa Nelson comes in for a cheeseburger. Once Farrah Fawcett's biggest fan, now she's nouveau punk, tastefully rebellious. She sits at the counter and watches Louise at the grill, creaking with hunger and general impatience.

"Little minibummer, Cocoa, love?"

"Midterms. Tomorrow."

"Which ones first?"

"Bio and gym."

"Gym?" Cocoa doesn't answer.

"Are you prepared at all?"

"Sort of. I totally scoped out the book."

"Do you understand it?"

"It's not that. It's the teacher's just like totally vigerent."

"What do you mean?"

"He's got an attitude."

"Yeah."

"He's like, heavily old."

"Totally. Like, how old?"

"I don't know, fifty."

"Good God, *you're kidding!* What! Does he hobble in behind a walker? Is he on life support!"

Cocoa smiles. Louise bends over the counter to kiss her on the forehead. "Your burger'll be done in a second."

"Okay. But I'm going to have to pay you like in *total* dimes."

Willie was like this when they first met, surly, lost, confused. Lou had just started working at the restaurant. Willie had not yet started waiting tables. He was fifteen. He used to come by after school, sit with Jessie and Georgia, and half-heartedly study his texts. Louise won his heart with milk shakes and because she could make him laugh. He was a frail and beautiful boy, he reminded her of the Little Prince.

"What are you doing?" she'd asked him one day, sitting down.

"Studying vo*cab*ulary. We get the words today, we got a *quiz* tomorrow. It's just so totally fucked, man."

"You want me to ask you the words?"

"I don't know. It's just *totally* hiddybones."

She smiled. "Give me the list."

He signed and handed her a mimeographed sheet of paper. It gave her a jolt, like déjà vu, the purple alcoholic smell of the letters.

"Pelagic."

"*Plag*gic?"

"Pel-a-gic."

"I don't know."

"Pelagic. Come on, think."

"I really just don't *know*, Louise,"

"Pelagic. Of the sea."

When Louise looks over at Jessie and Georgia, they look like they have both just sat down on cleats. "Jessie? Everything okay?"

Jessie glares at Louise, then goes all hurt and indignant. "I just told *Geor*gia where the cow found the cabbage."

"Pfffffttt."

"Oh, for Pete's sake!"

"Pfffffttt."

What the hell can they fight about, since Georgia doesn't talk? "Do you want me to bring you some tea?"

Jessie's eyes fill up with tears. Georgia closes her eyes and turns up her nose—three-year-olds in a sandbox.

Louise goes over to their table, collects their teapot and cups. "I'll bring you a fresh pot. And Willie's made macaroons."

"Pfft."

"Come on, Georgia. Lighten up. Both of you, think nice thoughts. Think about wheat fields."

Jessie sniffles. Georgia imperiously puts her left claw inside her right armpit, tilts her head up and back.

"What, are you doing your Napoleon for us now?"

Jessie dabs at her eyes with a Kleenex she keeps tucked up under the cuff at her left wrist.

"Jessie! Come on, sweetheart, tell me. What is it?"

Jessie sticks her bottom lip out all the way. It quivers.

"Georgia won't share."

"Share what, what won't she share?"

Jessie crosses her arms, won't say another word.

Louise shakes her head. "This is *nuts*." She goes to the back room and makes them a fresh pot of tea.

"The girls are being bad," she tells Willie.

"Grandma didn't sleep well."

She takes the tea to the two old women, with two special mugs, one with a band of ducks standing in bulrushes, one with kitties on it, which she places in front of Jessie, who gives a little bark of unhappiness.

"*Now* what's the matter?"

"Georgia *always* gets the duck cup."

Louise's shoulders sag.

"Georgia does not always get the duck cup."

Georgia brings one gnarled old hand out of her lap, lays the backs of her fingers against the duck cup, and slowly, evilly pushes it two inches closer to herself, with a prim, bratty set to her mouth, like an older sister tracing an invisible mark of demarcation down the back seat of a car.

"I give up," says Louise, and goes back to the grill.

Willie comes over and stands beside her, watches her mash black beans. "Cocoa really got pretty, didn't she," he says. Louise nods. "That girl I slept with that time, she looked like Cocoa, sort of."

"You never told me you slept with a girl."

"Yes, I did."

"No, you didn't."

"Well, I did. I slept with a girl one time."

"How was it?"

"Oh, it was all right, you know. But, it just wasn't the real thing."

She looks at him. "I love you so much," she says.

He goes to his grandmother's table and kisses the nape of Jessie's neck, peers into Georgia's empty mug.

"Are the ducks thirsty?" he asks.

"Pfft."

He fills her cup with steaming tea.

"Try to be nice to each other," he says. "It's hard on Louise when you aren't." Louise, at the grill, shakes her head.

Willie feels, he has told Louise, that Joe betrayed them all when he betrayed Louise, and hell hath no fury like a Willie scorned. "I really don't wish to discuss it," he says, but he does: "He fucked our whole family, Louise. He fucked you, he fucked me, he fucked my grandmother. A good person does not fuck someone's grand-mother—she feels *terri*ble, she misses him so much. So it's his loss, you know. I mean, like Grandma says, as you do unto others you are doing unto yourself. So he really just fucked himself and I hope he rots in hell."

God, they were all so close, Louise thinks, Jessie, Willie, Joe, Louise. Willie used to tease him just relentlessly and could get him to laugh at himself. Last year Willie made blackberry ice cream from berries Jessie had picked. It was perfect, rich creamy purple, full of seeds, but when Willie brought him a bowl, Joe turned it down.

"I'm sorry, Willie, I just can't eat ice cream anymore, I mean, especially with seeds in it. . . ."

Willie's face went blank with disbelief.

"I've just got these *extreme*ly delicate teeth."

Willie rolled his eyes. "What are they—*chalk*?"

Joe blushed, smiling. Really, he could be the sweetest shyest man, brimming with the eagerness to please.

Now, at the grill, Louise has started to cry.

"Willie? I want to call him."

"Why?"

"Because I just want to talk to him."

"Don't do it, Lulu. You're setting yourself up. Somewhere down the road, he'll break your heart again. You call him, man, that's like 'you fukker.' Or like me and speed."

"You fukker" is shorthand. Louise's beloved uncle Duncan had been sober three months when his younger brother, Louise's father, died.

"I need a buffer, baby," he told Louise.

"But drinking doesn't work for you—you end up in the toilet."

"Because I always drink too much. My liver can only metabolize one and a half ounces of alcohol an hour, so if I stick to that, more or less, maybe sometimes just a *little* bit more..."

He had tried before to limit himself to an ounce and a half an hour, and she had seen him too many times when he'd had just a *little* bit more, but he was determined to try again. Six ounces of wine equals one and a half ounces of alcohol. He would limit himself to one bottle, to twenty-four ounces a night.

He kept a journal of the first night and showed it to Louise when he was sober again: "6:00, scared, but breathing again. 7:30, calm, smart, may not need whole bottle. 8:15, feel I will *stride* again. 8:45, last glass, want to sleep soon." Then, in the scrawl of an angry child: "YOU FUKKER!!! YOU OPENED THE SECOND BOTTLE."

"Willie! God, I needed that."

"Back in the saddle?"

"Back in the saddle."

"Did the girls make up?"

"See for yourself."

Willie wipes soapsuds off his hands and peers out into the other room. *People of the Willow* lies open between Jessie and Georgia. Jessie is pointing out huskies and seals, Georgia is studying the watercolors intently.

"What are you going to make them for dinner?"

"Tamale pie, with blue-corn tortillas."

"Blue corn may push Georgia over the edge."

"Willie?"

"Are you crying?"

"Where is all the *cus*tomers?"

"What's the matter, Lou?"

"I'm *sad*."

"I can *tell*."

"My *feet* hurt."

Willie puts down the spatula he's using to frost an angel food cake. "What can I do? Want me to rub your feet?"

"I don't know."

"Don't cry, I hate it when you cry. Come on, let's go in the can—okay? Time for a little break." He takes her by the hand and pulls her out of the back room, calls to Jessie and Georgia that they'll be back in a minute. There is no one in the cafe. He pulls Louise into the bathroom and locks the door.

"Have a seat," he says, pointing to the door.

She sits down against it on the floor Indian style and covers her face with her hands. He sits in front of her, brings one of her feet into his lap, unlaces and removes her sneaker, puts it down, peels off her white cotton sock, and sniffs it.

"It smells like corn chips."

Louise sniffles, still covering her face.

Willie stares into his lap. "This is the foot of a Hungarian dockworker." He strokes her instep for a minute, then begins to massage the arch, pushing in hard with his thumbs.

"Does that hurt?"

"Hurts good."

They hear footsteps coming down the hall.

"There are people here now, and they're hungry," Jessie says.

"Hope they can cook, Grandma," Willie tells her.

"What did you say?"

"I said *I hope they can cook!*"

"Oh."

"Stall 'em, Grandma."

"What's that?"

"*Stall* them. Seat them. Get their drink order."

They listen as her cooing recedes back down the hallway.

"Lulu?" Willie asks. "Want me to sing you a song?" She shakes her head. "You sure? I could sing you 'San Antonio Rose.'" She shakes her head and finally uncovers her face. She looks at him and snorts.

"*Corn chips?*" she asks.

Joe Jones and his mother have spent much of the day together, and she hasn't yet driven him as crazy as she usually does. They read the paper in the lanai, went to her club and swam on its beach, and then to visit Alice, who called them in the late morning from the hospital, saying her blood pressure had rocketed again.

The last time he was in a hospital his father Edwin lay dying, and today when he reaches out to stroke the plump pink hand of his mother's friend his head is filled with snapshots of his father in defeat.

He brought Alice white tea roses and a jar of plum preserves.

She closes her eyes while inhaling the scent of the flowers, then adds them to the plastic water pitcher beside her bed that already holds daisies, begonias and a lily.

"Ira brought these this morning," she says. Ira is Husband Number Four. Joe has never met him but his mother says he is a shy, blushing hick who dotes on Alice, plays the guitar, and wears a cheap toupee. Alice outweighs him by at least fifty pounds.

His mother sits in a chair by the side of the bed and asks the questions one asks: How do you feel, how's the food, how long do they want you to stay? Joe stands at the foot of the bed, studying them, Alice and his mother. It is not the fear in their eyes that is making his heart sink as he smiles gently at Alice. It is that he cannot find one real ray of caring in himself. He swallows hard and feigns engrossment while thoughts of Louise and his father move through his head, slippery, gray-blue and cold.

There's something wrong with me, he says to no one on the beach. He stares out at the striated tropical waters with dejection. He sees himself at the foot of Alice's bed—Alice whom he likes so well—and inside his heart the needle doesn't move to the left or to the right.

He bows his head.

Later he reads the sports section of the evening paper in the kitchen while his mother broils sole.

He watches her bony back as she cooks, and reaches for his can of beer. After taking a sip he pinches the inch of tubing that runs around his belly. He ought to stop drinking beer—the roll is not bad yet but you let these things go and two, three months you look like Sydney Greenstreet.

He sighs and looks up at his mother. "Ma?"

"Yes, darling."

"I think I'll go back pretty soon."

She drizzles flakes of parsley over the fish.

"I mean, I need to get settled again. Whether or not Louise wants me to move back in right away. And I ought to call all the schools and see if anyone needs a coach."

Again she doesn't respond. Joe is getting terribly antsy. He can't stay here one more night. He has to get back home. He feels as if there is an unopened letter from a funny old friend in his back pocket and he has to wait to read it because somebody he doesn't care about is talking at him.

"Ma?"

"Oh, stick around a little longer, Joe. Maybe find a part-time job. Earn a little pocket money."

He looks like he has just inhaled a blast of ammonia—a little pocket money, a paper route perhaps? *You just untwisted my nuts like a lightbulb, then tossed them into the corner.*

He does not look at her while they eat. She talks about Alice's husband and the grandchildren of the girls at the club.

He is sitting in a piano bar two hours later drinking another Guinness. An old Hawaiian man with a ukelele is playing along with the black piano player, singing "Hanalei Moon," slow and haunting, melodic. Joe is fighting back tears.

Louise liked to say, "You're a psychopath who has made a reasonable adjustment. So am I." She said it with a smile, as if in exoneration.

Hearing her voice would be a cool drink of water.

He sees the old man play the ukelele for Louise, at the cafe, playing his song "Hanalei Moon"—she would probably cry. She used to love him so much, her love could make him feel like he was steady and loose on water skis.

"So okay," she tells Jessie and Willie and Georgia, with Joe sitting right there at the table cringing, but good-natured. This was maybe four years ago. "In the morning, when he's driving me home, he announces he needs an evening alone. Now, this is like the beginning of our second trimester—I mean, the honeymoon's over but we're really, really close friends. And we're together almost every single night, so when he says he needs a night alone, it's *soul* death. And I'm totally cool, you know, it's like, hey, I was just about to suggest the same thing, but on the inside I'm thinking, 'Sure, hey fine, everyone needs some time alone, give me a call Friday or so. No, no, I mean *next* Friday.'

"But then about ten the phone rings. It's Joe, and he's freaking out six ways from Sunday, coming apart like a two-dollar watch. You know how he gets?"

"He gets a *bee* in his bonnet," Jessie proclaims. Joe winces, he covers his face, embarrassed and happy.

"And he says his dog is having babies," and her voice becomes shrill and rapid, "'Bethy's having babies prematurely, and they're all dead, man, they're fuckin' ass dead, man. I can't deal with this—you oughta see the bathroom, man, it is covered with blood and afterbirth; *I can't deal with this,* Louise.'

"So I exhale in my commiserating sort of way and ask, 'What do you want me to do?'

"And he screams, 'HELP ME OUT, MAN.'

"Then he says to be outside and he'll come get me, and while I'm waiting for him, I'm pushing back my sleeves. Clearly it's gonna be an all-day cleanup, blood up to my wrists. He thinks Bethy's dying too—it's gonna be *Gone with the Wind*—no, no, the *Texas Chainsaw Puppy Massacre.*

"Joe stays in the car when we get to his house. It's the angriest I've ever seen him. I go into the bathroom, expecting ratty splattered corpses on the wall, but it's spotless. One pup's dead, two feet away from Beth—there's no blood, no afterbirth—"

"And what's Bethy doing?"

"Bethy, Jess, is nursing the puppies. Five little babies."

Joe, in the bar, laughs out loud at himself. *This!* this! is why he misses her so badly.

Hello, house, Louise says, stepping into her apartment that evening. De princess be home. How you doing. She looks around the cluttered, frumpy living room.

It is furnished with her parents' flea market antiques, the braided rag rug Jessie made sixty years ago, Duncan's wonderful old brown leather couch, and prints of the Old Masters taped to cream-colored walls.

The phone sits on an upturned produce crate, "Don't Worry Apples," it says. "When buying, Don't Worry"—a little blond boy is smiling at a shiny red apple—don't worry, don't worry, don't worry.

She should get the answering machine out of the closet, hook it up again. Why had she unplugged it when she made Joe leave? It used to make coming home exciting, like getting mail twice a day. Louise sees him on the day he brought it home, sees him hunched over it, recording the outgoing message, over and over, getting it right, like he's taping a demo for a record company.

She smiles.

She fills the bathtub with hot water and bubble bath and begins to undress. She is stiff and tired and old, but pats her round belly admiringly, king of a cannibal island. Gingerly then, she steps into the tub, moaning as she lowers herself: Ohhhhhh, hot, good. I am so sore tonight, my legs, my neck, my back. She lies moaning until she gets used to the heat, then turns on the hot water faucet with her foot: Ohhhhhh. He was crazy with aches and pains. Stiffness meant one of two things to him, flu or cancer. Give him a blister and you can watch poor crippled Amahl hobble about with an invisible branch-crutch. Never just a cold or the occasional hangover. "It's *bad*, man," he'd croak, raising a trembling hand to take the cup of chicken broth she'd bring him—he's Dulcinea at the end of *The Man of La Mancha*.

Louise laughs out loud. Joe. Maybe they can be friends. *Hail Mary, full of grace, the Lord is with thee...*

He used to call their house from the back room at the cafe, with Willie at the sink beside him, Louise in the other room, and listen to his own voice on the machine. "Hi, this is Joe Jones," as if this disembodied voice was some sort of proof he actually existed—was real, in space and time. Willie heard him do this once, heard him listen, rapt, to his own voice. It was Willie who told her.

It makes her melt, this fear of his.

When he was six, the Joneses moved down the block. He knew this, was told this, he was shown the new house. But after school, alone and confused, he went to the old one, went *home*, where he lived, and no one was there, nothing was there but an old black man waxing the floors.

In the middle of the night Louise dreams that she has awakened from a dream to find an enormous sloppy pink Dr. Seuss cake at the foot of her bed, and her leg lashes out in a myoclonic jerk, kicks it over onto the floor, and she's laughing and crying, thinking, in that microsecond, what a mess—a rat's wedding.

She wakes up.

Joe's father called a day when the sun was shining through drizzle "a monkey's birthday." When it was a gray drizzly sky, there wouldn't be clouds, so Joe would be confused, would think the rain would put out the sun as it fell to the ground.

"Did you ask your father, how that could be?"

"Yeah, yeah. He'd squint at the sky, shake his head and say, 'Must be a *mon*key's birthday.'"

"I miss him," she whispers out loud, meaning Joe, and she sits up in bed and begins to cry. After a while the middle-aged person who lives in her head begins to talk to her soul, the kid.

You're lonely, it's late. Go to sleep.

It's just that I don't understand.

Give it up. You've cleaned out the bird cage—you don't have to read the newspaper through the shit.

I'm sad.

Get angry. He laced the punch, lovey. Don't drink it.

Oh, God.

He's like—well, remember at Woodstock, the tent full of people who'd taken bad drugs, who were wigged out and watching bats fly out of each other's noses? And then Wavy Gravy comes on the PA system, booming almost cheerfully, "Do *not* take the brown powder. The *brown powder* is *not* particularly good."

Joe's not brown powder, the child says defensively.

Joe is *not* particularly good powder, though, the older Louise responds.

I need to talk to someone.

What am I, chopped liver?

It's so hard in my head right now.

It's hard in your head, and it's *cold* out there.

I want to talk to my Uncle Duncan.

One moment, please, miss, I'll connect you.

Louise pulls the covers up around her shoulders, wipes away her tears, sniffles, and takes a deep breath.

Duncan? You got a minute?

Lovey, I got all *kinds* of time.

My *broc*coli knows he's just not right for me. I remember what you said. If you see a fin in the water, there's only one thing to do—clear the area. And I know if we get back together he'll drop me on my head again.

So what's the problem? This broken heart will pass.

I've got so much invested. Five years, and now I'm so fucking alone again. I don't want to start over with someone else.

Too bad for Lou then, huh?

Yeah, I guess.

You bought the wrong pair of shoes again.

I know.

Buy a better pair.

Louise smiles in bed, gets it—four years before, she and Joe flew to Hawaii to meet his mother. The day before they left, Joe began to panic, about Lou's clothes, her weight, her shoes.

"You gotta buy some *san*dals. What if we go out someplace nice with my mother? Please? For me?"

"Yes, may I help you, ma'am?"

"Do those thongs come in brown?"

"In what size?"

"Eight."

"I don't think I have an eight—I do have a seven and a half."

"Okay, let's give them a try."

They are too small, her toes extending over the insole—still she almost buys them. She has to open the cafe in an hour, and they are not bad looking, and they're only twenty-five dollars, but then she shakes her head, sighs, and leaves the store.

Okay, look, Louise, she says to herself on the street. Maybe two dozen times in the past, you have tried on shoes that gouged your feet or pinched your toes, and you bought them anyway. And you hated the shoes every time you wore them and ended up hating yourself for owning them. So today, we aren't going to do this, are not going to buy shoes that may make our feet bleed. I mean, this is not so much to ask.

So she goes into another store and finds a pair of simple leather thongs. "May I try these in an eight?" The clerk returns with a shoebox, and she takes off her sneakers. The sandals are a perfect fit but she takes several steps, several more, and then there's something wrong, the sandals go "slap-slap-slap." She has to grip tight with curled toes to keep them on, and she walks around with a sick look on her face, listening to the clapping on the leather, listening to her broccoli cry, "Don't do it, Lou, don't do it," but somehow she knows that, barring divine intervention, she's going to buy these shoes.

She stops and stares at her feet. "They slap," she says.

"They look like they fit perfectly," the clerk says.

"They *slap*. I have to grinch up my toes to keep them on." She frowns at the store clock. It's eleven thirty—a half hour and she has to be at work. She walks around cramping up her toes to keep the sandals on, hears the percussive clapping, the slapslapslap-slapslap.

"Okay," she sighs, "I'll take 'em."

She wears them out to the car, carrying her sneakers in the box. She will break them in today. By the time she's gone three blocks, her feet are bleeding.

Behind the wheel, she gingerly slides the sandals off and finds bleeding blisters under the straps near her big toes. She sees herself tossing the sandals into a garbage can. You stupid jackass, Louise. I couldn't find a pair of shoes, she will tell Joe Jones. I tried, I really tried.

Then she throws back her head and laughs.

She tells the story to Willie, he roars. She tells the story to Joe and shows him her bleeding feet. He looks like he is passing a kidney stone. He covers his eyes with one hand and exhales wearily. "Oh, *light*en up, Francis," she says.

It is Willie's favorite line. He uses it on Joe Jones all the time, whenever he's ranting. In the movie *Stripes*, Francis is a hostile army recruit whose turn it is to introduce himself to the other members of Bill Murray's platoon. "My name is Francis," he snarls. "I hate the name Francis. No one calls me Francis. Anyone calls me Francis, I'll kill him. And I don't like to be touched," he continues, at which point the sergeant, Warren Oates, rolls his eyes and says, "*Light*en up, Francis."

The trip goes well, all things considered—that Mrs. Jones is such a dry stick, that Louise's feet bleed and require new Band-Aids every hour or so, and that because she gamely continues to wear the sandals, the cuts are infected by the second day.

Joe and Louise make love quietly in his bedroom late in the morning. There is a note from his mother on the table in the kitchen. She has gone to the club and will be home in time to make them lunch. "Let's go to the beach," he suggests.

"Oh, Joe, I mean, God." He strokes her neck. "I'm going to look *grisly* in my swimsuit."

"You've got a beautiful body."

"It's just gross—it's fat *and* my legs are short."

"No, you're beautiful and soft."

"That's so nice of you to say. But I have stretch marks, and Black Leg—"

"What's Black Leg?"

"Broken, spidery veins, from the knees up. I'm illustrated, I'm the *Ele*phant Man."

"How can you be so free with me here, so sexy and bold . . ."

"I have a behind-closed-doors sort of beauty," Lou tells him.

She dresses in the bathroom and emerges wearing a white cotton shift. He wears aloha trunks, T-shirt, and his baseball cap. They walk to the beach holding hands.

"Good God," she says. "It really does look like paradise." The incandescent ocean, blue, and then green, and then blue, lavender, blue, the islands near the horizon, the palms, the running curved band of blond sand. She stares out at the beauty while Joe looks around at the bare brown skin of slender girls in bikinis. When he turns to look at Louise, she is staring down at the ground with the small smile of a good-natured but slightly prim woman uncomfortable being teased. She is hugging herself, still staring at the ground. Then she closes her eyes, inhales loudly, and pulls the white shift over her head. It seems that she is having trouble breathing, but there is still a small smile on her mouth, and he watches her wait, round and shy, in a fraying old racing swimsuit. Her thighs are white above the fading tan line from the shorts she wore last summer, stretch-marked, dimpled, soft, and lovely. He is smiling at her gently now but she doesn't see. She looks at her feet for a minute more, smiles, then squares her shoulders, looks out to sea, and begins to walk like an Olympic diver towards the water.

"Lulu?"

"What?"

"Wait."

He tears off everything but his trunks and walks quickly to her side.

FOUR

THE NIGHT AIR IS FULL of gardenias and gulls. Louise sits smoking on the stoop of the restaurant, tapping the ashes of her cigarette into an empty Sunkist orange juice can. Willie steps outside as blackbirds pass like silhouettes across the face of the round white moon.

"Lou?"

"Hmmm?"

"I finished scrubbing the grill. Everything's done, more or less."

"Thank you."

"You ready to go?"

"Yeah, in a minute."

"You sad?"

"Sort of, you know, melancholy. It'll be too quiet at my house when I go home."

"Wanna stay with us tonight?"

"I don't think so. Maybe the quiet will be a relief. But sometimes the quiet keeps me awake."

"The quiet keeps you awake? That night I stayed at your house on the couch, Joe kept me awake from one room away. I swear he makes this boxy clomping sound all night. It's like he's clopping two *co*conut halves together."

Louise throws back her head and laughs.

"It's like you had Mr. *Ed* in there with you."

"I love you so much, ducks," she tells him when she drops him off at his house.

"You *bet*ter," he says, getting out. "See you tomorrow."

Over four billion people on earth, and something gave them to each other. Is that a miracle or what?

She makes herself a cup of peppermint tea, puts on her nightie, crawls into bed. She looks around at the silence. After a while she takes *The Book of Common Prayer* from the drawer of her night table, opens it, and reads.

> Thank You for the wonder and the beauty of the world; for the light of day and the splendor of the starry night; for the wide order of Your laws made known by science, and for all things pure and lovely revealed by art; for the powers of our reason, the freedom of our will, and the joy of our pure affection; blessed be the Creator of all.... Amen.

See You tomorrow. Pleasant dreams.

Willie is watching TV on his grandmother's bed, eating Parmesan Goldfish, when he hears a heavy thud from the bathroom.

"Grandma?" he calls, and, hearing nothing, bolts out of bed. "Grandma, Grandma?" he calls as he runs down the hall. He opens the door to the bathroom and finds the old woman crumpled on the floor. "GRANDMA, GRANDMA," he hollers, bending to shake her shoulders.

She opens her eyes, crinkles everything up into a smile.

"Oh, *hi*, Willie," she says.

Louise dreams that she has just awakened from a dream and she is sitting up in bed, straining to hear something, but it is the quietest evening the world has ever known. It is a vacuumy quiet. The bombs have dropped. Outside the earth is in ruin. Panic rises inside her, a desperation so great and selfish, she'll be the Shelly Winters character in the band of survivors. Now somewhere a phone is ringing.

She opens her eyes and sits up. The phone rings again.

"Hello?"

"Lou! Guess what happened! Scary *duck*, man! Jessie fell down in the *bath*room. She was un*con*scious, man."

"Whoa, shit, man. . . ."

"She's o*kay*, though. She's like just reading in *bed* now—I called the doctor, and he said she prawley just got up from the *toi*let too fast."

"Whoa! Maybe we should take her *in* . . ."

"He said if she's weak in the morning."

"Whoa!"

"Whooooaaa. Scary duck, man!"

"You sure she's okay?"

"Yeah."

"Tell her I'm on the phone. I want to hear her voice."

"Okay. Hold on a sec. I'm in my room."

In a couple of minutes Louise hears the click of Jessie's extension phone, hears distant peeping, and then her voice.

"Why, Lou*ise*."

"Jessie," Louise whined loudly, "don't *do* that anymore."

"I fell *down*."

"I *know*. Don't fall *down* anymore."

"All right, I won't."

"You promise?"

"Scout's honor."

"Good night, dolly. Pleasant dreams."

Please just let it be that she got up from the can too fast. Is that
so much to ask? I mean, why don't You go get the bad guys? But
keep Your mitts off Jessie. You want to know why kind people
with inquiring minds, who are desperate to believe in something,
anything, don't believe in You? It's because you're such an *ass*-
hole sometimes. I don't mean that the way it sounds. But these
syphilitic despots live forever, and You'll let Your sweetest sons
and daughters die. And don't give me that doo-dah about the
"appalling strangeness of God's mercy."

She lies awake in the dark. I didn't really mean that You're an
asshole. It's just that, as long as You're there, why don't You *act*
like You're there? You could reveal yourself. I mean, I know You
do in nature and whatnot. Music. I know Jesus was supposed to
do the trick, but that was just a little *outré*. I mean, really. Bach is
really pretty much enough for me, but I'm easy. What about my
friends? It is like, say you have a small child who wakes up from
a nightmare and wanders around in the dark, calling for its parents. And the parents won't answer. They hide. The kids are having nightmares, and You hide.

Then in the dark her head is filled with slides: Willie wailing
in mourning for Jessie, closing the cafe. What will become of
Louise? She watches these slides in the dark. Is this, then, my
secret? That way deep down I really don't care about anyone else
but me? I do, I do, I try. I'm trying to learn, it's just that old joke,
I've been *sick*. But guilt and shame flood through her stomach.

She sits up in the dark, swallowing hard, turns on the light by
her bed, and hails Mary, full of grace. Then she sees Jessie last
year, with her hands on her hips, glaring at a woebegone Louise.

"God is bored *shit*less with your guilt," Jessie declared.

Louise gasped, then smiled. "I've never heard you swear
before."

"Well, la-di-*da*."

Joe Jones is on the beach in the late afternoon, when the sunshine is safer, reading a book by his favorite writer, Gerald Durrell. Four years before, when he and Louise returned from Hawaii, Fay sized up their tans with a face full of somewhat disgusted pity. "A tanned skin is a damaged skin," she announced. Louise had laughed her head off—Joe just shook his head. But, ever since, he has stayed off the beach until at least three. He smiles, thinking of Fay.

You know what she's like, Joe Jones? Louise said once. I mean, I'm really sort of fond of her, but talking to her is like throwing out topics for an improvisational troupe, only, instead of a skit, you get "Gack, gack, gack." Like, for instance, last year, remember. On the Fourth of July when we're all on the porch, waiting for the fireworks at Chrissie Field to begin: you, me, Willie, Jess, Georgia, Fay, Sam, Dana, Boone, and the Rednecks?

He's got to remember to tell his mother this story tonight.

It had been hotter than hell, day after day, crazily hot for the Bay Area, but that evening was cool, lovely in fact. The sky was band after band of crimson, the sky redder than it had ever been before, and the moon a lemon yellow, *bright* lemon. And we were all looking up at the sky, like some brilliantly lit spaceship was descending, except for Georgia who squinted at it, like maybe it was going to drop out of the sky and conk her on the head. Well, Fay shook her head and said, "It's all because of smog."

Several yards away on the beach, a handsome old man in his eighties or so who could be John Glenn's father turns over on his side to face the ancient old woman who lies on a towel beside him. Joe cocks his head and watches as the old man smiles at the woman, who is wearing a swimsuit with an accordion-pleated skirt, and beige butterfly wrinkle patches beside her eyebrows. He watches as the man bends forward to kiss the old woman on the lips.

Joe turns over on his belly and buries his eyes in his forearm.

Poor old lonely Joe. His back is already starting to burn, but he doesn't want to go home. He can't spend too much time alone with his mother. Maybe he should go into town by himself, hit the bars, see a show. There's a broken-down old movie theater, where skid row begins. He's been there before, it is cool inside, and the winos don't eat popcorn.

Louise laughs at him, shaking her head in the loving, fatherly way she has. But it ruins the *movie* for me, he pleads to Louise, the rustle of popcorn, the rustle of ice. I'm a magnet to people with large tubs of popcorn, and the bigger the tub, the bigger the soda. It's like having someone play maracas beside you during the movie: shush-shush-*shush*-shush-*shush!* Remember that time we went to the Surf, and the place was practically empty? And I say, mark my words, the popcorn eaters will find me. And you laughed. And then that enormous woman sits down, two seats away, with a shopping bag from Petrini's on her lap, from which she removes the camouflage lettuce, and the whole fucking bag is filled with popcorn. She's smuggled it in. Shush-shush-shush, shush! Shush!

You are so crazy, Joe Jones. Willie was constantly amazed. You're so goddamn crazy, Joe Jones, Willie says, endlessly amused, and then crawls onto Joe's lap light as a feather, his brother, his son.

"Where ya been?" his mother asks when he steps into the kitchen. He smiles at her. His father and mother lived in Washington, D.C., for five years, right after their wedding and used to go to an elegant seafood place twice a week. The maître d' was Jeeves, rarely said a word. Then the Joneses moved to Hawaii with their infant daughter Mary.

Twenty years later his daddy went Back East to bury a brother. He dropped by the seafood restaurant to have a quiet drink by himself, and the stuffy maître d' glances up briefly from his clipboard, behind the podium by the entrance, and asks him, "Where ya been?"

"On the beach reading," says Joe. His mother, dark and gaunt, comes over to him in the doorway, kisses him on the cheek, smoothes the lanks of brown hair off his forehead. He smiles, then hunkers down to unlace his sandy tennis shoes.

"Alice isn't doing so well today," she says.

"Did you go in to see her?"

"Yes, but they wouldn't let me in."

She studies her reflection in the mirror above the phone, preening.

"You're a fine-looking woman," he tells his mother.

They watch a Lakers game in the den after dinner. The Lakers are his favorite team in basketball. Magic and Kareem Abdul Jabbar. He can remember when Kareem was Lou Alcindor and watches him now lumber in that graceful way of his up and down the court. I just love him to pieces, Willie said once. Especially since he got those funny goggles. He looks like an underwater Doctor Seuss dude.

He sees himself smile apologetically at Willie, sees the wrath of God in Willie's eyes. Joe's shitfuck soul cringes.

Louise mewls and moans while reading the front page of the *Chronicle*. The world'll break your heart. God, don't let Boone get stolen, don't let Willie get AIDS. She reaches for her mug of coffee. After taking a sip, she replaces it on the short stack of unpaid bills that she is using for a coaster and turns her attention back to the paper. A small voice suggests that she move the cup, that one envelope will suffice. She means to but doesn't. The small voice clears its throat: Really, if I were you, I'd move it.

Well, you aren't.

She looks up wearily at the opened package of cigarettes that lies within spill range of the coffee cup. She yawns and looks back down at the paper. Then she reaches for the handle of the cup and knocks it over. "God!" she shouts, as she watches the coffee pour onto the bills, then rights the cup and jumps to her feet and spends the next five minutes mopping up.

What a stupid jerk you are! You saw that one coming up 101. She takes the pack of ruined cigarettes to the garbage bag under the sink, dripping coffee onto the floor and down her nightgown. She hurls the cigarettes into the bag, then stands with her hands on her hips, rolling her eyes: You just do the same stupid things over and over and over. You've done this before, you'll do it again. Now we're going to have to walk to the market for smokes. That's *just great.* Nice go, Louise.

She puts on blue jeans and a sweatshirt, tennis shoes, socks, and heads out the door. She is barely speaking to herself.

She thinks: Being me is just so *time consuming.*

Dark, elephantine fog crouches in the hills above the bay.

Half a block from the market, she approaches an old Volvo that has pulled off onto the shoulder. Its back left tire is flat. There is a woman in the front seat.

I'm not going to help you, she thinks. I would, but I'm in a bad mood.

Pretend not to notice her, Lou. Walk on. But she can't help peeking at the driver, who is a rather pretty woman of thirty or so, with fine dark hair heaped on top of her head, this bun held in place with an ivory chopstick. She is staring straight ahead. She holds her hands palms down and splayed, between her chest and the steering wheel. Louise stops. The woman looks like she might have just been shot through the hair by a pestering Indian's arrow while waiting for her nail polish to dry.

Louise raps on the glass. The woman turns ever so slowly. Her

eyes are blank, the color of tea, and she looks at Louise, as if trying to grasp why this carhop has brought her a chiliburger and
fries, when all she ordered was coffee.

Louise makes the spirally motion of *Roll down your window.*
"Have you called anybody for help?"

The woman shakes her head.

"Do you have Triple A?"

The woman shrugs.

"Do you have a jack? And a spare?"

There is a jack, a spare tire and a lug wrench in the trunk of
the Volvo. There are also science texts, a soiled hand towel, an
empty yogurt container, a broken Japanese vase, a rudimentary
microscope and a box of slides with smears in the center, a small
telescope, and a jar of what looks to be pond water, teeming with
former life.

"Here you go," the woman says, giving Louise the jack. Her
arms are trembling. The jack is too heavy for her. She can't weigh
more than ninety pounds. Her fingers are long for hands so
small.

"Gee, you have nice hands," says Louise.

The woman immediately balls them into fists.

"I think they're awful hands," she says. "But thank you."

"No, they're like the hands in 'somewhere I have travelled,
gladly beyond.'" Louise takes the lug wrench from her. "'Nobody,
not even the rain, has such small hands.'"

The woman smiles.

"My name is Eva. Eva Deane."

"My name is Louise."

"I can never thank you enough. I'm just helpless. I really can't
do anything at all."

Louise puts the jack in place.

"Sure you can," she says.

"No, honest, not one single thing."

Louise pumps the car off the ground, then turns to smile at Eva, who is watching intently, pigeon-toed, wringing the belt of her blue silk dress.

"Can you use a can opener?" Louise asks.

"No."

Eva is smiling at the ground, shaking her head.

Louise removes the hubcap, drops it on the ground where it circles and chimes, and starts loosening the lugnuts.

"Can you work a *lightswitch?*"

"Not very well."

"Are you a scientist or something? I noticed the microscope in your car. And the slides with googe all over them."

"I teach science in high school."

"What a wonderful job." She drops another lug into the hubcap, then turns and looks at Eva, watches for awhile. "You're just about the squirmiest person I ever saw." Eva smiles at the ground.

"Do you have a job?"

Louise pulls off the flat and lays it down.

"I didn't mean that the way it sounds."

Louise gets up off the ground and glances quizzically at Eva. She goes to the trunk for the spare.

"I mean, maybe you don't have a job, and you would just as soon not be grilled about it by a perfect stranger." Eva has a lovely, soft, clear voice.

"I have nothing to hide," says Louise, returning with the spare. "I work in the food industry. I'm the cook at Jessie's Cafe—you ought to stop by sometime." She puts the tire in place and dusts off her hands. When she bends down for a lug nut she notices Eva's shoes. They are fine, black, very high heels, glamorous. Louise shakes her head. "I wish I could wear shoes like that. I can't, though. They're like trying to walk around in ice skates. I guess I have weak ankles or something."

"Oh, you get used to it. You don't even think about it."

Louise is tightening the nuts with the lug wrench now.

"I bet you've got thousands of shoes."

Eva covers her mouth.

"You do?"

"I have sixty pairs."

"Wow! It's a *kink*, isn't it?"

"Yes."

When Louise is done, she gets up and wipes her hands on the sides of her jeans. Eva watches. Her face has fallen.

"Your hands are all nicked," she says.

"Oh, that doesn't matter. You get used to it when you work in the food industry."

"Thank you so, so much."

"You are so welcome."

"She had this teeny little nose," she says to Willie. "Slightly pug, in a becoming sort of way."

"That was so nice of you, Lou."

"Yeah, well."

"You're like the Good Samaritan. I mean, that's the sort of thing that gets you into heaven."

"Oh, yeah, sure, St. Peter will toss me a bale of hay, say, 'Here, you horse's ass.'"

"Lou."

"How's Jessie? When's she coming in?"

"She didn't say."

"I mean, is she totally fine?"

"Totally."

"What's she doing?"

"Prawley still hanging around the house, walling up the cats."

Louise smiled.

"Did that lady give you anything?"

"Who, Eva Deane? Nah. I told her to bring a bunch of her fattest, hungriest friends by for dinner."

"Eva Deane, Eva Deane. It sounds like something you give babies when they're teething."

Eva Deane, in front of her first-period class, feels like she is going to faint. "The Milky Way, as you know, is four starry spiral arms embedded in a disk of hydrogen gas...."

She has a can of tomato juice before second period and feels somewhat stronger. "One of the first abstract concepts a child learns is that, when its mother leaves the room, the mother still exists."

"She *does*?" someone asks.

Eva Deane smiles.

She's so weak again by third, her hands are trembling.

"Barry, what's a hormone?"

Barry Luchessi looks around, as if the answer is written on one of the walls. "Well," he asks, "it's like that *thing* that your body makes that—you know?—let's you know yer a *guy*."

Eva Deane smiles shyly, folds and refolds a slip of paper as if she's doing origami. She nods to Terry Weber, who clicks the next slide onto the wall.

"And here it is, ladies and gentlemen. A crystal of adrenaline. This is the emergency hormone," she says. She then walks slowly to her desk, sinks down into the chair, casually wipes the sheet of sweat off her unlined forehead, begins again to fold and unfold the slip of paper.

"Pfffffffftttttt."

"Be with you in a second, Georgia." Louise scrapes scrambled eggs from a pan into a bowl, turns to Georgia, and holds up a finger. "Just a minute, darling. Hey, Boone!" Boone is pushing his chair around the cafe with purpose and alarm on his face, muttering darkly. "Go sit with your daddy, my love. I've made you some *lovely* eggs." Boone pushes his chair over to the empty space at the table beside his father, who sits sketching a double-chined boat in his notebook.

"You're so good, Sam."

He smiles, this man of few words, fair and weedy, kind. He helps his son into the chair. Louise sets down the eggs, and Boone pats them with the back of his spoon. "What's that, duckie," she asks, pointing to the emblem on his polo shirt. He looks down at his left breast, ever so slowly, as if there's a big bug crawling towards his neck. "What is that, Sam? Running Jesus Sportswear?"

Sam smiles. "It's an eagle," he says.

"Where's Dana?"

"Visiting a friend in L.A."

"Pfft."

"Excuse me a minute. The chairman of our entertainment committee wants to see me."

Louise goes over to Georgia, who is standing unsteadily by the cash register. "Come with me. I'll show you to your table." Georgia stares at her—she's not going to budge—with eyes full of an almost superhuman intelligence. "What's the matter? Oh, *I* know. You want to know where Jessie is, huh?"

Georgia blinks.

"She's on her way. Willie just talked to her. Come and sit down. Give me your hand. And then I'll bring you some tea." Georgia's hand in hers is stiff and dry.

It's a long walk to the table Georgia shares with Jessie by the window—she keeps freezing, like a fawn in the middle of a midnight road.

"Kisses!"

"No!"

"KISSES FOR LOUUUUUEEEEEZZZZ!"

Louise is at the cutting board dredging cubes of lamb in flour for stew, when she first hears the squeal of brakes from the far end of the parking lot, then silence. Then what sounds like an outboard motor starting up, various vehicular screams, and as she stares out the window, Jessie's old Plymouth lurches and bucks into view.

Louise grabs the back of her neck, which is already stiffening up. It appears that the car is trying to throw Jessie, rodeo style, but she's got the wheel with her left hand like it's a pommel, and she stops the car in its tracks by throwing it into reverse.

"Willie?" Louise clears her throat. Willie appears from the back. "Your grandmother's having a little trouble parking." He comes to stand beside Louise, and they peer out cautiously at Jessie and her car, as if there is some possibility she is going to open fire on them.

She gets the engine running again. The two watch, spellbound.

"She's going to hit my car...."

"No, I think she'll miss it...."

"She's goin' to fuckin' ass *broad*side it—watch this."

Jessie has backed up enough to take another pass at parking alongside Louise's aged VW Beetle.

"I'll go out there and help...." Jessie is moving in reverse rather quickly, with that crazy-intent look on her face.

"You nuts, Willie. Fuck, man, she'll mow you down."

"I can't watch."

"SHE'S GOING TO RAM MY CAR."

The car creeps inexorably forward.

"Don't speed up, Jess," Louise coaxes. "Hit it *soft*."

"She's gonna ram it, Lou, you're right...."

At almost the very last second, right before she would plow into the passenger door, Jessie pulls the wheel hard right and eases into the space next to the Beetle. After a moment she steps out, both proud and humble, about to bow, as if to wild applause.

"Willie? I am simply not well enough for Jessie to be driving."

"Yeah, well, you want to tell her?"

"You've gotta tell her, and you've gotta tell her before she starts ramming *people*."

"I know but, goddam it, why now? I got *plenty* on my plate right now."

"Wellll, have a little more."

Jessie struts in, in her jerking jutting way. Georgia is giving her the eye.

"What's *that* look about?" Jessie asks, self-righteously horrified. "Do you have a *bee* in your bonnet today?"

"Hi, Grandma."

"Hello, Willie."

"I'm making shortbread for you and Georgia, today."

"Georgia, he's making us shortbread," Jessie intones, and she lowers herself into the empty seat beside her friend. She gazes lovingly at the dour old woman, then turns to Willie and exclaims, full of pride, "This woman eats like a horse!"

"When is *Dana* coming back?" Willie asks Sam several days later. Boone has been a brat, whining, crying, and sullen. Yesterday he threw a ball of Play-Doh at Georgia, hitting her square in the back, causing her to silently cry. Jessie took the boy and held onto him squarely, "Naughty, naughty boy!" And Willie took him into the back room for a conference: "Make nice with Georgia, Booneville. She's our friend." Boone glowered.

"I'm so sorry," Sam told the old woman, stroking her shoulder. Georgia continued to look pained and surprised, as if Boone had launched a javelin at her that had pierced her breastplate. Jessie fawned over her, peeping and cooing, all the rest of the afternoon.

Sam says he doesn't know when Dana's coming back, and then he shrugs nonchalantly.

"Darling? Mr. Mailman just came."

"That's nice, Lou."

"I mean, will you go out and get it? My hands are sort of full."

Willie gives the bills to Jessie on his way to the grill, where he hands Louise a white Crane envelope, postmarked Hawaii.

"At Alice's funeral, he heard the wet moan
of Alice's husband: *We was only married a
couple a years, but I'm sure gonna miss
that woman. We done everything together.
We was together every day.*
Behind dark glasses
He was safely crying
But not for Alice
Or her husband.
I sure do miss you, Louise."

"Lower than *worm sweat* man. That is *not* playing fair." Willie hands the letter back. "I refuse to discuss the matter any more."

"Willie? I want to live with a man for a long, long time...."

"So wait for a *good* one."

"I'm getting old."

"I'm laughin', Lou."

"Fifteen years older than you."

"Look, *I* want to live with a man. *I* don't want to wake up some day and be this old Liberace type, with a house full of *lap dogs!* and African violets. But you don't hear *me* mewling and puking about it. Maybe it's not in the cards. Maybe you'n *I* will end up growing old together. We'll sit on our porch and whack people on the shins with our canes."

"And can we get a doggie?"

"*Two* doggies."

"And will we live in canyon country?"

"If you stop crying we will."

"And we'll just read and be quiet and happy?"

"Happy as a bucketful of bunnies."

"And I can keep being Miss Takeover Broad? And you'll make me custards and strudel?"

Willie nods solemnly.

Jessie and Georgia sit bathed in a broad shaft of sunlight, watching tiny birds bounce around on the sill.

"You two want to make yourselves useful?"

Both of them look around for the sound.

"Will you two shell these peas for me?"

"We certainly will."

"I'll get you a bowl for the empty pods and a bowl for the peas."

Jessie pushes back the sleeves of her red cardigan, rubs her hands together in a conniving sort of way, and then gauges the peas for a moment as if they are a pool of water into which she is about to dive.

Georgia regards the peas, snorts at them.

Louise returns with two large bowls. "Put the peas in one, pods in the other."

"Peas in one, pods in the other."

After intense study, Jessie singles out a pod and lays it in front of Georgia, who nudges it with one finger, the way you might nudge a caterpillar to see if it is alive, then looks away.

"Take your time," Louise hollers from the grill. "Friday'll be fine."

Georgia looks at the pod in front of her and then around the room, like an eight-year-old left alone with a box of Band-Aids. After a moment she sighs and studies it, as if under pressure, *as if* she alone has the skill to dismantle this one particular pea pod. In very, very slow motion, she shells the peas, then holds the empty pod up to the sunlight, studying the veins like she's contemplating a slide of a cathedral.

Then she holds it out to Jessie.

"Pods in the other!"

After a moment, Georgia drops it into the pod bowl.

Jessie is on her third pod. Georgia, a job well done, reaches for her pack of Pall Malls.

"Shoemaker?" Jessie cries. "Stick to your last."

"Jessie's got a bee in her bonnet today."

"So would you, if you'd woken up on the floor of the bathroom."

"You gonna water, or should I?"

"I'm not into the plants today."

"It's your baby, Will. You put in the gardenias, you put in the wisteria, you put in the jasmine. *You* made our porch a real fairy dreamland...."

"*You* brought in those huge potted plants."

"So?"

"So, I'm not into 'em. It's like having a bunch of horses milling around on the porch. They give me the creeps."

"You gonna go out after work?"

"Maybe, yeah, prawley."

"Prawley? You gonna go to Smitty's?"

"Yeah."

"Gonna do a heart?"

Willie shrugged. "I hope not."

"You fukker."

"I *said* I hope not."

"But if you go there, you will. And I tell you over and over again what Duncan used to say: If you see a fin circling around in the water, there's *one* thing to do. Clear the area."

"Oh, fuck you, Louise."

"Fuck me, baby? Uh-uh, fuck *you*." She smiles. It is her favorite joke. The Pope is walking through the back streets of Rome when a ragamuffin approaches and asks for a light. "Oh, my *child*," the Pope exclaims, "you're much too young to be smoking." "Oh, fuck you," says the little boy. "What?! I am the spiritual leader of one billion people? The Bishop of Rome, the Vicar of Christ, the Successor of the Prince of the Apostles? And when I say, you are too young to smoke, you say to me, 'Fuck you'? Uhhhhh-uh, baby, fuuuuuck *you*!"

"That's us, isn't it," he says, somewhat later. She is at the grill, seasoning chili. He is fiddling with a Batman PEZ candy dispenser that she gave him for his last birthday.

"What is?"

"Anyone says to me, or you, or Joe, 'Fuck you,' and we go, 'Fuck *me*, baby? Uhhhhh-uh—"

"Fuuuuuck *you*."

She smiles.

"Pretty half-baked species," he says.

She is watching him wistfully when he sidles up to Jessie and Georgia, brandishing his PEZ dispenser, debonair as David Niven. "Can I interest you two ladies in an after-dinner PEZ?" Jessie's face crinkles up with love. Georgia at first looks alarmed, as if he is holding a squirt gun, and then she reaches a gnarled brown spotted claw out and tugs at the piece of candy that juts from Batman's neck. Then she lets her tongue slide out and receives the candy as if it is the Host.

Louise turns, smiles at the chili.

An hour later, opera on the radio, Jessie has stopped off at the bar on her way back from the bathroom and is flirting with the Rednecks. Willie is in the back, washing dishes. A shy fat nun named Sister Peter-Matthew sits by herself reading Gerard Manley Hopkins, absently picking at her second *crème brulé*. Louise is sitting on the porch with a cup of tea, smoking. She looks over her shoulder, through the window, into the cafe. Georgia, the old barn owl, gazes out at her. Louise winks. Georgia, owl-like, blinks. Louise assumes that Georgia had a stroke. Joe thinks she has taken a vow of silence.

Willie asked his grandmother once, Why won't Georgia speak?

I don't know, said Jessie, she's never told me.

A breeze blows in off the sea, bearing traces of gulls and seals, algae, boats, and fish. She closes her eyes to sniff it, imagining Joe beside her, she is crying, safely, behind dark glasses.

She turns to look at him, sighs.

The lights on the buoys blink red, green. She listens to the night birds, takes a sip of tea. Her eyes are full of tears. The moon tonight is the color of light-pink toy pearls.

She still dreads going home, dreads how quiet it will be, now that Joe is gone. She will go home and put on her pajamas and crawl into bed with a book, and will look up with a start from time to time. It is like when the bell has been ringing outside your window for years and suddenly stops, and you look around puzzled and wonder, What's that?

FIVE

J OE IS LYING ON THE COUCH listening to "Hungry Heart"
and eating Mint Milanos. He looks sad and slightly feverish, but there is also latent meanness in his face, like that of
an aging Doberman pup. When the cookies are gone, he caresses
the thick blond hair on his arm, blows on the hair like you'd blow
on a burn, but his own breath on his skin is too subtle, so he bites
himself on the wrist to make sure he is really there.

Every time I start to get comfortable, someone pulls the rug out
from underneath my feet. *Whap*, down again. Through high
school, for instance, my audience always cheered. I was an ath-
lete, the clown. Girls desired me. We went steady. I gave them my
ID bracelet: Joe Jones. I could get up on stage with my juggling
balls, shy but in slap-shoes, and juggle away, dazzle the crowd
and make them laugh. When conflicts came up, I knew what to
do; my daddy taught me to yield. It means two things, he said:
(a) to give way or give up, and (b) to produce and bear fruit. But
then, when high school ended, I get up there on stage, in my slap-
shoes, holding my juggling balls, and just as I am about to toss
the first one into the air, someone in the first row barks, "Wait a
minute. Enough *jug*gling already. We're in the mood for some-

thing else. Do you know any, say, German *lieder?*" And it's whap, down again.

Now the sky is European, the high clouds backlit by the sun, low clouds heavy and dark. The glassy jade bay could be reflecting grass. Small waves shingle the shoreline, slanting leftward in a smooth ripple like the legs in a chorus line.

Georgia keeps a directorial eye on the ducks, pelicans, egrets. Jessie watches a robin bob around on the sill outside the window, which is closed. "I love their little voices," she says, happy as the blind old man in *The Children of Paradise,* who loves mime.

"Darling, we don't need more desserts. The less people we have, the more desserts you make."

"Less people gives me more time."

"But it just doesn't make financial sense."

"I just feel compulsive, okay?"

"Okay."

"Lulu, don't touch the *pouf* paste."

"Lou?"

"The *pâté...à...choux!*"

Louise goes through the refrigerators, removing Pandorian jars and containers of dying angry former foods from the back. Her mind wanders from the task at hand.

You're afraid of commitment, Joe accused her, the second time she asked him to move out, three years ago. Just because I'm afraid of commitment doesn't mean we're right for each other, she said. No, look, Louise: You've got this *Muppet Movie* sense of life. Well, life ain't like that, baby. Life is messy. Life is blue. She looked about to cry. It wasn't that I went out with another woman, it's that you were waiting in a crouch for me to blow it *one more time,* as if I already had five personal fouls, one more and I'm out of the game. Because behind all your cute and your love and your faith is this garbagey passive aggression.

This hits her full in the belly and she jerks back from the shelves of the refrigerator, looking as if someone has just caught her reading his mail.

"Willie?"

"Yeah? Keep your mitts out of my frosting."

"Do you think I'm secretly bad?"

"I think you have more secrets than you like to cop to."

"But do you think I'm bad?"

"Yes, I do, Louise."

"Honest?"

"I think you're the Antichrist. I think if we shaved your head, your scalp would have *sixes* all over it."

"*Really?*"

"Get out of here, Louise. Leave me alone. I'm busy."

"Being mean to me won't increase your peace of mind."

"I have plenty of peace of mind. I'm just edgy."

Life is a rich old lady in a white beaded turban and pearls, who stares into her cup of tea like it's her move on a chessboard, who splutters, likes birds, and smokes Pall Malls.

Georgia looks up at Louise with dark marble eyes.

Louise has a memory of childhood, where her mother is in the kitchen, cooking up a storm, in the last minutes before the dinner guests arrive. Her mother's face is steaming, red. Louise is four years old. Her mother finishes basting a roast, pushes it back in the oven, closes the door, and dashes away, to *put on my face,* she says. Her daughter gets the chill. She sees a mask in her mother's vanity, which her mother will put on for the guests. Louise seeks out her father, who is hunkered down in front of the fire, jabbing the logs with a poker. Above him, on the mantel, framed ancestors peer down at her with disapproval. She wishes he would turn around and smile. She hears her mother's footsteps come, and doesn't want to look, but does, and sees the mask of thick flesh-covered makeup, the darting marble eyes lined in blue.

She remembers this only now, as Georgia turns away and stares at an oblivious Jessie, who is reading Emily Dickinson. Then she raises her hand to pat her beaded turban, the way you pat your hairdo into place. Louise bends down to kiss the nape of Georgia's neck. It smells like wildflowers pressed long ago between the pages of an old book.

She is standing at the grill stirring black bean soup, hailing Mary, wishing Joe would call. She hears Fay greet Jessie, warmly for Fay, and she turns from the grill to say hello.

"Hello, Louise."

"Fay," Jessie implores. "Willie's making cream puffs!"

Fay tries unsuccessfully to mask her disapproval. Louise smiles. This should be good—it always is with Fay, like some perverted word-association game. Mention oysters, fresh from Johnson's Oyster Farm, and Fay won't miss a beat: "Too much uric acid." Laugh happily at the hoodlum antics of the gulls, and she'll tell you about the diseases that lurk in seagull poop. Louise finds Fay strangely endearing.

"Sit wherever you like, my friend. Here's a lovely cup of tea." Fay smiles and sits down by herself near the bar.

"So, no cream puff today, huh?"

"Just my usual wheat toast."

"Is there some ugly cream puff incident in your past?"

Fay looks down into her lap, injured and prim, then twiddles the charms of her bracelet.

"I'm sorry, darling. Never mind. I'll go get your toast."

"I know I'm an easy target, Louise."

"You are an easy target, Fay, and I tease you too much, but I can't help myself. I mean, it's like, you know, you mention Willie's cream puffs to anyone else, and it's like, they think it's the reason they were created human beings instead of rain boots. But you mention them to you, and it's like they're carcinogenic."

Louise looks into the plain middle-aged face. "I'm sorry," she adds.

"I know, I know," Fay says.

"Was it a really, really bad experience?"

Fay manages an affable snicker. "Pretty bad," she says.

Boone lurches in wearing overalls and an Oakland A's cap.

"Weee!" he demands crossly.

"Willie's in the back, love. Kisses for Aunt Lou." She lifts him into the air, kisses his ear, and sets him down. He promptly falls over, and she sets him back on his feet. "Willie," she calls, "there's someone here to see you."

In a plaintive whisper, Boone asks her, "Weee?"

"*Boone!*" Willie lifts him into his arms, kissing him. "I made you *cream* puffs." Boone reaches toward Willie's blond lashes as Willie closes his eyes.

Sam sits down with Jessie and Georgia. When Louise looks over, the three of them are staring in silence out to sea, almost huddling. They might be in the waiting room of a hospital, waiting for surgery to be over.

"You okay, Sam?" Louise asks.

"Oh, yeah, just sort of . . . logy."

"I'll get you some coffee. Want one of Willie's cream puffs?"

"I don't know."

"Did you have bad sleeps?"

"Terrible sleeps." He sighs. "How come it's so slow today?"

"You got me, man. But I say don't look a gift horse in the mouth. I'm logy too—so is Willie."

Five minutes later twenty young sea scouts arrive for lunch.

"What can I get you," Willie asks, seating them at four tables.

Eighteen hamburgers. Three well done, nine medium, three medium well, three medium rare, twelve with American Cheese, three with cheddar, one with jack, two plain. Two on English muffins. One chili dog, one quesadilla. Nine Cokes, one with lemon, four chocolate shakes, one strawberry shake, one Mountain Dew, one Seven-Up, three milks, one root beer float.

"Anything else?" Willie asks, scribbling feverishly.

Thirteen orders of french fries, four onion rings, one bag of potato chips, one barbecued chips, and one Fritos.

Willie and Louise work in a well-oiled frenzy, tear back and forth like two balloons that are rapidly losing air, grilling, deep-frying, delivering condiment cups and mustard pumps and bottles of catsup, flipping burgers, draining fries, zizzing up milkshakes, pouring sodas, and—either from cream puffs or overstimulation—just when the orders are ready, Boone throws up.

When everyone leaves but Jessie and Georgia, Willie and Louise sit on the stoop in the sun with very strong cups of tea. Willie massages his temples. Louise stares at the birds and the boats on the bay, smoking one of Georgia's Pall Malls, puts her head on Willie's shoulder, and closes her eyes.

Has she gotten today's letter? Joe wonders.

In the garden, wine-red orchids glisten.

He puts a trigger nozzle on the green garden hose and turns it on. Water springs forth pyrotechnically, almost white, and he backs away from the orchids as if they are a petrified bank teller, turning to spray from the birds of paradise. "Spraaaay me," he and Mary cry on hot summer days, and their father turns from his orchid bushes and whips the nozzle up and down so his children can chase down and through the atomized rainbow. Squealing, they slip on the wet green grass, and Edwin hoses them down, hoses muddy rivulets off their skinny brown legs.

Joe remembers pitchers of pink lemonade, pitchers of Kool-Aid, slapping mud into patties, dirt-clod wars.

He can remember the design on a glass container in which his mother used to pack potato salad for their picnics, and he can remember perfectly what his third-grade teacher's Guatemalan purse looked like, and he can remember the smell of Mary's freshly starched dresses being ironed, but is now straining to remember the name of his mother's father.

He turns the hose on the tree ferns. Underneath are the pink ginger, torch ginger blue. I honest to God can't think of my grandfather's name.

It's been replaced, says Louise.

Lou? What's the difference between a second cousin and a first cousin once removed?

Used to know, Joe, but it's been replaced.

I used to know all this stuff about planets, she says, all this stuff about the Peloponnesian War, like how to spell it, for instance. But that stuff's all been replaced with more immediate data, like, you know, to remember to take off my socks before I get in the shower.

She shakes her head.

"Dear Louise: there is a terrifying new group of people around who've just come to my attention. I saw them first in a piano bar and grill on Diamond Head. Now I see them everywhere I go. I can't guess at their numbers. They always sit in groups of five, and they look like blind people, but aren't. They almost never wash their hair, and *all they eat is French bread and Coca-Colas.* I call them the Mole People.

"They're everywhere, dolly. Be careful out there. You take a shirt in to be dry-cleaned, say, and no one's behind the counter. You ring the bell for service, and out they come, sipping on Coca-Colas, with French bread crumbs in the creases of their mouths.

"I worry that I will come in from the beach, open a beer, go to the lanai, and the Mole People will be sitting there sipping Cokes. They won't hardly bother to look up, chawing down my mother's French bread.

"I love you, miss you, need you, and I am sorry. Joe Jones."

"Vaguely funny," Willie says, handing the letter back to Louise.

Louise and Willie are playing gin around four at Jessie's table by the window. Jessie is reading poetry aloud to Georgia, Emily Dickinson's "A Narrow Fellow in the Grass." "There Came a Wind Like a Bugle," "That Love Is All There Is, Is All We Know of Love." Georgia listens reverentially, with her eyes closed and her head thrown back, an emaciated empress dowager whose face is being pummeled by hurricane winds.

There is a sudden knocking on the porch. Louise looks up. Eva Deane is walking up the steps of the cafe and then across the porch, staring down at her pigeon-toed feet in gorgeous white high heels. "That's her," she says softly to Willie, "Eva Deane, the woman I fixed the tire for."

Eva appears in the doorway and stops, stands wringing her hands with shy Woolfian dignity, so *sorry* to be such a bother.

"Eva?" Louise inquires. Eva looks up and smiles.

"Hello. I'm sorry, I...uh..."

"Why should you be sorry? Come in and meet my friends." Eva looks up at all of them apologetically and begins to trace the lifeline of her left hand. Louise stands and pulls out the empty chair on the other side of Willie, then goes to stand by Eva.

"I, uh…" Eva reaches into the purse that hangs from her shoulder, then changes her mind and looks beseechingly at Louise. "Hi," she says.

"Hi! Listen, I would like you to meet Georgia—Georgia, this is my friend Eva Deane."

"Hello."

Georgia blinks and looks over at Willie with an expression that suggests they've got a real lulu on their hands here. "And Jessie, this is Eva."

Jessie claps her hands together once. *"Eva!"* she enthuses.

"And this is my best friend, Willie, Jessie's grandson."

"Hey," Willie smiles. "Nice to see you. You want me to get you a cup of tea, or'd you rather have coffee?"

"I can't stay."

"Honest?"

"Those are such beautiful shoes," says Louise.

"Why can't you stay?" Willie demands.

"I have to be somewhere in fifteen minutes."

"Where?"

"Willie! Mind your own business." Jessie glares at him.

Eva glances unhappily at her purse and begins to squirm. Louise watches her patiently. Then Eva begins to stammer and stutter, is trying to blurt out the reason she is here. Willie says— after Eva leaves—that he guessed she'd come to tell Louise that her flat tire had given Louise gonorrhea.

She has brought Louise a small box wrapped in cranberry silk the way Buddhists wrap the ashes of their dead. Louise removes the silk and lifts the lid a crack, peering in as if maybe the box houses a frog.

"Apricot lotion," she says. "That is so nice of you."

"*To*tally nice," Willie declares.

Eva smiles.

Frail, rangy, she stands worrying the cupped palm of one hand with the finger and thumb tips of the other, like she's speaking to the blind, deaf, and dumb. Georgia watches this with wide penetrating eyes, waiting for Eva to fling up her hands, freeing the canary.

The next time she comes in, several days later, Eva brings tulips and stays for a cup of tea.

She sits with Jessie and Georgia, making a pleated fan with her napkin, glancing over at Louise at the grill, as if to assure her that she will be leaving soon.

Willie minces over, drying his hands on a towel. "I just *love* your shoes; oh, they are *totally* to *die* for. Can I sit down with you?"

"Of *course.*"

"So tell me. What'd you have for lunch today?"

"Willie?" Louise calls. "Don't do the Senate Investigating Committee routine on her."

"Bug out, sluthead. Stir your soup." Then he smiles prettily at Eva. "So, tell me. What'd you have?"

"Yogurt?" she asks.

"Brand?"

"Yoplait."

"Flavor?"

"Lemon."

"Anything else? Anything else you might wish to declare?"

Eva smiles into her lap. "Raisins."

"Sunmaid? In a little red box?" Eva nods. "Those are like your pick of the litter raisins. The grape growers had a horrible season this spring. Too much rain—all the grapes got *bunch* rot. That's what they really call it—*bunch* rot."

Eva covers her mouth as she laughs.

Later Willie tells Louise, "That's what Joe has, *bunch* rot." Louise smiles. "You know why I like Eva so much, Louise? Because she's like *to*tally a lady. She's just so *neat*, you know, she makes me want to start being shy."

Eva is in the shade of an old oak tree, hiding behind its trunk with a pair of binoculars hanging from her neck. From time to time she wipes the sweat off her forehead, raises the binoculars to her eyes, and leans around the trunk to peer at the activity in the park. At the seesaw where a mother croons "Seesaw, Marjorie-daw" as she and her young son go up and down. At mothers and children, fathers and children, in swings over bark chips, in circles doing "Ring Around the Rosie," crumpling to the ground like their bones had turned to dust.

A middle-aged man in gray flannel walks by, wearing a young woman on his arm like an expensive watch. Eva ducks behind the tree, wipes her forehead, closes her eyes, tries to catch her breath. When she opens her eyes, a royal black girl of three or so is standing two feet away, solemnly sucking a melting Missile Bar—swirls of red, orange, yellow. The girl's eyes are as black and shiny as French roast coffee beans.

Eva says hi. The girl turns away and bolts. Eva closes her eyes.

Eva sits in a waiting room, drumming her nails on the coffee table. She hears the basset hound in *Montenegro* clicking his way across the linoleum towards the bowl of poisoned milk.

"Mrs. Deane? Right this way."

Forty-five minutes later, she steps outside again, with dumb awe on her face like a kitten who is staring out the front door for the first time, gaping at the infinite dome of sky, at trees, flowers, shrubs, and birds.

The Mole People arrive at eight.

Five of them trudge into the cafe. They have dirty hair and sleepy eyes. Louise can smell marijuana from across the room, it smells like a burning sofa.

Willie's eyes widen in alarm. Louise smiles. The cafe is almost empty. Willie lumbers over to their table.

"Some Cokes to start out?"

Three of them have already grabbed for the French bread, Willie reflexively licks at the corners of his mouth.

They order a pitcher of beer, and five orders of fries.

Willie goes to the back room after bringing them the fries. He peers around the doorway from time to time and watches them eat—it's like they're consuming their own fingers.

Later he asks Louise, "Could Georgia be their leader?"

"Worldwide?"

Louise shrugs, then seems to notice for the first time that Willie is stirring batter.

"Now what are you making? I want to close *up* pretty soon."

"Peach cobbler. Hand me the vanilla."

"You're compulsing out, man."

"You're right."

Louise watches him work. He's getting so good with puff pastries and Danish, he can't stay at Jessie's forever, a couple more years, he'll be at L'Etoile.

The possibility blind-sides her. Her eyes fill with tears—she couldn't cope without him.

When Willie doesn't look up, she sniffles.

"Oh, God! No more! Enough already! Jesus, Louise, he's not fit to drink your *bath*water. He's—"

"That's not—"

"Hand me the sugar tin, please. God it was a *drag*. The guy was *al*ways in pain and stop toying with your hair, Louise. I don't want a bunch of *follicles* in my batter."

"I wasn't—"

"It was just babyish overreaction, every few days, it was like 'Wolf here again, Joe?'"

"I WASN'T EVEN THINKING OF JOE JUST THEN."

"Then why are you crying?"

"We've still got half the cream puffs left."

"And you're crying 'cause I'm making more desserts?"

"I don't know. Everything's off right now, all right? All this weird shit is happening all at once."

"Like what?"

"I don't know, it's just *off*, I can smell it. It's like smoking with your left hand. It doesn't *feel* right."

"You prawley just need to get laid."

"DON'T YOU DARE EVER SAY THAT TO ME AGAIN."

"Okay."

"I really can't *stand* men."

"Oh, you *wor*ship the ground on which I walk."

Louise sighs, tucks her belly back down into the top of her pants.

"I think I'll try to go on a diet again."

"Don't go on a diet. Hand me the cinnamon."

Louise looks over her shoulder and down at her ample bottom.

"I've got steatopygia."

"No, you don't have steatopygia."

"I look like a fuckin' *Hot*tentot," she says. Willie rolls his eyes, stirs his batter.

"I could carry *cock*tails around on my butt," she says. He smiles. "'Here you go, sir—you had the Keoki coffee?'"

"Ohhhh," Willie moans. "I made you be *fun*ny again."

Louise drives Jessie home that night. Willie stays behind to finish his cobbler.

"I'm tired, Louise," Jessie says.

"I'm beat, too."

"We did well today, didn't we."

"Yeah. The sea scouts pushed us over the top."

"Will that nice thin woman be back?"

"Eva, you mean? I think so."

"I haven't seen her in *so* long."

Louise smiles to herself, drives along. The bright new moon hangs over the city.

Louise, in a long flannel nightie, rubs apricot lotion into her hands and crawls into bed. She is asleep in four or five minutes. Three hours later she is dreaming of Joe when the phone by her bed begins ringing.

No, she thinks. Don't be ringing.

It rings.

Please stop ringing, she thinks, but when it doesn't, she grog-gily reaches for it.

"Hello."

"Hi."

"*God*, Willie. It's after one. What's wrong?"

"I'm sorry."

"What do you want?"

"I've got a heart."

"Well, throw it in the toilet, for Chrissake."

Dead air.

Louise sits up in bed, rubbing her eyes.

"What do you want *me* to do about it?"

"I don't know."

"Where are you? Why is it so loud?"

"Smitty's. I just came to play a couple games of pool."

"You fuckin' asshole, Willie. You knew you'd get some speed tonight. You fukker."

"Don't be mad."

"Well, I *am* mad and I was trying to sleep."

"Call you tomorrow."

"What, are you going to take it?"

"I don't know."

Louise kneads her forehead, sighs, gives the finger to the ceiling. "What, are you loaded?"

"Sort of."

"You want to come over?"

Willie, on the other end, exhales noisily.

Louise's shoulders sag.

"Take a cab. I'll leave the door unlocked."

Louise's front door opens ten minutes later, she hears Willie's footsteps in the hall. He steps into her room a minute later, bedraggled, drunk, sheepish. Louise is sitting up in bed, arms folded across her chest, scowling, but shaking her head, so he knows he's already forgiven.

"I can smell you from *here*, man. What've you been eating?"

"Lou?"

"I'm not kidding, my love. You smell like African *goat* cheese."

Willie shuffles over and sits on the corner of the bed. He looks like a little boy, he looks like a very old man.

"Come get under the covers. It's cold out there."

He kicks off his shoes, not yet meeting her eyes, crawls into bed beside her, and covers his eyes with his hand.

"What are we going to do with you, ducks?"

"I don't know."

"Did you throw it out?"

"Yeah."

"Honest?"

"No."

"Where is it?"

"In my pocket."

"Go throw it in the toilet."

Willie tugs at his cowlick.

"Give it to me then. I'll do it."

He reaches in his pocket and hands her the tiny pink heart.

She stares at it, climbs out of bed, and walks down the hall to the bathroom, where she almost drops it in the toilet.

Then—*what are you doing, Louise?*—she stands studying it for a minute, looks over her shoulder to make sure that Willie isn't standing in the doorway watching, and drops it into a drawer. She reaches to flush the toilet and closes the drawer.

She goes back to her bedroom and crawls into bed. Willie turns over on his side, watching her. She looks away at first.

"So. Shall I make you a cup of tea?" He shrugs, sad and dissipated. "Or you want a beer?"

"Want to split one?"

"Yeah. I'll be right back." Walking to the kitchen, she imagines that she can hear the heart beating softly in her bathroom drawer, boomp-boomp-boomp-boomp-boomp, can hear it in the hallway, can hear it when she's back in bed with Willie, the tiny pink heart of speed that she doesn't want but did not throw out. She takes a sip of beer and passes the can to Willie. Then she stares off into space for a minute.

"I'll be right back," she says, "I have to pee."

When she opens the bathroom drawer the heart goes BOOMP-BOOMPBOOMPBOOMPBOOMP, and she picks it up gingerly, rolling it between her fingers. She hasn't had one of these since her early days with Joe. After a minute, she puts it back in the drawer, turns to leave, and then, shaking her head with exasperation, picks it up again and flings it into the toilet.

"All day it was like this gremlinny *mag*net. I couldn't cook it away."

Louise nods.

"I'm just so fucking weak, Louise."

"No, you're not, my love."

"Yes, I am. Sometimes."

"You ever try praying? For willpower, strength?"

"No. I'd just be faking it. Talking to the walls."

"Is that what you feel?"

"Uh-huh."

"Well, you've never had a child who was really, really sick."

Silence.

"That's when I learned to pray, my love."

"But it didn't do any good. If there was a God, why didn't He let your baby live?"

"I don't know. I can't answer that."

Willie bows his head and starts to cry.

"I just get so fucking *sad*, Louise."

"Oh, I know. I know, Willie, I really do."

"How did you keep on going when he died?"

"I don't really remember now. It was so long ago. I guess it was just like someone said, you know—patch, patch, patch."

S I X

"COME HERE, COME HERE," the Rednecks call from the bar. On TV there's a tape of a bar mitzvah that had been videoed live.

Behind a candle-lit altar, a chubby cherubic boy reads from the Torah. His father and the rabbi stand behind him. Off to the side are his mother and sister, both in formal white dresses decked with lace, and—in a suit—his little brother, a scrawny boy of maybe ten with an elongated evil Mona Lisa smile and a dodgy look in his shifty eyes.

"The little guy is Herschel," one of the Rednecks says.

The camera pans the family as the older boy continues reading: first the father, then the mother, then the sister, then Herschel, who hooks his baby fingers into the corners of his mouth and pulls a jack-o'-lantern smile.

The camera jump-cuts away.

Now there's a close-up of Herschel's older brother, who innocently keeps on reading, until a bony branchlike arm reaches into the screen and lands on his yarmulke. The boy freezes as Herschel's hand slowly pushes the yarmulke down over the brother's forehead and down past the tip of his nose.

Louise and Willie howl.

The Rednecks have wonderful, burbling laughs, like wine being poured from a bottle.

She has seen the Herschel look before—the protracted Mona Lisa mouth, the artful shifty eyes—has seen it in Georgia, has seen it in Boone. Now, looking back, she also sees it in God, sees how He effects his Rube Goldberg machinations with a sweetly evil leer. She thinks that God was smiling this way when she knocked the cup of coffee over onto her cigarettes several weeks ago, at about the time He had Eva's car tire go flat.

Coincidental? her Uncle Duncan used to ask, waggling his eyebrows.

Eva has been coming to the cafe nearly every day at three. She stays about an hour drinking tea, grading papers, and poring over science textbooks. Willie and Louise listen for the knock of her high heels on the porch. She's like a wild kitten to them, with her feral shyness, her amber eyes, and those busy, busy fingers. They're taming her, by teasing her, by little and by little.

"So whadjew have for lunch today?" Eva makes a ring with a napkin. "You had yogurt again, didn't you. I can tell these things. Lemon again? Gack! It's the most screaming nellie flavor in the world."

"Willie, leave her alone."

"Why don't you ever eat a more *manly* yogurt, like boysenberry?"

Eva's a good sport. When Jessie asks, "Did I do alligator pears for you?" Eva shakes her head and smiles at her encouragingly, even though she's got a stack of tests to grade.

"It goes 'IIIIIIIIIII've got algator pears.' *Al*ligator pears, you see. Avocados."

Eva picks daintily at imaginary lint on her sleeve until the street vendor call is over, then shakes her head in wonder.

The books that she brings to study are full of amazing pictures. "Wow, what is *that?*"

"Oh." Eva looks up from a textbook, busies herself by folding a napkin into a duodecimo. "It's the surface of Io, one of Jupiter's moons. The black spots are volcanos."

"Too much, man. Willie! Come here! Eva's got a photograph of the volcanoes on one of Jupiter's moons!"

Another day it is a photograph of a wasp's nest.

"It looks like paper."

"It is, Louise. They make their own. They chew up wood fibers and make a paste from them."

"Too much."

"Is honey really bee barf?" Willie asks.

Eva smiles, nods her head.

"See, I told you so, Louise."

"It's a miracle."

But a wild show-stopping confusion passes over Eva's face all the time, a look Louise has seen on Joe when he has a major attack of Heart Awareness. The first time she saw it on Eva, they were on the porch, on the shadowy sunlit porch. The bay was the soft dark gray of Willie's eyes, and when a great blue heron passed overhead, Louise applauded for a minute and then said, "Shouldn't this just be enough, to live in a land where herons fly by, where there are herons and egrets and pelicans?" But on Eva's face was a look as though she were both immobilized and bolting.

"Is something wrong, Eva?"

"No. No." She blinks and takes a deep breath. "I just remembered something."

"Something's really bothering Eva."

"*Please* don't touch my meringues. *I* don't know where your fingers have been. Tomorrow or the next day I'm going to make Eva a Key lime pie. She seems to like citrus-y things."

"Did you ever notice how sad she looks sometimes?"

"She's just shy."

"No. There's some major sadness in there."

"Well, maybe—I didn't really notice."

"She looks like Joe does when he's having one of his heart attacks—that abrupt panic."

"It's really bad," Willie says, perfectly mimicking Joe. "It's really bad this time, man. It's like, *heart* cancer."

Louise smiles.

"Remember that time he started to get a head cold, he calls here and I go, 'How you doin', Joe,' and he goes, 'I'm sick as a dog, man, I've got a cold—I've got like *two* colds, man.'" Louise smiles. "He gets a *head* cold and he's like in the Near Room."

"*Eva* goes to the Near Room. I can see it in her face."

"You think it's that bad?"

"Uh-huh."

Muhammad Ali went to the Near Room, when he had been hit too hard in the ring. Through a half-open door he saw a room with orange and green neon lights, where alligators played trombone and snakes were screaming.

Joe Jones sits waiting for a bus on a bench outside a doughnut shop. He looks like he is terribly late for something. He sniffs the doughnut fumes, looks over his shoulder at the shop, and five minutes later boards the bus carrying thirteen doughnuts in a pink box, a baker's dozen.

He gets a seat by the window in the back, across the aisle from a little girl who is sitting on her mother's lap.

He opens the box, selects a jelly doughnut, and gobbles it down. While chewing the last of it he reaches for a maple bar. The little girl tugs on her mother's sleeve.

"Don't stare," the mother says.

Now he's eating a glazed doughnut, and a minute later, another jelly.

The little girl watches him lift the lid of his box. She looks like she thinks there's a decapitated head inside, her mouth hanging open.

He reaches back into the box for another glazed, as casually as if reaching for a potato chip, and devours a chocolate-covered doughnut before the little girl's bugging eyes.

She tugs on her mother's sleeve.

Her eyes begin to loll around in her head when he reaches for another jelly. She and Joe are both beginning to overheat rather badly by now. He wipes the sweat off his forehead with one hand, reaches for another glazed with the other. Joe Jones' eyes are begging to cross—it feels like there are twenty pounds of putty in his trunk.

Several mornings later Louise is at the grill going, *Agnus Dei qui tollis peccata mundi... dona nobis pacem*, but every time she gets to *peccata* she sees a pan of veal. She is wishing Willie would arrive. It is nearly noon. She pours a cup of pearl barley into the soup and adds a dash of cumin, sees herself sneak out to the pay phone to call Joe, lying by not mentioning it to Willie. It's nuts to be wanting Joe, it's like Willie wanting speed. I'm tired of sleeping alone. I'm tired of doing the same thing all day every day, not making that call.

"One must imagine Sisyphus happy."

Oh, fuck You.

Fuck Me, baby? Uh-*uh. Fuuuck you.*

Well it *is* like that, trying to get over him, like pushing a rock uphill all day, knowing it will roll back. Can't You make it not roll back on me?

I can send you some people to serve, Whatever It is says. That's about all I can do.

"Morning, Fay."

"It's awfully cold in here."

Louise bristles. *You want me to go catch a dog and cut it open so you can stick your hands inside?* Wait, wait, wait! *There isn't anyone out there who isn't Seymour's Fat Lady.*

"Let me get you a cup of tea."

Don't you know that goddamn secret yet? Don't you know who the Fat Lady really is?

"Here, Fay. Put my jacket on."

"Thanks, but no—"

"Fay? Put it on or I'll break your nose."

After a moment Fay puts on the proffered coat.

"Better?"

Fay nods.

A morbid hunger to call Joe beats inside her. It is really bad today. She stirs the cassoulet, she waits for Willie.

"Hey, lovey. There you are."

"Sorry I'm late, Louise."

"Where's Jessie."

"Out in the car, brooding."

"What's the matter?"

"She's just got a big bee in her bonnet today."

"Kisses for Lou."

"David called."

"Give me a kiss. Thank you. Who's David?"

"That Gays Against Brunch guy."

"Oh, right. Good!"

"He's talkin' about getting tickets for Charles Pierce. At the Venetian Room."

"Willie, God, you lucky duck."

"They're late shows, I can go after work."

"Oh, boy, are you in heaven?"

"More or less."

"I'm so happy for you."

"I don't have a *thing* to wear."

"Wear the red taffeta, dolly."

"Oh, but it pooches out around my hips."

"Well, the burgundy tulle, then."

"He's really neat, Louise. He's really gentle, and he laughs at all my jokes. And he kisses just like me."

"How do you mean?"

"Well, I think I kiss like a fat person."

She smiles. "How do fat people kiss?"

"Oh, you know. Slow."

Jessie is still out in the car half an hour later, with her bottom lip jutting out all the way and her arms crossed across her chest. She is tapping her foot with impatience when Louise slides in on the driver's side.

"What's the matter, Jess?"

Jessie sticks her lip and jaw out even farther.

"You could dislocate your jaw if you keep that up."

Jessie is blinking back tears.

"Tell me what's wrong."

"What's Willie doing," Jessie sneers.

"Making potato salad."

"I could brain him."

"What's he done?"

"What?"

"What's Willie done?"

"*What?*"

"Why are you mad at Willie?"

"I'm not mad at you, Louise, I'm mad at Willie."

"Why?"

"Did you say something?"

"*I asked, why are you mad at Willie?*"

"I can't hear you, Louise. I can't hear you because Willie *rushed*

me this morning and I forgot my hearing aid. So you can sit there
chattering like a monkey for all I care."

"Let me go get Willie's keys, I'll run you home."

Louise has been sitting in the car for fifteen minutes, at the curb
in front of the big cottage where Jessie and Willie live, feeling
more and more exasperated. Finally she gets out and goes into
the house.

Jessie is lying on her bed, looking up at the ceiling, with a
Siamese asleep on her chest and three mongrel cats lying beside
her. The room is flooded with sunlight, pale yellow gold.

"Jessie, are you napping?" Louise approaches the bed. "Jessie?"

Jessie stares at the ceiling as if through a window at something
far away.

"*Jessie.*"

"Is this where they bring you when you die?"

"No, darling, this is your *bed*room."

"Louise?"

"Yes. I'm right here."

Jessie finally locates Louise and squints at her.

"Is this where they bring—oh, wait. Oh, dear." She glances
around at the dresser, the photos of her family, the plants, the cat
on her chest. "Am I as crazy as I think I am?"

"Oh, Jessie, my love."

"Oh, Willie, guess what happened," Louise whispers in the back
room.

"Joe called."

"Nooo. I went in to get Jessie because she'd been in the house
for like ten minutes, and I found her on the bed, and—she
seemed like she was asleep, but she was awake, and she thought
she was in the room where they bring you when you've died."

"Is that what she said?"

Louise nods. "She's fine now. She insisted she wanted to come back here. As soon as her hearing aid was in, everything seemed more or less back to normal. But maybe we should call her doctor."

"Yes, I guess. Shit." Willie looks away, exhales noisily. "She was prawley just napping, dreaming."

"Yeah."

"I should call her doctor."

"Yeah. Call him, now."

Willie reaches for the phone, begins to dial.

"Joe really did call, Louise. He said he'll try tomorrow."

"Joe really called?" The elevator has stopped too quickly.

"The doctor said to watch her for a couple of days. To bring her in if she, you know, seems extremely tired or disoriented."

Louise licks her lips, nods, raises her brows in relief.

"So, uh, when did Joe call?"

"About ten minutes after you left."

"What did you say?"

"I said if he ever called again..."

"No, honestly."

"I said you were taking Jessie home to get her hearing aid and you'd be back in like fifteen minutes. But he said he'd try again tomorrow—he was headed out the door or something."

She bites her bottom lip.

Louise sits on the stoop at four eating a cheeseburger. A grand old bag lady of a houseboat chugs slowly past. It is an old tugboat with a big hat of rooms built on, one the greenish blue of Hubbard squash, one orange, one purple. It has a tall red smokestack and lace in the windows. On the deck are oilcans, oars, potted plants, a hound dog, and a little red wagon. That's how I want to be, a bag-lady tug on the green bay.

There's a streak of mist in the sky, a ladder. Remember Mrs. Turpin in Flannery O'Connor's story "Revelation" when she sees the purple streak in the crimson Georgia sky? She sees a bridge, remember? Souls rushing up to heaven. First in line are the white trash, Negroes in white robes, freaks, and psychopaths, and they're hooting and hollering and whooping it up, and the last to go up the ladder are people like the Turpins, the respectable people, the people with virtues, who march sadly in a quiet orderly file up the ladder, their moral excellence stripped away as they climb.

Joe fills her head.

You're like Mrs. Turpin, Lou.

I can't help it, I've been sick.

Lou? Let me ask you something. My mother says most women don't enjoy sex, that most of them pretend to, but that—

Joe, yo mama lied.

He said he'd call tomorrow, call tomorrow, call tomorrow. I'm going to go nuts, though, God. You fukker. She smiles.

Eva walks in a pigeon-toed tiptoe up the dirt walkway to the stoop where Louise sits smoking.

Louise gasps. "*I* know you."

"Oh, hi, Louise," she apologizes.

"How you doin'? How come you're so late? Georgia's half out of her mind."

"I left my purse at school. I had to go back."

"How could you forget your purse? I mean, God, it's like leaving your uterus somewhere."

Eva covers her mouth and laughs.

"Here, have a seat." Eva sits on the step beside her, and they stare out at the bay. "It's so pretty right now. Did you have a nutty day?" Eva nods, smiling. "There's something in the air. It was *King of Hearts* around here. It's finally quieting down."

"What happened?"

Eva listens with her hands folded in her lap as Louise tells her about Jessie and the room where they bring you when you die.

Eva moans, soft and low.

"Did you take her to the doctor?"

"No. She hates him. She calls him Old Stone Face."

"How does she seem now?"

"Fine."

"I could run her in to my doctor. He's wonderful."

"That is so sweet of you, Eva, but I don't think she'll go."

They stare out at the water for a while.

"Okay, then what happens is, Willie makes two Key lime pies for you, and Boone totters over to watch them cool, and the next thing we know he's planted a grove of cigarette butts in one of them." Eva shakes her head and chews on her bottom lip. "The Rednecks have been swilling down beer all day, waxing philosophic."

"What do they say?"

"They say, 'Don't cost no more to feed a purdy girl than an ugly one.'"

"Ah."

"Nope. And then, moving right along, about an hour ago an extremely tense Muslim arrives, tosses down some sherry, then starts *raving* at Jessie. She's sitting there with Georgia, reading Thomas Merton. Georgia's keeping watch over the ducks outside the window, and suddenly the Muslim shouts, 'Hindus are vapid!' Well, Jessie looks up from her book, peeping and cooing, and he hollers, 'They are water! And you Christians are *fire*.' Jessie's peeping and going, 'Oh, dear.' And the guy shouts, 'We Muslims take the fire, pluuuunge it into water. WE MUSLIMS ARE STEAM!' And Jessie's looking at him like, how mad *is* this guy— then she looks to Georgia for help, but Georgia's sitting there looking like someone's just jammed something up her *boom-boom....*"

"Then what happened?"

"Well, then Jessie starts to tell *him* where the cow found the cabbage with *righteous* indignation, but he just dusts off his hands and leaves."

Eva shakes her head, smiling.

"Eva, darling." Jessie puts down the book she is reading, tilts her head, beams at Eva. Georgia looks at Eva as if she might burst into derisive laughter if she didn't have such good manners. She has to concentrate on lighting a Pall Mall to keep from laughing. Louise smiles, shaking her head, rolls her eyes.

"Tea! I'll get you some tea."

"Thank you."

Jessie raises her closed book in a toast to Eva. "Can you sit with us today?"

"I've got a lot of reading to do. I'd better sit alone."

"No, I won't hear of it. We'll be quiet as church mice, won't we, Georgia?"

Georgia slowly turns to give Eva the Herschel look.

Eva sits down at the table.

"Eva, guess what, I made you some Key lime pies and Booney put cigarette butts in them."

"Oh, I heard," Eva moans, clasping her hands to her chest.

"But there's a couple good pieces left, you want some?"

"Maybe I could take some home with me?"

"She's trying to read," Jessie says.

"Oh, bug out, Granny. So whadjew eat for lunch, Eva?"

"Cottage cheese with pineapple."

"God! That's like so Tricia Nixon. I heard this comic go, 'Who invented cottage cheese—and how'd they know when it was done?'" Eva closes her eyes when she smiles. "So don't leave without a piece of pie or I'll be very, *very* angry. Okay?" Eva smiles, nods. Willie turns and leaves.

"Hey, Lulu," one of the Rednecks calls from the bar.
  "Hey, what."
  "We need some more brewskis."
  "Okay."
  She heads over to the cooler behind the bar.
  "You're a great-lookin' broad. I *like* 'em big."
  Louise smiles, she opens three bottles of Bud.
  "And baby?"
  "Yeah?"
  "S'long as I got a smile on my face, you got a place to sit down."
  Louise throws back her head and laughs. She puts the bottles on the bar in front of them, instantly imagines telling Joe, then catches herself and frowns.
  She lowers the heat under the black turtle beans, tastes the cassoulet, shreds lettuce for quesadillas, makes Green Goddess in the blender, hailing Mary full of grace.

Louise makes herself a cup of tea and takes it to the table where Eva sits pondering a picture in a book about the human body.
  "Can I sit down with you for a minute?"
  Eva nods, and pushes the book across the table to Louise.
  "Oh, Louise, look at this photograph. This was taken from inside an eye, looking out. This big circle of blue is the *sky.*"
  "Good Lord."
  "See the wispy white clouds? And the rest of the page, this round amber frame, is the interior side of the iris. This is just so beautiful to me. It's like the I, you know, the me, behind our eyes, the viewer who looks out and sees the movie."
  "God." They shake their heads. Eva's eyes are the color of tea.

She leans forward until her nose is nearly touching the page, peering into the blue circle of sky.

It is a quiet evening at the cafe. Eva and the Rednecks leave before dinner. Louise feeds Georgia and Jessie cassoulet and sends them home in a cab. There are hardly any customers, and no one at the bar. She and Willie sit down with beers, plates of black beans and rice with salsa and sprigs of cilantro.

"I don't feel like being interesting and funny."

"Good. I don't either."

"You want another beer, Louise?"

"Sure."

"Do we have to clean up tonight?"

"Well, we could do it in the morning. No, we better do it now. God only knows when the Health Department'll drop by."

"Will you do the grill for a change?"

"Sure."

"Let's just sit outside. *Then* we'll clean, okay?"

A silver star-shaped moon reflection shimmies on the bay. They sit drinking Kronenbourgs, listening to the night birds, the sea breeze, and the waves.

"Will you still love me if I tell Joe he can come back?"

"Is that what you're going to do?"

"I don't know. Maybe. Yes—not move back in with me—but I just want him to be some part of my life."

"So be pen pals."

Louise smiles, stands, and goes inside for more beers.

"I think he ought to be with us," she says when she returns. "I'm so *used* to him. I really miss his friendship, Willie. And I've been *wait*ing these last two months because he's not around. You know what it feels like, darling? When I was young, like twenty-three, and poor, I had to have an abortion. And I'd always wanted babies, but this one time I knew I couldn't have it, and I had to walk around for a month knowing I was pregnant and wouldn't be having the baby. It was so hard. That's how I've been feeling for the last two months."

"Well call him then. I don't care."

"Yes, you do. And, Willie, I know I went around mewling about what a pain in the ass he could be, but now, since he's been gone, since I sent him away, it feels just like what I said, being sad pregnant. You can't know what it feels like. It's like your belly's this big goldfish bowl—you keep looking down at it, imagining the funny little baby."

Willie stared out at the moon's reflection on the bay. After a minute, he said, "Did you show? When you were twenty-three?"

"Oh, yeah. Every time in my whole life when I got pregnant, I'd start showing about three days after conception."

"Was he a creep, the dad?"

"He'd taken too much acid. He was cool at first—then he started getting crazy. *Way* too much acid. Oh, Willie." She takes a sip of beer. "I remember how crazy Joe is, how dramatic. I can see him, you know, when he's sick, or exhausted, or depressed, the way he sits slumping backwards, eyes barely open. I mean, he looks like Manet's *Dead Christ*, without the angels."

Willie smiles forlornly.

"But, Willie, now, thinking I can talk to him again, that he can be our brother, I feel like I'm getting out of this terrible box I've been in. I mean, it's like when you've been depressed for a really long time? And then all of a sudden, the plates of the earth shift and you get a big rush of something that feels like self-esteem. Like, you get bouyant again."

"So if you get to have him around again, do I get to take a bunch of hearts?"

"Nope."

"I think you're a fool, Louise. But it's your life."

"So I'm a fool, so who cares. I'm doing the best I can. And I know that what I do is to make silk purses out of sows' ears. So fuck me, man, that's the game. That's what you have to do. That's where the body's buried."

"It's not all sows' ear."

"Well, baby doll, it mostly is. *You* read the paper every morning. I mean, it's a *jungle* out there, Jane."

SEVEN

WHEN SHE FIRST WAKES, the sky is black with golden glitter like the space behind closed eyes, but some time later dawn breaks through. Red pillows fill the dark sky, and across the bay behind the fleecy hills is a shoot of white yellow light. She wallows under the covers for another half hour, dreams that Joe and a tortoise are in bed with her. The tortoise turns out to be the weight of the book she was reading before she fell asleep.

The sky is bleak, primeval. She pulls on the nightgown Jessie gave her for Christmas, Lanz of Salzburg, tiny lavender flowers. She puts on a green zippered sweatshirt, baggy gray wool socks, and pads into the kitchen to put the kettle on for coffee. After doing so, she stands looking as if she had just remembered that there was something she had wanted to remember to do.

They will be so shy when they first crawl into bed again.

Handel is on KKHI. She sits by the window to wait for the water. A great dark dragon of fog slides down the mountain out to sea. What if with Joe—no, watch the dragon, Louise. Sufficient unto the day and all that, sufficient unto the morning.

Behind her eyes, out of nowhere, a phantom comes into focus. There she is at eleven years old, hunched over the table in her parents' kitchen, writing one hundred times, "I will never again make, throw, or have in my possession spit wads at this school."

She smiles, remembering the victim of the spit wad attack, a substitute teacher named Mrs. Phillips, with a moustache and sheer black stockings. She was wearing a red and black dress on a Friday, and if you wore red and black on a Friday it meant you were a whore. Louise and her friends stoned the woman with spit wads.

Louise hadn't even been caught. She had turned herself in. The ones who were caught were the popular kids, her friends the popular kids, and she wanted to complain with them about having to spend a weekend writing one hundred times, "I will never again make, throw, or have in my possession spit wads at this school."

It is like thinking of a much younger cousin, to remember herself at eleven.

She gets up to grind French roast beans. Now a movie clip plays in her head. She is in the bathroom at school on the last day of eighth grade. They'd been given cheap yearbooks and she's in a stall, forging someone's autograph, that of the cutest boy in school, Andy Williams. "You are the prettiest girl, Louise." That is *verbatim* what she forged, and here she isn't really sure that Joe called yesterday.

Louise walks into the cafe several hours later with two big bags of produce. Jessie is at her table by the window, glowering at the front page of the *Chronicle*. Her chin and bottom lip are jutted out so far that she looks like a toad in song.

"What's the matter, lovey?"

Jessie crosses her arms.

"JESSIE'S HAVING AN EPISODE," Willie yells from the back.

"Jessie? What's the matter?"

"Willie's being fresh."

"I am *not* being fresh," he says, stepping into the dining room with a yellow mixing bowl, whose contents he stirs with a wooden fork. He looks rosy and amused.

"Hey, Willie, love, give me a kiss." He comes to the table to kiss her, and she peers into the bowl.

"Apricot upside-down cake." Louise waggles her eyebrows.

"He *rushed* me again."

"Grandma, for *God's* sakes, you're up at six every morning. We leave at *quarter* to *twelve*. By eight you've soaked your Grapenuts, fed the cats—that gives you *three* hours and forty-five minutes to dress—"

"Don't you talk to *me* that way, Mr. *Fresh* Mouth."

"Grandma."

"I may just have to tell you where the cow found the cabbage."

Louise and Willie grin at each other. Jessie stares at her lap.

"*Don't* make the Ubangi lip, Grandma."

"What, uh, started all this?"

"Well, we've got a new pussy," says Jessie. "And this morning—"

"Grandma," Willie says wearily, slipping into the chair next to her. "We've *always* got a new cat. We get new cats like other families get *magazines*. People must think we're like those nutty *Bouvier* aunts." To Louise: "People take their cats out to the dump, chuck 'em out the window. They stay a night or two— they're these *junky*ard, wino cats—and then this social worker cat comes by. She's Harriet Tubman, you know, and she looks at her clipboard, finds our address, locates the North Star, and leads them to our home—"

"That doesn't have anything to do with—"

"Oh, yes it does, Grandma. The new cat's why you felt rushed. 'Cause you were at the *last* minute giving it the garden tour." To Louise: "It's like 'Tripping with Terwilliger.' It's like, 'Why *here's* our *friend* Mr. Spiiiider.'"

Jessie makes a terrible face, as if a fly has just flown up her nose.

Willie rolls his eyes, and pushes up from the table, and with his nose in the air, takes his bowl of batter to the back room.

Louise bends to kiss the back of Jessie's bony neck.

"You've never *lived* with an old person, Lou. It's *nuts*." Louise nods and picks an apricot half out of the can. "And all those god-damned *cats*. They're like these snooty faggoty *arch*dukes." He covers the bottom of a buttered tin with apricots, carefully pours in the batter, then rubs his eyes with the back of his arm. "I mean, I *get* it, man: she took care of me, and now she kind of needs me to take care of her. I mean, I *get* it, dude, okay. But, boy, some-times I feel like I have a *sad*dle on."

Louise nods, then shrugs. Willie looks away.

He's the best person she's ever known. She watches him ambush Jessie on her way back from the bathroom, lift her off the ground in a bear hug, Jessie seems dizzy when he sets her down—you can almost see the dents popping out of her tiny body. He's back in her good book; you can tell by the way she twitters, primly, with secret pleasure, on her way back to the table.

"Well. When I was a kid she'd put calamine on my poison oak and blow on it." Louise nods. "And she put me into cool baths when I had a fever. I mean, you know? That's pretty heavy shit, man."

"Yeah."

Georgia arrives just before the rain begins, wearing a red velvet crown.

Louise leaves the grill to pull out the chair beside Jessie, who looks up in reverence at the rickety sour dowager, as if she is the last person one might ever expect to enter Jessie's Cafe— as if Katherine Hepburn has just walked in. Maybe Jessie is a star-fucker: Georgia is rich, her husband was a famous painter. Georgia sits down in her tentative, rocking way, aided by Louise, as if she is stepping down into a rowboat. Louise slides her in close to the table.

It starts to rain at one. Louise listens to the rustling scratchy drum on the roof. When it becomes clear that there will be virtually no one to feed, Willie starts making crème brulée. Louise cleans out the refrigerator, silently cursing Joe. He may not call until dinner, even though he knows it will keep her waiting all day. It's passive aggression, Joe. Get me by not doing anything.

What a hypocrite you are, she thinks. It's passive aggressive not to answer his letters.

I was confused. Duncan used to say that when you'd left a man, *any* contact at all was a come-on. If you went up to him on the street and kicked him right in the old giblets, *that* was a come-on.

Louise smiles, wipes off a jar of raspberry jam.

That was *guts*ball for Joe to call. Admit it.

But he's such an uptight asshole.

So are you. You just fake it better. You're a better sport.

But there's that thing Duncan always said, that a good marriage was one in which each person in the couple thought they were getting the better deal. I think Joe's getting the better deal, she thinks. He's a psychopath who's made a reasonable adjustment.

So are you, the voice says. You're cut from the same cloth, you just have a cuter act.

I'm so fucking confused right now.

What does your broccoli say?

It says, I want to hear his voice. But I know, I *know* that he'll be sweet and good, at first. And then the episodes will start. Like Willie said, 'Wolf here again, Joe?' I mean, *maybe* it's all just a joke. Maybe we're just a big ball being batted against a garage door in space by a sullen child as big as the sun. But we can *still* try to do the best we can. I mean, look how graceful Willie is. Willie is a giver. Joe is a taker. I don't know what to do.

Give up. Let go.

It's just so *hard,* being an uptight asshole. It's *hard.*

So? Try to be a little easier on yourself.

The rain is a billion pricks on the murky green bay. When she goes out to the porch to watch it up close, each prick makes a radiating whorl. After some slow deep breaths, she turns and sees the pinched, staring, apple-doll faces of Jessie and Georgia on the other side of the glass.

Louise sits down with the two old women for a moment and bums one of Georgia's Pall Malls.

Georgia is watching the ducks near the shore, rowing around in the rain. Jessie is reading *By Little and By Little,* by Dorothy Day. Neither of the women seems to notice Louise. By little and by little... according to St. Paul it is by little and by little we are saved, or fall. But it all goes so fast. Looking back, it's like turning the crank on forty years' worth of microfilm: whoooosh!

Louise gets the chill, gets up, and shuffles off to find Willie.

Still no one calls. Louise is eating her third custard cup of crème brulée as she and Willie play gin.

"I may eat like *ten* of them," she says.

"Be my guest."

The phone rings, Willie leaps to get it. Louise composes herself, clears her throat, but Willie keeps talking. It is his new friend David, the Gays Against Brunch guy, calling to shoot the breeze.

When the phone rings again at four, Louise glares at it. Willie takes the call.

"Jessie's Cafe. Oh. Hi, Joe. Pretty good, yeah, look, wait a sec.

I'll get Louise." He holds the receiver out to her. She clears her throat.

"Hey, Joe."

"Lou!"

"How you doin'?"

Mournful, wistful, "I don't know, Louise." His Dog-Loved-Him-But-She-Died voice. "I spent all morning at the dentist's. Root canal." Louise stares off into space. Nothing she thought earlier applies. It was all fiction. He was at the dentist. "So I'm all right though now. How are you? You got a lot of people there today?"

"Me, Willie, Jessie, Georgia. Slow as molasses today. It's been raining, though, that's why it's so slow."

"But is business mostly good, most days, I mean?"

"Yeah." She shrugs. "Can't complain. What's the use."

"I'm writing you a song. It's about the cafe."

"Yeah?"

"It's called 'A Wallet Full of Ones.' It's about . . . tips."

Louise smiles. "I like the title."

"Actually, that's all I've written so far."

Louise's mouth trembles.

"Look . . . uh . . . I'm flying back on Friday. I'm just going to get a room in the city for a while, like on Lombard. And see if I can get another coaching job. And just, you know, play it all by ear?" Louise nods. "Louise? Are you still there?" Louise nods. "Lou?"

"Yeah."

"And I'll sort of get settled in, and then, you know, give you a call, and see if you want to, you know, meet for a drink?"

"Yeah?"

"Yeah. Okay?"

"Yeah. Of course."

"What's the matter?"

"I'm just. Scared."

"Yeah, well, so am I. Think of the Louis Armstrong story."

Louise takes a deep breath. "Yeah."

This is one of Joe's father's stories—Joe told Louise on the deck of a ferry to San Francisco, five years before, just when they were moving in together:

When Louis Armstrong was a little boy, as poor as they come in the South, his mother sent him down to the river one morning to get a pail of water. Lounging on the bank was an alligator. Louis tore home, nearly in tears, and told his mother what he saw. "Louis," she said, "that old alligator is just as scared of you as you are of him." And he replied, "Then, Mamma, that water's *not safe for drinking!*"

Or so the story goes.

Joe takes another codeine, washes it down with a beer.

Daddy, he asks, what's a billabong?

It's a channel, flowing out from a river.

What's a swagman?

A hobo.

Who's Matilda?

There was so much singing then. At every celebration there was singing. Songs about cowboys, hobos, pirates, sailors, shanties. Carols and rounds. Mary could do harmonies, their father played guitar. Joe was loud and tone-deaf, still is.

He's on the couch in the lanai. An unopened *Playboy* lies on the floor beside him. It went well with Louise, he thinks. He will call Sunday or Monday—make her wait a couple days. When he first steps into the cafe, they will both be short of breath, but then they will both look like Diane Keaton in *Reds* when she first sees John Reed after their long separation. He practices the look on the lanai. It's his wistful Windsong look, quiet, sad, full of intense longing.

He will bring long-forgotten memories as gifts, to make her laugh, make her love him again.

When I was nine, Louise, my dad and I spent a weekend in Sausalito with an old Navy buddy of his named Palmer. Me and my dad shared a bed upstairs on this houseboat, in a sleeping loft. On the first morning, we woke up really early, at dawn, and Palmer was climbing the ladder with two cups of coffee and a cup of cocoa for me. And we all sat on the bed, waiting for the sun to rise. Ducks swam in the water right below our window. There were hundreds of white masts in the harbor, reaching way up into the sky. And a huge red flattened ball of sun glowed behind the masts, as if it was jailed, and then it started to rise like a marionette. And Palmer started singing "Lloyd George Knows My Father"—you know? to "Onward Christian Soldiers," but it's "Lloyd George knows my faaaahahther—Father knows Lloyd George?" And Dad started singing along. They were like Volga boatmen, hoisting steins of beer, and they sang it until the sun rose above the masts.

There was another memory I meant to tell you—wait a minute, it'll come back to me.

He practices the Windsong pose some more, then sleepily reaches for the *Playboy*. First he opens it to the last page, to the "Next Month's Listings." Then he flips through it backwards, pulling out the cardboard subscription inserts. Then he reads the Table of Contents, the movie reviews, the captions under the interview.

"Part of me thinks that I'm a loser, and the other part thinks that I'm God Almighty." That was in *Playboy* a long time ago. John Lennon, I think. He closes the magazine, does a bemused variation of the Windsong face, nuzzles his shoulder like a mother horse, feeling his soft warm breath on his skin. Oh, *I remember now*. He smiles and clears his throat. It was my father's favorite story:

"Later that same year, when I was nine, Dad took me and my best friend, Stevie Gronewald, camping. He was the wimp skinhead weirdo nerd with the air rifle, remember? Well, Stevie adored my daddy; his own dad was like this *replicant*, and my dad was like Judge Hardy. So we stop at a store on the way and buy all of our favorite foods. Weiners, cans of chili, Oreos, potato chips, cocoa, salami. Sugar Pope. Bushmills for my father, Mountain Dew, Delaware Punch for us. *Glop*. My dad used to call soda *glop*. 'What kind of *glop* do you want?'

"He puts down the back seat of our Chevy Malibu station wagon. Stevie and I are stretched out, using our sleeping bags for pillows, and we start driving up the mountain, singing cowboy songs. And then my dad says 'Boys? This is *our* weekend. This one is just for the guys. No women are going to tell us what to do or when to do it. You can eat whatever you want, whenever you want to eat it. You can stay up as late as you want. You can stay up all *night* if you want. You can wash if you want, but you don't have to. And you can say anything you want, anytime you want. Okay?'

"And Stevie says, 'We can say *any*thing we want?'

"'Yep,' my father says, nodding gravely.

"'THEN SHOVE IT UP YOUR ASS, EDWIN JONES.'"

"Do you think I can lose twenty pounds by Friday?"

"Gee, I don't really *think* so, Louise."

"I look like *Sumo* Cook."

"Lou, you look great, don't worry."

"I am *blank*eted in layers of *avoir-du-pois*."

"What's that?"

"Fat."

"Gin."

"God, again? Lucky for me Joe's an adiposephile."

Willie smiles, collects the cards, and begins to shuffle.

"I'm pretty nervous about him coming back."

"So that's okay."

"It's so crazy in my head."

"Yeah."

"It's like I'm dreaming half the time. Most of the stuff in my head is fiction." Willie nods. "And my conscience is so bad. I think I had a bad conscience about five minutes after I came out of the chute."

Willie nods.

"I mean, it's like a three-level chess game in my head."

Eva appears in the doorway at five, soaking wet.

Jessie sees her first and stares with such concern that Eva might be covered with blood instead of water.

Georgia peers down at the pool of water forming beside Eva's red rubber boots. Willie dashes over and helps her off with her Burberry raincoat. Louise brings her tea in the duck cup and leads her to a chair at the table nearest the fire.

"Let's all sit here," she calls to Jessie and Georgia. "By the fire." Eva has dark circles under her sad amber eyes, she hasn't said a word. When she lifts her purse to hang it on the coat rack, her arm trembles. "And, Willie, make us a little snack, will you?" Eva's dark hair is piled into a wet haystack on her head.

"You've already *eaten* everything that isn't nailed down."

"Well, make us little toast points or something."

Jessie lurches over, cooing, to inspect the damage. She studies Eva from several angles as if trying to decide if there's any point at all in taking her to the vet.

Willie prepares a plate of toast points with cream cheese and chutney. Louise helps Georgia, still in her red velvet crown, make the painstaking journey across the room and seats her so she can follow the plot of the fire.

KKHI plays a stone flute concerto. One imagines mountain goats on rugged slopes and ledges, above the rustly drum of the rain on the roof, the windy crackle of the fire.

"Pffffft."

"Will you stop with that ba*zoo*?" Jessie cries. Eva and Louise smile at each other shyly. Eva begins to corrugate her napkin.

"So whadjew have for lunch?"

"Ohhh...?" It is like a plea. "Barley soup?" Jessie asks her about her day.

"I told my third-period class today that I'd looked up 'blue' in my dictionary? And the first definition was 'the pure color of a clear sky.' And I thought that this must surely be the dictionary's finest moment. But I looked into their faces and could see that all they were thinking about was whether or not it would be on the final."

They listen and watch with such obvious pleasure, watch her busy fingers as she talks. She corrugates everything in reach: a napkin, a matchbook cover, a receipt. They watch her spindly fingers as she toys with the red plastic ribbon from the package of Georgia's Pall Malls. Georgia is staring spellbound at the ribbon as if in a moment Eva will unfurl the final dazzling bridge of a cat's cradle.

"Are you going out for dinner? Why don't you ever eat here?"

"Willie? Mind your own business," Louise says.

"Oh, butt out, you gas hose. I can ask her anything I want."

"As long as she knows that she doesn't have to answer."

"Yeah, well, that's *really* polite, Louise, to sit here and talk about her in the third person *invisible*."

They both smile over to Eva, shaking their heads, and Eva looks so sorry for all the trouble she's caused, and then, all of a sudden, her eyes fill with tears.

Mouths drop open, time stands still. She bows her head and covers her eyes with a shaking hand.

"Oh, Eva."

Louise covers Eva's hand with her own. Willie searches Louise's sad face for an answer. The two old women hold their breaths.

"What's the *matter?*"

Eva shakes her head.

Willie gets a box of Kleenex and brings it to the table. Louise licks her lips, kneads Eva's hand.

"What's the *matter*, lovey?"

"Oh, I'm sorry."

"Don't be sorry."

"I didn't sleep at all last night."

Louise nods.

"I should go home and just sleep."

"Stay with us awhile."

"No." She shakes her head. Her eyes are droopey and wet.

"Oh," Willie says, "you seem so *sad.*" Eva nods. "You look like *basset* death."

Now at eight Jessie and Georgia finish dinners of gumbo and cornbread, crème brulée. Nine people showed for dinner, and Willie is in the back washing their dishes. Louise has the jim-jams, premonitions of disaster, and chants to keep the fear at bay.

Don't be afraid, Louise. Only fear can rob you of your grace. She stands scouring the grill with pumice, thinking sad and fearful thoughts.

Years ago at dusk, on a boat with friends, in a wind-shadow of the Golden Gate Bridge, she scattered the ashes of her lover. Anchovies leapt, silver flashes out of the water. Gulls swooped down on them, crying. Louise held the gold cardboard box inside of which was once her friend, and she strew the ash and bone into the mild wake of the sailboat, and her lover's father read the

Twenty-Third Psalm, and his mother tossed red flowers into the water after each handful of ash, as mad in her pain as Ophelia. The sun was going down behind the Farallones, and in her despair Louise was thinking that Unamuno was right—when the last person who knew her dead lover died, he would be dead forever. But in the face of this, after each handful of ash and bone, she prayed, *Blessed be the name of the Lord. The Lord gave and the Lord hath taken away, blessed be the name of the Lord.*

She gently scours the grill, hailing Mary.

The two old women sit nursing crystal cordials of the beautiful red port the Gristdancers, Sam and Dana, brought from Spain last year.

"Let me know when you're ready for your cab."

"Loooouuueeeze?" Jessie intones. Alcohol brings out the preacher in Jessie. Several sips and she begins to sound like Martin Luther King, Jr. on helium. "Weeeee will let you know."

Oh, Jessie and Georgia, I love you, she thinks, as she helps them on with their coats. A car pulls up in the parking lot, and Willie in the back room wipes soap off his hands and arrives to help the women to their cab.

He takes Georgia's arm. Louise takes Jessie's hand, and the four leave the cafe. Willie and Georgia walk like father and daughter coming down the aisle, where every second step is meant to catch up with the first, marking time.

The air on the porch is crisp and clean, smelling as green as a freshly mown lawn. They take the porch stairs slowly, the older women on the outsides gripping the railings. And coming up the walk in her pigeon-toed tiptoe is Eva Deane.

"Eva, for God's sakes, welcome back! We thought you were their cab." Louise thinks for a minute. "Look. We'll go out to the parking lot and wait for the cab. Eva? You go in, help yourself to anything you can find. There's wine behind the bar, and there's a *lovely* port from Spain. We'll be back in a second."

"Eeeeva, as I live and breathe," Jessie intones. "And *how* are you tonight?"

"Oh, fine," Eva says, wringing her hands.

Louise smiles.

"Getting about on what stumps you have left?" she inquires politely. Eva nods solemnly.

Eva skulks into the cafe, as if she shouldn't be there. She's the woman who won't transfer sunglasses from the top of her head to her purse in a department store for fear of accusations of shoplifting, the woman who stands in the empty cafe posing shyly as if a photographer has just entered the cocktail party. But there's something much less arthritic about her shyness tonight.

It takes Louise a few minutes to figure out she's been drinking. Eva sits down by the window, looks over her shoulder at the dying fire, turns back to look at the white sickle moon that hangs over the bay. She hears a car pull up, hears two doors open and after a moment two doors close. She licks her lips.

"So. May I have a sip of this port?" Eva asks.

"Well, sure." Louise pours some into a cordial glass, sets the bottle in the middle of the table. "Help yourself. I've got to do the receipts and set the tables for tomorrow. Willie's gonna sweep, then we'll join you."

Eva sits sipping port, infinitely calmer than Louise has ever seen her before. She does not fold or spindle napkins and matchbooks, and appears to be concentrating on the clarinet line in the Mozart quintet that plays on the stereo.

But something is off, Louise thinks. When she's up close to Eva, stopping by her table to comment on the slowness of the day's business or the pearly white moon, or when she's at a distant table, wiping it down, arranging place settings, filling the napkin dispenser, it's wonderful to have elegant Eva there. She can do what Joe can do, can be a calm warm presence.

But when Louise is at a neighboring table, within Eva's territorial air space without actually being at Eva's table, there's a current of something static. Louise notices this again and again. It's similar to tuning a temperamental radio: You can fine-tune it with your body close by, but when you turn to leave, the static begins. So you sneak up on the radio, fine-tune it again, and start to tiptoe away, and then it sees that you're leaving, and goes into its Herschel mode, staticky and lost.

Louise is surprised when she hears the clattering of a bottle against the rim of a glass and sees out of the corner of her eye that Eva is sloshing more port into the glass. Louise looks away, like she does when she sees a cocky teenager botch a wheelie on a bicycle.

By the time Louise has finished her chores, Eva sits looking like a poster child, eyes droopy with sorrow and hunger. Basset death.

"Heyyy. What's the matter?"

Eva looks off, concentrating on a sad thought. She looks like someone who is trying to figure out how many people will be at her funeral. Louise used to see this look in Duncan, when he was in his cups and had decided he was dying. If you asked him what he wanted he'd say, "Cab fare to the Bridge."

"I'm done," Willie calls from the back room and comes out wiping his hands on a dish towel, smiling.

"Hey." He glances at Louise. "What's the matter, Eva?"

"I just need some fresh air. Maybe I'll sit outside for a minute."

"You want to be alone?"

Eva shakes her head.

"Well, then, why don't we all sit outside," says Louise. "It's really sort of warm. We'll all have a bit of port—it's been a long, crazy day."

Several ghostly clouds now hang in the black-blue sky. Several gold planets too, a sprinkling of stars, the white sickle moon.

They sit at the picnic table on the porch. Willie has switched off the porch lights and lit the lantern that hangs beside the door. Eva and Louise sit with glasses of port on the side of the bench that faces the bay. Willie straddles the bench across from them, and they study the lights of the city, the lights of the bridge, the stars, flickering moonlight on the bay, the blinking green light of the four-second buoy. Louise glances at Eva to see if she feels like talking, but Eva seems to want to be quiet.

Louise counts the seconds between the blinks of green light. She remembers rowing out to it with Joe once at twilight. On it lay a barking seal, huge and dark, and beside him a small copper-colored female who seemed shy, maybe even sick. Do you remember that Scottish ballad about the nurse, with her baby— her *bairn*, young son—singing by the water to the father, who is a man on the land and a silkie, a seal, in the sea? Joe had never heard it. Louise sang the words she could remember. Joe rowed, and the seal barked, and every four seconds the green light blinked.

Eva starts to cry again.

"Oh, Eva, what's the matter?"

Eva shakes her head and looks at Louise. Louise has seen this look before, this look of a person suffering a great narcissistic injury—one night last year when Joe was drunk Louise found him slumped on the floor with his back against the refrigerator, crying, and he looked up at her with those eyes. Willie was right: basset death. Joe whispered, imploringly, "I just wanted her to love me."

Eva holds out her hands in frustration.

"I feel violent!" she says. Louise nods. "I feel like breaking things. I feel like *swearing* at you."

"You can swear at us," says Willie.

"I have never once in my life shouted. Goddamnshitfuckpiss." She looks into her lap.

"Wow," says Willie.

She smiles into her lap, but then, after a moment, pulls her mouth down in the way a man tightens his mouth downward when he is going to shave off his moustache.

"Pour me another port, Willie."

Willie dutifully fills her glass, then glances at Louise, who shrugs. Eva downs half the glass in one gulp and lets her head drop onto her chest. Then, as if someone behind her has found Eva floating face down in a pool and is pulling her out by the hair on the crown of her head to see if she's still alive, her head raises. She looks at Louise blearily, then shakes her head and smiles. "I'm not a very good drinker." Louise nods. "I mean I get like a roaring four-ton hippo, galumphing-out-of-the-water, drunk, shit-flying-everywhere drunk." She crinkles her eyes up at Willie. He looks inquiringly at her. "You had much experience with shitty drinkers?" He shakes his head and smiles nicely at her.

"You're pretty much the shittiest one," he says.

"Have you, Louise?"

"Well, my Uncle Duncan used to be a pretty shitty drinker."

"I don't drink very often."

Louise nods.

"And sometimes when I do, if I just sip, you know, it's fine."

Willie toys with his cowlick. Louise fiddles with her bangs.

"Did he stop?"

"Duncan? No, he died."

"Of drinking?"

"Or just of general ruin."

"Oh."

"His nervous system went all cuckoo on him. He'd sit around shaking like a dog shitting peach pits, and he'd figure maybe a drink would calm him down. He'd be all right for a coupla drinks, and then he'd, you know, start coming apart like a two-dollar watch."

Eva appraises the moon.

"Go on, then, tell me more about your Uncle Duncan."

"What do you want to know?"

"What'd happen after he got all falling apart?"

"He'd drink a little more, and then he'd pass out, then he'd wake up a few hours later, shaking again and hung over. So he'd have another shot, you know, just enough to get all the flies going in one direction."

Eva starts to cry again. Willie sighs and looks over at Louise, who winks.

"Why don't you just tell us what's so sad."

"Oh, God." Willie and Louise sit waiting. Louise is getting bored. How bad can it be? It is probably one of those things that the world will *little* note nor long remember.

"Darling? Get us another beer, will you?"

While Willie is gone, Eva pours herself another splash of port.

"Will you tell us when Willie comes back?"

"I don't even know you two from Adam's off-ox."

"Who is Adam's off-ox?"

"I don't know. I just heard it somewhere."

Louise reaches out and strokes Eva's cheek with the back of her hand. Willie steps onto the porch with two Guinnesses.

"So I'm going to tell you," says Eva.

"All right."

"There are two things going very badly wrong." Eva sniffles, but she is no longer crying. "One is that my husband left me for someone else. Several months ago. Out of the blue. I was *so* in love, Louise." Louise nods. "It was like living next to the sun I didn't even notice the planets." She grimaces. "He did. Notice the planets, I mean."

"Joe, too."

"It, well, one night, I was lying by the fire grading papers. And he came home, looking funny. And I said, 'Come lie with me by the fire.' He looked at me and shook his head. I said, *teasing*, 'Don't you love me anymore?' And he shook his head and said, 'No.'"

"Oh, boy," Louise says sadly, and squeezes Eva's shoulder.

"And, I mean, that's the *good* news," Eva says.

Willie looks like he could cry. Eva bends forward and stares blearily into her port. "I'm very, very sick," she says. Louise cranes her head forward, peering at Eva.

"Really?"

Eva nods.

"What is it?"

"I don't want to tell you."

"All right."

"It's not cancer. But it's just as bad. I was better for awhile, but now I'm getting sick again."

"Oh, shit."

"It's . . . I don't want to say. But I'm so *angry*, I can't handle it. That everything else will go on, people coming and going, here at the cafe, everywhere, eating, singing, the tides, but it's going to go on without me."

Eva hunches forward with her shoulders in tight protecting her head. It is clear to Louise that she doesn't want to be touched.

Louise lifts her face, listens to the sea lions bark, to a distant foghorn, to the pounding of her heart, remembering something Richard Pryor had said after his near-fatal burns: he thought he was going to die, and it was like being at the Sunday matinee as a child, watching a double bill, engrossed in the second feature, when the usher comes along, and taps you on the shoulder, and says, "You have to leave." And you cry out that you want to watch the rest of the movie, and the usher sort of shrugs, and says, "I'm sorry, time to go."

"We'll protect you," Willie says.

"How can you protect me from *death*, Willie?"

"Maybe you'll get better."

"No, I *can't* get better."

"Are you sure?"

"Uh-huh."

Louise sighs. "Boy," she says.

"Boy yourself." Eva shuts her eyes tight, then covers them with her hand. "Can you give me one good reason why—*now*—before it gets really bad, why I shouldn't just take a bunch of pills? One good reason, Louise?"

Willie looks at Louise, whose face is blank, and then he turns to Eva, who now looks angry, defiant. "Well," he says to her gently, "*Mornings* are nice."

EIGHT

JOE IS LYING ON THE COUCH biting himself on the shoulder. Every so often he stops and practices his Windsong pose. "I Went to the Animal Fair" keeps playing in his head, only he can't remember all the words—they've been replaced. He thinks that the giraffes and the monkeys were there, in the first stanza, still he isn't sure. It is driving him nuts. His plane ticket is on the coffee table in its folder. So far this morning he has read it eight times. He leaves for San Francisco in less than twenty-four hours and is already in a panic. The last time he came to Hawaii, four years before, he and Louise had stayed up the night before snorting Methedrine. He had slipped a bindle with a quarter ounce of the powder into his suitcase, and when, on board, with his seatbelt on, the pilot announced a delay in takeoff, he saw the belly of the airplane filled with frenzied snuffling bloodhounds, baying at his suitcase.

He is waiting for his mother to come home from the bank. She is going to lend him five thousand dollars, enough to set him up in case he doesn't move right back in with Louise, enough for a cheap car, enough to live on until school begins in the fall. (He has told his mother that he plans to call all the Bay Area high schools and see if anyone needs a basketball coach, and his mother asks, "Why not *Cal*? Why not call *Stanford*?")

He reaches for the airplane ticket and reads it again.

He hates to fly, knows each time he will die, that the plane will plummet on fire into the Pacific Ocean, or collide with another plane, or plow into the terminal. He hates the suspension in time and space, the lag and the warp. And it's a double warp. Even on the ground when he hasn't flown for months, he goes around feeling that he's been in a pressurized chamber and is waiting for his inner ears to pop, after which he will be able to experience reality with some sort of steely edge, instead of with the sense that he is a figure in someone else's clairvoyance.

His mother returns. He hears the front door open and close, reaches for a magazine, pretends to be reading.

"Hello, Joe."

"Hi, Mom." He looks up pleasantly, smiles, prays that she won't sit down, but she does, of course, settles into the easy chair as if to hatch an egg.

She begins telling him a gleeful story of the woes of an acquaintance she ran into at the bank, a rich middle-aged woman named Sandy Baker who has bad teeth and a coke-head lesbian daughter whose dog was recently run over by a car.

Joe looks like he is listening but in his head he is telling Louise stories about his mother. This one time, when I was eight, me and Stevie Gronewald got caught stealing a package of Fizzies, and our mothers had to come get us at the five-and-dime. And when we got to the car, my mother slapped me and said—I'll never forget—"Once a thief, always a thief." So I was always afraid of policemen after that 'cause I thought that they could tell. I mean she sealed my fate that day! I'm white, I'm male, and I'm a thief, so let's just get on with it. Then, you know, this is like the most satisfying moment of my life so far. I'm fourteen years old, and I've shot up during the summer: All of a sudden I'm five foot ten, and one day she winds up to slap me, and I grab her by the wrist and say, quietly, "No more."

Friday rain clouds and blue sky are mirrored on the bay. Louise has arranged to pick Willie and Jessie up, and they'll all do the shopping together. She sits in her car outside their house and honks. In a minute, Willie comes out the door, across the lawn, and climbs in.

"Hello, lovey. Give me a kiss. Thank you. Where's Jess?"

"She's gonna take a cab. Let's go.

"What's she doing?"

"She's lying on the couch, covered with cats. They're like the Harmoniums in *Sirens of Titan*. They feed on her pulse. No, they're like, have you ever left for a week during flea season? And when you come back, a hundred fleas jump onto your shins? That's what it's like every time Grandma lies down." He shakes his head. Louise smiles and looks him over.

"So what else is new?"

"David called, just to sort of shoot the breeze."

"You still on for Charles Pierce?"

"Yep."

"Have you told him a lot about me? What've you said?"

"I said you're my best friend, and that you're totally crazy. No, I said that you were maybe just a *little* bit left of center, and that you're totally devoted to your work in the food industry."

"Ohh. And does he know that I'm the princess?"

"Yep."

There's a lot of traffic in the downtown area. The yellow Volkswagen bus in front of Louise has a bumper sticker that says, "I hate your dog." She points it out to Willie.

She pulls into a space in front of the butcher shop. "Run in and get me a chicken," she says. "I'll go get the produce."

"How come Eva doesn't come in anymore?"

"I don't know. It hasn't been that long. She's probably embarrassed because she got so drunk last time. She'll be back."

"Joe still coming in tonight?"

"Yeah, I think so. Now I sort of wish he wasn't."

Eva sits at her desk at school with a pocket pencil clenched between her teeth. The tendrilous bun on top of her head is pierced with an ivory chopstick, and her hands, holding a scientific journal, shake. The students are hunched over their finals, sighing, scribbling, tearing at their hair. The article she is reading claims that there is an unexplained loss of one or two ounces of body weight fifteen minutes or so after death. It's not fluid, and it's not breath. Scientists do not know what it is. Louise loves this sort of thing. "It's enough proof *for me* there is a God," she'll say. "It's enough proof *for me* there is a soul."

Eva smiles, she looks up to see if anyone is cheating.

When Louise returns from the market, she finds Willie sitting empty-handed. She appears to ponder the situation.

"I see no bloody feathers about your mouth."

"They're out of chickens."

"How can a *butcher* be out of chickens?"

"Don't ask me, man. They think they'll have some by noon."

"Well, we'll go to Safeway, then."

And so it is that they end up on the other side of town, and pass a silver-blue Cadillac in the front seat of which a fat middle-aged man appears to be shouting at Georgia.

Louise brakes one car length in front of the Cadillac. She turns to look at a bug-eyed Willie. They both slowly turn to look over their shoulders, then whip their heads back.

"Look in the rear-view mirror."

"I wonder who the fat guy is."

"Must be her son."

"This is *wild*. Now her lips are pursed."

"She's prawley making the bazoo."

"I think he's yelling at her. Wait, wait: She's opening the door, she's getting out. She's getting out. She's still getting out, still getting out," Louise glances at her watch, "still getting out, she's *out!*"

Georgia shuffles over to the curb, leaving the door open. The fat man gets out of the car, puts his hands on his hips, and speaks with a stern expression on his face. Georgia turns away from him, her nose in the air. The man shouts some more, then throws up his hands and gets back in the car. He closes both doors. After a minute he drives away. Georgia stands swaying and then adjusts her beaded turban; she seems lost in the ozone.

Louise backs up, and Willie rolls down his window. "Hey, Georgia!" Georgia looks away. "Hey, Georgia, it's us, me and Louise!"

Her mouth drops open, then yanks closed, like a ventriloquist's dummy, and she looks at the two waving people in the car as if she has been waiting for them for ages and was in fact *just about to leave.*

Willie gets out of the car. "Come on. We'll give you a lift." He walks over and takes her by the elbow. She cranes her neck to peer around him, sees Louise, then turns away with the perfect Herschel smile. With her nose in the air, she allows Willie to escort her, one together, in marked time, to the car.

Trying to get Georgia into the front seat, trying to duck her head and bend in appropriate places, takes a good two minutes. Willie goes around to Louise's side of the car and crawls into the back seat. Louise smiles at the stone-faced old woman, studies the trellises of skin, the gnarled elegant liver-spotted hands, wonders if she's KGB, and if she had been talking. "Okay," she demands, crossing her arms. "Who's the guy?"

Louise has fed several dozen people by three.

"I am as happy as a bucketful of bunnies," she tells Willie. "I could chase down an airplane today."

He is making chocolate pudding for his grandmother, who is reading at her table with Georgia. Jessie is being a curmudgeon today and has been complaining all afternoon—that the taxi driver drove too fast, that it's much too hot and muggy, that Georgia is smoking too much, that the three fans are probably going to give her consumption, and that most of the people she knows are dead.

Boone lurches around the cafe pulling a wooden train on a string. He is no longer the fat little furniture mover who had to be fed. He still looks like a howler monkey, and he still walks stooped forward, like an old man walking against the wind, but now he can bend at the waist and the knees, can turn the doorknob, and run fast.

"Boone! I've made you a *lovely* peanut butter sandwich. With strawberry jam, at *enormous* personal expense and inconvenience. And I want you to sit down and eat it immédiatement— eee-meee-ja-mow."

"No."

He drags the train off towards the back room. "WEEEEEE."

"BOONE?" Willie thunders, off-stage. "I think that with *proper* planning and adequate cash flow, we could turn this into a *damn* fine library."

"What did he say?" Sam asks.

"He said that with proper planning and adequate cash flow, we could turn this into a damn fine library."

"Oh."

"It's from *Chinatown*."

"Ah." Sam pencils in a corner of his napkin with latticework.

"Sam? Is Dana really not coming back?"

Sam shrugs and then shakes his head. He looks wistful, and dazed, as if he is trying on this answer for the first time.

Willie told Louise right after Dana left, that she was never coming back, that she had jumped ship; and that if this is the case, he hopes she rots in hell.

Willie has the basic emotional range of the Old Testament God, the God in whom Willie does not believe.

Louise brings Sam a beer and a bowl of stew. In the back room, Boone clings to Willie like a starfish.

After Sam and Boone have eaten and left, Jessie resumes reading Emily Dickinson. Georgia is smoking, watching the tide come in. Their combined age is somewhere over 160. Together they weigh only slightly more than Louise.

Louise is at the grill hailing Mary, full of dread. She never wants to see Joe Jones again. Maybe his plane will crash.

Don't hold this against me, she prays. She looks over at Jessie reading in the window, wishes Jessie still had the wherewithal to throw on the lights for Louise.

What if I end up being cruel to Joe, in my secret, evil confusion? How could God love me then? "He has to," Jessie told her once. "I told you, That's His *Job*."

"Even when I'm fucking someone over, when I'm full of faults and failure? When I'm at my most disgusting?"

"Yes," the old woman said. "Even then. Especially then."

Jessie has laid down her book and is dabbing at her brow with the handkerchief she keeps tucked up under the cuff of her blouse. Louise ambles over with a fresh pot of tea.

"You two duckies fine?"

"I'm hot, I'm bored, and Georgia's being about as much fun as a *shrub*."

Georgia might have just swallowed a brimming tablespoon of castor oil. Jessie crosses her arms across her chest.

"Well, shall I get you two a project?"

"What sort of project? I'm just sick of everything."

"Hey, *light*en up, Francis." Louise smiles. Jessie doesn't. Louise strokes her chin. "You want to take the strings out of some green beans for me? And I'll cook them for your dinner."

"Isn't there anything even slightly more interesting?"

"What, do you have your eyes on making the radish roses?"

"The what?"

"The radish *roses?*"

Jessie looks away.

"I'm going to get the beans and set you both up, okay? If you don't want to do it, don't."

"We *want* to do it. But Georgia's as slow as a *swamp* turtle."

"Listen, you. The *ox* is slow but the earth is patient."

This coaxes a very small smile out of Jessie.

"Boy, Jessie's in a mood today."

Willie, washing dishes, shrugs.

"She's not feeling all that great these days. And she doesn't even get to drive anymore. It's like Boone's growing up real fast and Jessie's growing down."

"Yeah."

"Fast."

Louise walks down to the water at five. Two red-tailed hawks hang in the sky. Near the shore, a young egret stands with her back to Louise, poised as if she has her hands in her pockets, then leaps into the air and flies low, in an arc skirting the water. When she reaches a patch of rushes, she wafts slowly up several feet, and then floats to the ground. Louise sits on a rock.

Poor old Jessie. Louise sees her only six months before, helping Joe wash the windows of the cafe, slugging one of the Rednecks when he used the word "nigger," bicycling to a meeting of the Audubon Society. *Oh, boy, Jessie. Hang in there, love.*

Jessie is the only devout Christian Louise has ever been able to stand. Wouldn't that be interesting to be able to believe that Jesus Christ *rose from the dead?* I mean, in your *heart?* It must bring on the sort of security one imagines in an infant marsupial. I'm more like—who was it who said that Unitarians are atheists without the courage of their convictions? I mean, I'm sure that Jesus was one of the Truly Sweet People, like Willie—I'm sure He stepped high over bugs. But that He *rose from the dead*? Jessie thinks so. But then again, Jessie believes that toasting a piece of bread reduces its calories by about one-third.

"Hey!"

Louise, at the grill, looks up from the stew she is stirring to find a little girl of five or six standing on the other side of the counter. She has red hair, a red E.T. shirt, and red shorts. Louise glances above the little girl's head and sees a tired young woman who must be the mother.

"Hey, yourself."

"GUESS WHAT MY NAME IS."

"Tell me, I don't know."

"A*man*da! What's your name?"

"Louise."

Willie pokes his head out from the back room. He and Louise exchange smiles, and she juts her head towards Amanda's mother. Willie dries off his hands and goes to take her order.

"Guess how old my brother is?"

"Seven."

"No, stupid, he's an infant."

"Six months."

"Wrong! You only get eight more guesses."

Louise squints, pretending to think. She feels terribly depressed, about Eva, and Joe. It's all hopeless. Snoopy this morning told a fallen leaf, "Don't stay here. They come and get you with a rake." Then as another leaf floats slowly to the ground, Snoopy thinks to himself, Nobody ever tells them about the guy with the rake.

"Come *on*!" the girl demands.

"Ummmm . . ."

"Take it by months."

"One month."

"*Three* months!"

"*Mornings* are nice," said Willie. God, he knocks my fucking socks off sometimes. Louise smiles. She has a small sad attack, stirring stew. Sees in her mind's eye Eva in the doorway, hanging her head, grinning at her feet. We'll protect you, Eva Deane.

At six the bay is red with sun. A lone dark goose flies past. The Mole People sit eating cheeseburgers and fries. Sister Peter-Matthew, the fat nun, dawdles over a bowl of black bean soup. An elderly couple sit flinching at Georgia's occasional bazoo, eating stew and white bread. An Italian family of five talk softly, sharing a plate of nachos with extra cilantro, and the Rednecks sit at the bar watching *Star Trek*, drinking beer.

"Eva's coming up the stairs." Knock knock knock knock knock-knock knock-knock knock-knock.

For Willie and Jessie and Louise, it is like the mailman has just arrived.

Eva steps inside, straining not to bow her head, with her arms hanging stiffly at her sides, and her knees knocking. She looks like a shy girl modeling her first prom dress.

Jessie looks proudly at Eva. Willie hugs her, kisses both sides of her mouth. Louise hugs her and closes her eyes. Eva is all skin and bone, trembling, and Louise holds her tight.

"So. Wha'd you have for lunch?"

Eva lowers her eyes and begins tying imaginary knots. "I had to eat at Denny's." Her fine hair, brushed back into the bun, comes over her forehead like the brim of a muffin when you've poured too much batter into the tin.

"You ate at Denny's? Good grief, man, wha'd you do, like, have them rustle you up a cor*ral* burger?"

"It was our secretary's baby shower."

"At *Den*ny's?" Eva nods. "So wha'd you *or*der?"

"Oh, I had this thing, a *sal*ad, with four big shrimp in it."

"Oh," Willie says, with a nellie flick of his wrist, "that would be like Prawnettes of Salad."

"I'm going to get you a *love*ly cup of tea," Louise announces, but Eva waves her head: No, no, she's fine.

Louise gets up to see if the Rednecks need more beer, which they do, because, as one of them said, it's hotter'n a two-peckered goat out there, musta lost two quarts a sweat, and Louise gets them some beers, stops by each table to make sure everybody has everything he or she needs. Soon, Joe will call to say he's back.

"Is it really fun being smart?" Willie asks Eva.

"Anyone can teach science, really."

"No, you're really ex*treme*ly smart. You're like, *heav*ily smart. We're just like a bunch of old *brain* destructs, sitting around trying to grasp these simple ideas. Aren't we, Louise?" Louise can sense rising panic in his chatter. "I mean, *she* didn't even finish high school," he says, jerking his thumb over his shoulder at Louise. "I mean, okay, look, she's read everything. Me now, I was very, very smart there for a while, and then in *high* school I did like vast quantities of drugs, I mean, anything that wasn't nailed down I injested. But definitely, I've lost a *lot* of ground in the last five years."

"Oh, Willie," Eva says, apologetically.

"Oh, no, it's okay; I mean, I was *too* smart then. I couldn't *han*dle it, man. I mean, now I think I've got my brain cells down to a more manageable level."

Eva looks at him as if he is a magic trick. Slowly, shaking, she picks up her cup of tea and stiffly brings it to her lips as if it is much too full. What do you *have*, Eva Deane? Are you sure you're going to die? Maybe you just don't want to burden us: Hi, my name is Eva Deane, thanks for fixing my tire, let's be friends, I'm dying. But I'm going to ask you tonight, going to say, *What do you have, Eva?*

Louise honestly believes that God sent Eva to them, thinking that they could help. Or maybe God sent them to Eva. Or maybe none of it means a thing, except that it's warm and cozy inside the cafe, and the food is pretty good.

"I have a story," Jessie declares, and begins to compose herself for its telling. Then she looks at Louise for the go-ahead.

"One day, in the spring, Frances Mae Colley and I went for a ride on our horses. We were young girls then, twelve or thirteen." She looks off into the distance, straining to see. "And, *oh*, I loved my horse, Louise. She was a bay with a black mane and tail.

"We used to ride to an apple orchard, on gently rolling hills. And Eva, my dear, one day we rode toward the orchard and, even from a distance, could see waves and waves of golden yellow—a yellow carpet of daffodils beneath the apple trees."

Eva is tasting the picture. Louise stares out the window at the water so Eva and Jessie can be alone together in the moment. *Jessie, my love. Big sickness, big medicine, right?*

Joe Jones sits in a window seat on the Death Plane watching the preflight activity on the ground. He has a bag on his lap that contains seven magazines: *Esquire, Newsweek, Time, California, Rolling Stone, New York,* and *Sports Illustrated.* His seat belt is already buckled. He is not blinking very often.

An old businessman nods once in greeting to Joe before he sits down next to him and starts reading graphs. He has manicured nails and sheer black hose.

Joe sighs deeply and begins unwrapping pieces of cinnamon gum. He puts three in his mouth at once and sits in a masticatory trance, waiting for takeoff.

The plane, he feels, is in trouble from the word go, and almost right away he begins overheating badly. His heart acts up during takeoff, but he begins to relax when the plane levels out. He looks down at the clouds and then orders a beer from the stewardess. He pulls down the tray in front of him and takes his magazines out of the bag, sets them in a neat pile on the tray, and begins.

He picks up the top one, checks out the contents page, flips to the back to see next month's features, and then, with a look somewhere between glee and annoyance, begins ripping out the coupons for subscriptions and merchandise.

There are eight in the first magazine, nine in the second. They fall out onto his lap like leaves, and he's muttering away, shaking his head with irritation, amputating the coupons faster and faster and sticking them in the sleeve on the back of the seat in front of him.

It is while pruning the fifth magazine that the businessman first speaks up.

"Want some help?"

Joe flushes, smiles, shakes his head. "Jeez. There's like *ten* of these in every magazine."

The man commiserates with a nod, and then his eyes seem to track a slow insect that flies in an arc off to his right.

Joe finishes his lunch of sirloin tips in the time it takes the businessman to dress his salad, pepper his meat, butter his roll, open, pour, and sip his wine. As soon as the stewardess clears his tray, Joe orders another beer and, while waiting, picks his magazines off the floor and sorts them into two piles: the five without coupons on the left, the other two on the right.

Rip, rip, rip. When he finally tears out the last coupon, he collects the others from the seat pocket, arranges them in a neat stack, and deals them to himself, counting.

"Sixty-three," he announces to the businessman.

The man shakes his head and makes a sympathetic sound through his nose, like air escaping from a valve or blowhole, and then once again tracks the slow insect as it flies off to his right.

"ATTENTION, DINERS," Louise hollers from the grill.

All of the cafe's fifteen customers, with the exception of Jessie and Georgia, look up. Eva now sits alone, grading finals. "Everybody okay? Anybody need anything, 'cause I'm going to make me and Willie some food. Table one?" she asks, pointing to a cheerful blond family of five who had bowed their heads in prayer before dinner. "Table two?" A shaggy bohemian writer type and an elderly gypsy, both eating stew, shake their heads. "Rednecks, help yourselves to beer if you run out. Jessie? *Jessie?* Do you and Georgia want more pudding? No, okay—hey, you at table three—do you need, anything?" A young man and woman shake their heads. "Eva? You want some pudding or something?"

Eva shakes her head. "I'm going to leave in a minute."

"You stay *right where you are.* I'll be there in a sec." Louise goes to the back room where Willie is silently grumbling at the dishes in the sink. "I want to talk to Eva for a minute, okay? Then I'll get us some dinner." He nods, then yawns.

"So okay, Eva Deane," she says, sitting down beside her. "I want to know how you are. I want to know how you really are."

"I don't know."

"Do you hurt? Does it hurt, whatever it is?"

"Oh, no, it doesn't hurt. It's disagreeable, like having the flu. I'm stiff. And I'm tired." Louise nods. Eva bites her bottom lip.

"Well, doesn't your doctor, I mean, are you on medication?" Eva nods.

"And can you control the—whatever—discomfort?"

"I've been able to, to a certain extent, up til now."

"And do you have others to help you, family, and friends?"

Eva scratches the butt of her palm. "I have a younger brother I love near Seattle, and his children. I'm crazy about them all. And it's very pretty there."

"You got *us*, too, you know." Eva looks down at her fingers and ties imaginary knots. "Do you *pray* or anything?" Eva shakes her head.

"I don't, you know, really believe in God."

"Not even some vague sort of higher power thing that's going on inside you?"

Eva shakes her head, clearly embarrassed by this line of questioning.

"Well, why don't you just pre*tend* you do, as an experiment," Louise says. "I mean, why don't you go around pretending that you believe that some higher power is having things turn out exactly right. Could you just pretend that God made your tire go flat and made me be walking past you, and now you're like our favorite person, and we'll take care of you—you know, pretend that God sent you to us? Do you think I'm just full of shit?"

"No, I don't. No. It's just that I don't believe in God."

"*Fake* it, Eva. Just for a day *pretend* you do. Pretend there's some sort of nebulous higher power inside you and outside you, something you can talk to, who can help and protect you."

Eva has done a double take. She laughs softly, as she talks softly, bemused. "That," she says, "is a wild idea."

Louise smiles.

"Go around pretending I'm talking to some higher power, that I'm being protected by some higher power."

"Right."

Eva covers her mouth. Hers is a smiling face of crowsfeet.

"Talking to the old H.P., huh."

Louise feels a tremendous relief.

"Okay. I'll try it for a few hours." She looks up at the ceiling, as if she sees her higher power there.

"My old H.P.," she says, thinking. She looks off into space, then back at Louise. "My old Hewlett Packard."

NINE

SHE SHUFFLES TO WORK blue and antsy in the muggy heat, homesick like she's been away at camp too long. Church bells peal, and she's hailing Mary full of grace to keep her mind off Joe, who hasn't called. Look at the hills, the mountain, the bay. Look at the trees, the city, look at the ducks. It's going to be all right, Louise. Give thanks for Willie, and remember what the poet said: "Yearning is blindness." Hail Mary. Get a grip.

Ten feet from the shore, near the cafe, she stops to watch three old Japanese fishermen, one of whom has caught a stingray. It lies upside down on the sand, with a wispy fan of blood on its gray belly, and tenderly, stopped over it like surgeons, the fishermen work on disengaging the hook. Then they flip it over. It slaps the wet sand, and they push it out to sea with the butt of a fishing rod. It floats off towards deeper water, then disappears.

They turn and see Louise. She gives them the thumbs-up sign and walks on.

Willie has turned on the grill. "Sgt. Pepper" plays, the coffee is brewing, the fans are blowing, banana muffins are baking, and all the tables are set. He's in the back room making a cherry pie.

"Holy smoke, Willie, how long you been here?"

"Oh, I don't know. Forty-five minutes."

He is cutting dough into strips to make a lattice top for his pie. "Kisses," she says closing her eyes. "Eee-mee-ja-mow."

"Mee-ja-mow," he says, kissing her.

"You're really happy today, aren't you."

"Yeah, I am. I think I'm in *love*."

"Honest to God? With David?"

"Uh-huh. We went out last night, after work."

"Well, when do I get to meet this young man of yours?"

"He might come in today."

"Have you deflowered him yet?"

"Get your head out of the *gut*ter, Louise. You're throwing your life away."

Willie gets the phone when it rings at noon, and Louise at the grill holds her breath. Willie in the back room keeps saying, "Oh, no, you're kidding." Then he laughs and says, "Just get in a cab— we miss you."

"That was Grandma," he says. "You know what she just did? She went to the sink to wash her stockings, but she poured salad oil on them instead of Woolite. So she turns on the hot water to rinse the oil out of them, and then she turns on the garbage disposal so the oil won't clog up the pipes, but the *gar*bage disposal sucks them down into its blades. Now it's broken," he says, and laughs so hard that he has to hold his stomach.

The stockings were knee-highs. Pantyhose are in her archives now, as are garter belts, heels, and dresses that zip up the back. Several times a year, when they drive over the mountain to the beach and sit with their picnic on the sand, Jessie rolls the knee-highs down into little inner tubes around her ankles.

"Lou?"

He is watching her dice celery for the tuna salad.

"Yeah."

"I think I have a tapeworm."

"Why do you say that?"

"Because I ate about thirty-five waffles for breakfast—and I'm already hungry again."

"I think you're just high-strung. I mean, I think you *vibrate* off about two pounds a day."

"I feel really fragile," she tells him later.

"I'll protect you."

"Why hasn't *Joe* called?"

"Because the guy is *dogage*, Louise."

"And you'll baby-sit me today?"

"Uh-huh."

"And you'll help me kill some time until I feel better?"

"Uh-huh. And I'll help you kill him, if he doesn't call. I'll bake him a poisoned pie."

The motel on Lombard at which Joe has been staying since Friday is run by East Indians. Everything smells like curry. The water in the shower smells like curry, the sheets smell like curry, even his forearms are starting to smell like curry, he notices, as he raises one arm to his nose to sniff it out.

When he first saw the lights of the city, her buildings and bridges and boats, he felt like a person arriving at Ellis Island. He got all choked up. He felt like kissing the ground. It was late and he bought a hamburger at Clown Alley and took it back to the motel. *Saturday Night Live* was on the tube as he ate. It was terrific, Louise, I was laughing out loud. Do you remember when Father Guido Sarducci did the "Find the Popes in the Pizza" contest? When he asks the viewer to cover their TV screen with wax paper, which shows a large pizza, and to circle as many faces of popes as you can find? I read somewhere, in an interview with

Sarducci, there was really only one pope—Pius the Twelfth, I think—and that all the rest were pepperonis.

He falls asleep soon after, dreaming of Louise.

Saturday morning he showers and shaves and calls the cafe. No one is there, and he calls her at home, but she doesn't answer, and the answering machine isn't on.

He goes to Upton's for bacon and eggs and blueberry muffins, and reads the box scores in the Sporting Green over and over. He strokes his chin as he reads, creating a goatee of newsprint that he discovers when, in the phone booth outside of Upton's, he bends to study his reflection.

He calls the cafe at noon from a gas station on Van Ness, but the line is busy—busy when he tries again a minute later.

So he heads down Van Ness until he gets to Market. The street is bustling with shoppers, dirt-bags, breakdancers, Jesus-Come-to-Get-You revivalists, musicians, bag ladies, winos. Much of the street is being torn up, as usual. Don Sherwood used to say, "It's gonna be a hell of a city when they get it finished."

You could take BART out to the Coliseum—the A's play at one. No, the Transbay Tube gives him the willies.

Now he looks like he is watching a TV set behind his eyes, and what he sees is Willie behind the wheel of the old Plymouth, Jessie in an A's cap riding shotgun, him and Louise in the back. Jessie had made deep-fried chicken—the smell filled the car. They parked next to the most elaborate tailgate party Joe had ever seen. It was like *Satyricon*, Willie said, with everything but an ice swan centerpiece.

It was Diet Pepsi Gym Bag Day at the Coliseum. The A's lost.

He ends up walking to North Beach and spends the afternoon in Gino and Carlo's watching the Cubs clean the Padres' clocks on the wide-screen TV. He is drinking Anchor Steam Beer. From time to time he glances over at the pay phone, scratches himself behind the ear, and pinches his ear lobe, hard.

"Can you say brontosaurus?" Willie asks Boone. They are in the back room, sitting on the floor, pushing a big plastic brontosaurus on wheels back and forth. Willie pushes it to Boone, Boone pushes it back.

Louise sits nursing a cup of tea at Jessie's table. Georgia, in her red velvet crown, seems sad today. She's staring at the birds on the shore gloomily, looking like Eeyore when he stares out the window thinking, "Somewhere out there, someone's having a birthday party." Jessie is reading a book on Japan. She is wearing a blue silk blouse the same color as the sky above Mt. Fujiyama, which is on the cover of her book. The top three buttons are undone, so you can see several inches of her pearly washboard chest.

Off stage, Willie says, "Brontosauruses were the bee's knees of dinosaurs, Boone. They were heroic. Like *planets*."

Sam smiles at Louise. "Planets," she says, and laughs. "You want anything? Well, let me know if you do. Georgia, you want a muffin, sweetheart?" Georgia doesn't take her eyes off the bay, but shrugs. Louise gets up and returns with three muffins on plates.

"Oh, my *dear*," Jessie exclaims. She takes off her glasses, which are on a necklace, and lets them fall against her chest, where they jut out, perpendicular, like a ledge. They fill up with crumbs as she eats. When she is done, Louise reaches out, cups her hands under the lenses, and tips them, so that the crumbs fall into her hand.

Louise is treading air today, like a hummingbird or the arctic terns who migrate to these shores in the autumn and the spring. White, with long Egyptian black eye patches, boomerang wings, and tail feathers split like fish fins, they hover close to shore, in the sky, treading air.

Three teenage girls sit huddled together at a table, as if for warmth, looking tearfully at the inscriptions in their yearbooks.

Boone has fallen asleep on the floor, clutching his blankie, sucking his thumb. Jessie has resumed reading and Georgia stares
wistfully out to sea. A man in his late forties, bandylegged and
scrappy, with a mane of white hair and black high-top Keds,
comes in off the porch from time to time to get another Dos
Equis. He's as nervous as a badly abused laboratory animal, first
kept awake for too long, periodically electrocuted, then given
large doses of dangerous drugs and placed in a maze with no exit.
He is a writer. He makes the rest of them nervous.

Yesterday for the first time, Louise saw rashes on Eva's arms and
little sores around her fingernails. Eva sat with sad grace alone at
a table grading finals, until Willie went over and plopped down
beside her.

"So what are these papers today?"

"Biology finals."

"So test me, give me a question."

Eva licks her top lip and studies the top mimeograph. "Okay,"
she says. "Why is the ovum so much bigger than the sperm?"

"Oh, I *love* it when you talk dirty."

"Willie!" Addressing her lap, she asks, "So, do you know?"

"Why the ovum is bigger than the sperm? No. Why?"

"Because, you see, when the fertilized cell first begins to divide,
the ovum has to provide nourishment for it."

"Oh. And then what happens?"

"Then the cell mass travels down the tubes—"

"Those would be your fallopians—"

"Right! And it, the fertilized egg, gets a footing in the walls of
the uterus where the blood vessels there start feeding it."

"And then it grows into a baby."

"Uh-huh."

"And it grows itself little feet? And eyes, and a heart?"

"Yes. Pretty smart little baby."

"*Really*. And when does the heart start beating."

"Oh, so early, Willie. Like, by three or four weeks. I mean, right away. It's a primitive heart, but it's *beating*—probably often even before the mama knows she's pregnant."

"Wait'll I tell Louise. She *loves* that kinda stuff."

Last night, for the first time, Eva stayed for dinner. Louise sat down with her whenever she had a chance, watched the young woman pick at the lamb and buttered noodles.

"Eva, how are you feeling these days?"

Eva bandages her forefinger with a napkin. She speaks softly. "Unnerved, like I felt in first grade, when I first understood that there were other continents besides America. When I first really got how huge the planet was. And how tiny my town really was. I remember feeling affronted."

Louise nods. "I remember that too. It felt like you were being ripped off."

"Yes, exactly. It's what Copernicus, Darwin, and Freud did to us, too, stole all that thunder from our egos. It's terribly hard to think about."

"Of course it is."

Eva looks away, pale and exhausted. Louise wishes she would eat more. Willie brings her a tiny piece of Key lime pie, which he has made to please her. *Strengthen me with raisin cakes, freshen me with apples.*

People wander in and out all day, complaining of the mugginess—people who work on the waterfront, families, fishermen, bird-watching couples, kids. Sister Peter-Matthew in her white habit and standard-issue black nun shoes sits reading sacred poetry, gently turning ancient pages. Every so often she smiles, looks up, and takes a sip of tea from the duck cup.

"So, Sister," says Louise, "guess what Willie made this morning? Cherry pie."

The nun's gray porpoise eyes widen and she leans back in her chair. "Oh, I really shouldn't," she says, then goes ahead and does.

"Sister? Before you go, may I ask you something?"

"Yes, of course, Louise."

"Where is 'Strengthen me with raisin cakes, freshen me with apples'?"

"*Song of Songs*—'Song of Solomon,' to be precise."

"Oh, that's right, I remember now."

"Chapter Two, where 'The flowers appear on earth, and the time of singing of *birds* is come...'"

"'And the voice of the turtle is heard in our land.'"

"'And the fig tree putteth forth her green figs.'"

"Princess?"

"Yeah."

"I was alarmed by that Bible talk."

"Oh, don't be, my love."

"Well, I can't help it. I don't want to have to *pay* to have you deprogrammed."

"I'm not that far gone."

"What if you become a *Christian*?"

"I'm not going to become a Christian, Willie. I wish I could."

"So what do you think a turtle's voice is like? Would it be like a really soft gritching kind of sound?"

"Turtle meant turtledove there."

"If you don't become a Christian, I won't sleep with Haitians."

"It's a deal, my love."

A man comes in around three—tall, gaunt, shy, maybe thirty, in faded 501s, a black and orange Giants cap, and a T-shirt. He stands scanning the room from the doorway.

"Hello?" says Louise at the grill.

"Is Bill here?"

"Bill?"

The man looks blankly at Louise, when Willie steps out from the back room.

"*David*."

"*David*," says Louise, smiling.

"Hi, Bill."

Louise walks behind Willie toward the blushing man in the door. He has Lenny Bruce eyes, dark and hooded, high cheekbones beneath which the skin is pocked rather badly. His T-shirt says "Kevin Hicks Construction—Guys and Trucks."

Willie is all but wagging his tail as he introduces his friend to his family. David takes off his baseball cap. "*David*, this is Lou, Louise—Lulu, this is *David*. And this is my grandma, Jessie—Grandma, this is my new friend *David*."

Jessie coos. "*Davey*, darling."

"And this is our friend Georgia."

"Hello, Georgia."

Georgia suppresses a laugh and straightens her red velvet crown.

Willie and David go out to the porch and sit on a bench, talking. Louise spies on them from time to time. First Willie seems coquettish—good God, she sees, they're holding hands—and then Willie's face becomes blank, then surprised and angry. He storms inside a minute later.

"What's the *mat*ter, love."

"Just leave me alone, Louise."

"*What?*"

There is a pinched concentration in his eyes.

"How come you won't tell me?"

"'Cause you'll try to say something *use*ful."

He slams through the next hour, in wound-up silence, ignoring eye contact with Louise, who blithely goes on making meals that Willie then slams down in front of customers, as if they have already sent them back twice.

She wishes Eva would come in now. It would cheer up Willie, and Sam said something she wants to tell her.

She goes into the back room to check on Willie. His cheeks are flushed, his eyes are red, and he's breathing like an asthmatic.

She takes his hand, leads him into the bathroom, and locks the door behind them. He sits with his back against the wall and cries.

"He's *leav*ing, in a couple *months*. It's like we're out there on the porch, and he's being really *ador*able, and *flir*ty," he's choking on the words, stammering through tears, "and then he goes, like totally casual, he says, 'Oh, I got this like great job in New York.' It's like this big *break* for him."

"Oh, love."

"Don't be *nice*—it makes it worse." Louise nods. "He was just so *cas*ual about it, it's like, oh, la-di-da. I'll tell you *one* thing, Lou: I'm not going to Charles *Pierce* with him."

"How come?"

"Because I'm not an *es*cort service. Fuck him, man. I'm not going to let him *use* me all summer, whenever he wants to get laid, or he needs a cute little bunny rabbit escort for some stupid show."

"Oh, lovey—"

"*Don't* say anything useful."

"Okay." What she was going to say was that they let themselves be in love with Eva and she's going to leave them, too. But she doesn't say anything. She lies down on the cool tiles, with her hands clasped behind her head, as a pillow, and she stares up at the ceiling, like you lie on the earth and stare at the clouds.

Life is hard and then you die, but there are people to serve food to all day. Willie's eyes are rimmed in red, but he manages to be kind to the customers, if not exactly friendly. "I just wish it were six months later and I was already over him," and Louise can only nod because all she can think of are useful things.

"Boy, I'll tell you *one* thing, Louise. The fucking you get is not worth the *fuck*ing you get."

"*Willie's* got a bee in his bonnet," Jessie announces in alarm. Louise nods.

"That friend of his, David? Who asked you what you were reading? He's leaving for New York."

"Oh. And Willie's sad."

"Yeah."

"Tell him I want to see him."

Louise goes to the back room. Willie's washing dishes.

"Your grandmother wants a word with you."

He sputters and scowls and wipes off his hands, then trudges over to Jessie's table. She pats the empty seat to her left. He folds himself down into it, stares into his lap, frowns.

"Willie, look at me. Now then. Try not to take this so hard."

"Grandma, I'm bummed. It just sucks."

"Of course it does. But you have me and our *Lulu*. And don't you remember when we went out to Green Gulch Farm?"

"Yeah, I remember. *Please* don't say anything useful."

"At sunrise?"

"I re*mem*ber, Grandma."

"It was a very wise thing that the Buddhist said. He said— remember? He said—someone said, what can you do when something *so* sad happens, when something happens that makes you hurt *so* bad. And he said," she stares out the window for a minute, then turns to Willie again. "He said, you just grit your teeth and try to get through it."

He looks at her with great sad resignation.

"I *knew* someone was going to try to shoehorn something useful into my afternoon. I just *knew* it."

KDFC plays a Haydn quintet at twilight. The Rednecks sit at the bar with their brewskis, watching *Wonder Woman* on the silent TV. Jessie is still reading her book on Japan, Georgia in her red velvet crown is sadly watching the birds outside, pelicans, ducks and egrets. The cafe is half full of strangers who sit eating, talking quietly. Eva still hasn't arrived.

Yesterday, over tea, Louise asked her how the experiment with her old Hewlett Packard was going, and she said, well, not really all that well, and besides, she thought, it was something of a copout. Like Anne Sexton said, you can't build little white picket fences to keep out your nightmares. "But you *have* to," Louise thundered. "Oh, you *have* to, or you go around with your *head* up your ass all the time. And you pretty much have to make up a God for yourself, too. You have to make up a God who will be amused by you, who is laughing at you, in a friendly way."

Willie overheard and shook his head at Louise. "Miss *Take*over Broad," he said."

Eva's car pulls into the parking lot. Louise watches her from the window. She gets out of the car, stiffly, as if she's creaking.

She doesn't look up to see Louise waving from the window. She walks with her head bowed. Her bookbag over her shoulder seems to pull her forward and down.

She needs to sit by herself again, she explains. She's still grading final exams, essays on cellular organization. It is a difficult exam. She smiles. One of the students called her a murderess, and she looks at them all apologetically and limps to a small table by the window at the far end of the room.

She sits grading papers for an hour until Willie shuffles over with a beer, scowling.

"Can I sit with you for a minute?"

"Yes, of course." She tucks her tooth-marked pencil behind her ear, stares into her lap, and then up at Willie's sad face.

"Oh, Willie. What's the *matter?*"

Willie growls softly and tugs at his cowlick. "I got *dropped* on my head today. By this guy I was sort of in love with."

She waits.

"It's like he's in love with me too, right? And then he goes, 'Well, la-di-dah, be leaving for New York in a month.'"

Eva licks her lips.

"It's so hu*mil*iating. I wish the guy would just fucking *die.*"

"Of course you do, I mean, you *have* to, all things considered."

He looks at her, sad and expectant, then drops his eyes. She rubs her forehead, thinking.

"I would take that sadness, instead of you having it, if I could." He nods. "I know it makes you sick, in the pit of your soul's stomach...." He nods again and looks up. "I mean, we all know from humiliation, Willie."

She looks away, at the floor off to her right, and clears her throat. "I could give you a humiliation story if you want."

"What for?"

"I don't know."

They shrug at each other and look down, smiling.

"Okay," she says. "When I first fell in love, with the man I ended up marrying—the one who just left me recently?" Willie nods. "We were together every night. Mostly, we stayed at his house— it was bigger than mine—and I'd bring a change of clothes to wear to school. And, well, my clothes started piling up there. I'd leave a little something every few days—stockings, you know, and teddies?

"And it's clear that we were madly in love, night after night after night. We just assumed that we would—that I would come to his house after work. And when he did his laundry, he washed my things, too. Oh, Willie, is this boring?"

"Are you crazy?"

Louise is at the grill straining to hear. Eva wraps a fist around her forefinger, as if to stem its bleeding. Then, flustered and dainty, she wipes at her forehead and tucks a tendril of hair back behind her ear before continuing.

"He said that he felt all mushy when our clothes came out of the dryer and he got to fold up my little . . . underclothes. And I was, well," she covers her mouth for a second, "*sort* of aware that by letting a pile of clothes amass there, I had some sort of claim on his house." Willie nods. Eva smiles. "This is really embarrassing."

"Do you want me not to look at you or something?"

Eva shakes her head. "But then, you see, what happened was, one night, about two months into our romance, he took me to a bar, and he was in a foul mood, and I said, 'What's the matter?' And he looked at me, and shook his head, and said 'Eva? We are not living together.'

"I don't think I've ever been so humiliated in my life. But I said very casually, 'I know.' And he said, 'I just wanted to make sure we both know where we stand. Because you seem to be moving in slow-motion.' And I shrugged and pretended that it was no big deal."

"Oh, God, Eva."

She chews on her baby finger a minute. "But, so, the next morning, full of wounded pride, I waited for him to shower, and then I stuffed a clean pair of my socks in my purse, and some of my underpants—like I was a kleptomaniac. And little by little, over the next few weeks, I brought my clothes back home. I'd *shang*hai a skirt—wad it up and stick it in my purse when he wasn't looking, or I'd tie a sweater jauntily around my neck, you know? like I was accessorizing?" She throws back her head and laughs into her cupped hand. "I was so furtive, Willie, like some old convict tunneling out of jail. There I was, swiping my own clothes, when I thought he wasn't watching. Oh, Willie, I know I'm chattering on." Willie shakes his head back and forth, smiling. "But it was like when you move a cat's new litter? And one by one, she carries them by the neck, tiptoeing, back to the nest where they were born."

Louise watches Eva, hunched over her final exams. She feels ever so slightly jealous. Willie let Eva be useful. Louise, dishing up tamale pie, enchiladas, black beans, wishes she was like them: small and shy and smart.

"ATTENTION DINERS," she hollers from the grill sometime later. "Anybody need anything?" People look up from their meals. "Okay, then," she announces, "the Princess is going to take a break." She wipes her hands off on her pants and ambles over to Eva's table. "Can I sit with you for a minute?"

Eva looks pleased, and begins knitting with tiny invisible needles.

"We had a bitch of a day here. How did your day go?"

"What happened?"

"Here? Well, you heard what happened to Willie. And that man I've told you about—Joe—is back in town, has been for several days, and he was supposed to call and?" Louise throws up her hands, "Shit, I don't know, man. Jessie's in good shape, Boone is a joy, business is good, so I don't know. And *Sam* said something sort of interesting."

"Sam."

"Sam is Boone's father."

"Oh, yes."

"He's a painter, you know. He does a lot of these sort of John

Constable landscapes, very peaceful, golden, pastoral. And I asked him if he saw a finished painting in his head before he started it, and he said, well, yes, to a certain extent, he has a sense of what the painting is about, the forms, and colors and shadows, so he starts. Works on one patch of the canvas and paints what he thinks he sees, but as often as not, that wasn't it. So he covers it up and tries again—maybe it's closer this time, but it still isn't it. So he keeps on finding what it isn't, until he finally finds out what it *is*."

Eva nods.

"He explained it more—eloquently than that, but . . . ?" Eva nods. "And you, what did you learn today?"

Eva touches her lips, briefly. "I'm finding, with my kids, with these students," she says, pointing to the stack of exams, "that they're much more comfortable—oh, I don't think this would be interesting, unless you were a teacher—but they're much more comfortable with the infinitely small than with the infinitely large."

"Why do you think that is?"

"I don't think they have to take it seriously. It doesn't unsettle them. The size of outer space unsettles them. But I tell them that, say, between two letters of the alphabet, between, say, the 'a' and the 'n' in 'and,' there is an infinity. And they nod, very agreeably, but it's as though they're going along with my dementia. It's like, 'Right, Mrs. Deane—and thanks a lot for stopping by.'"

Eva smiles. Louise studies the lesions around Eva's fingernails, the raw patches on her fingertips, the rash on her stick-figure wrist. Eva hides her hands in her lap.

After a minute, Louise asks, "Shall I leave you alone, so you can work? Or get you something to eat, or what?"

Eva shakes her head, looks up.

"Could I please have a glass of wine?" she asks.

Inwardly, Louise groans—Eva got so drunk the last time she drank here—but went to get a glass of Merlot.

Eva sips it, and Louise sits with her, and color comes into Eva's cheeks. Her shyness becomes more composed. "I was trying to talk to my Hewlett Packard today. And I had a second of being electrified with remorse, that I'm now, towards the end, getting some sense of things, and some most important stuff, and then I thought, well, better late than never. And I felt, briefly, very grateful."

Louise smiles sadly, nods. God, Eva's such a lady, and with a bit of wine, sexy, like the Sphinx.

"Sometimes, Louise, lately, I mean, the more I read I get a hazy sense that even though I may not be here when the snow melts, that somehow there's going to be a certain all-rightness about it." She begins to make a fan with her napkin. "That wherever I am, you'll be there, too. And that will make it better. I'll have had you and Willie. And Jessie."

"And Georgia."

"Yes, of course Georgia."

"But where would you go? Why wouldn't you just stay here?"

"My brother wants me to come see him and the kids. I don't actually know where I'm going to go."

They sat in silence a moment. "My doctor was examining my eyes. I have certain retinal problems. And so she was peering through my pupil with her ophthalmoscope, it's got a light in it, you know, and I said, 'What do you see? What is it like?' And she said, 'I see cytoid bodies on your retina, I see vessels, muscles, I see your optic nerve—it's rather like peeping through a keyhole into a room that isn't very well lit.'"

Louise shakes her head in wonder.

When Eva asks Willie for a refill, he glances at Louise at the grill, then shuffles off, like Emmett Kelly, to the bar.

"I hope she doesn't get drunk," Louise whispers to him in the back room. "We're not well enough for her to get drunk."

"I just hope she doesn't start *cry*ing." But she does, midway through the second glass, her mouth turns down, like a man about to shave his moustache, and the tears fall into her lap.

"Evaaaaa? Why do you do this to yourself? Why do you drink, if you're going to get so sad?"

Eva goes into the throes of basset death and whispers: "All I ever wanted was a little self-respect."

"But *don't* cry, lovey. It tears Willie apart."

"Oh, fuck Willie."

Louise's mouth drops open. "Oh, good, now you gonna do your Flaming Slutmouth of the Amazon routine?" She smiles. "Huh?"

Eva covers her mouth and laughs so softly you can hardly hear her.

"The problem with drunks," says Louise to Willie, "is that they leave you and go off to Pityland."

They are on the porch. It's terribly muggy, the night sky is filled with clouds.

"What a creepy day, man. Something's in the air," Willie says.

"My Uncle Duncan used to get all weepy when he drank, and he'd get nasty too, in the blustery way, like Eva does. There is some *ang*ry kinky stuff stored away in that brain pan of hers, I'll tell you that, dude."

"You think so?"

"Count on it, babe."

When her Uncle Duncan drank, he liked to listen to the world's most beautiful mournful music. Then the weeping would begin.

An American in Paris was his favorite; it just tore his heart out. He'd get so whispery, so hangdog and tremulous in his pain, that Louise would almost burst out laughing. "Ira was just a little boy," he'd say, "whose mother didn't love him. Listen to that clarinet, my love."

She just adored her Uncle Duncan, her dad's baby brother. Sober, he was funny and wise, but, good God, he used to drive her crazy when he drank. One time she went to his apartment on Nob Hill, and he was on the couch having wine, listening to KDFC, with the world's greatest view of San Francisco. He was chatty, and cheerful, and feeling no pain. All of a sudden, the first lonely notes of *An American in Paris* began, and Louise prayed that somehow he wouldn't notice, but he froze, like a bloodhound getting its first whiff of the rabbit, and he started revving up for a great broken-hearted cry, and told her "Turn it up."

Louise and Willie have just stepped into into the cafe when behind them a giant shutter closes outside and the sky is a white flash, like silence. Mouths drop open and then there's a boom, an apocalyptic boom of thunder.

"HOLY MOLY," cries Louise. She dashes to Eva's window. A lightning bolt, a hundred miles long, cracks the sky in half, thunder crashes into the cafe, and the rain begins.

"*Hoo*, hah!" Jessie cries. It looks like the beginning of the world, or the end, the Big Bang, or nuclear war.

"Never a dull moment," Louise tells Eva when it's over. "Was *that* enough proof for you that there's a God in heaven?"

Eva is on her third glass of wine, looking sly.

The rain stops around eight. Louise bums a cigarette from Georgia and goes out to the porch to smoke it, standing in the shadows. Willie comes out with wastepaper baskets from the bathroom.

"We'll be out of here early tonight. I'll take you guys and Georgia home."

"Okay." He walks down the porch steps and off to the right, and just before he disappears around the corner he stops, abruptly, freezes. The hair on Louise's neck stands up. The movie speeds through her head of the time she saw him stop this way before, paralyzed with fear. They were hiking along on a great long hill in Colusa, a huge shaggy blond beast of a hill, when Willie suddenly froze. Stopped short, bristling. Six inches away, a long fat granddaddy rattler blinked. With the cracking speed of a lariat the snake could have coiled and struck. Willie was shivering. Ever so slowly, ever so slowly he stepped back, stepped away. The rattler raised his head, doubled back over himself, and slithered off through the short dry grass.

Bristling, holding her breath, she waits on the porch, wondering what on earth it could be. Men with guns or knives?

"Hello, Willie," Joe says. Willie looks back at Louise.

She is silent, shocked, swaying like a frail old man on a narrow pier who is watching two frolicking dogs approach.

Willie clears his throat. "Hi."

Louise steps backwards, into the shadows.

"How you doin'?"

"Who fucking *cares* how I'm doing—you were supposed to *call* before you came. This is like an *am*bush."

Joe, standing ten feet away from Willie, sighs deeply.

"Why don't you just tell—"

"Why don't *you* just go away, and call, some other time. I mean, fuckin' A, man, piss me *off*."

"Willie," Louise says softly.

Willie whips his head around and snaps at her, "*What.*"

"Lou," Joe beseeches.

The elevator has stopped much too quickly again. She takes

two steps forward and her insides gasp at his face: Robert de Niro and Ratzo Rizzo rolled into one. He's wearing a 49ers cap.

"Lou."

"You said you were going to call," she says.

"I know."

"I really think it's arrogant to just show up like this."

"What do you want me to do?"

"I don't know."

"I really fucked up, didn't I?"

"Yeah."

"Sometimes you're really a *louse*, Joe Jones."

"Willie," says Louise, "it's okay."

"Tsss."

"I was just so fucking confused," says Joe. "I got on a bus in the city, and on the bridge, I knew I was making a mistake, and when I got to town I was going to call, but I got in a cab instead, and now I'm here and I'm just so fucking sorry, Louise. And I'm going to go in a second. Maybe you could call me a cab."

"Maybe you should just *hitch*hike," says Willie.

Louise smiles, shakes her head. "I'll call you a cab, okay? And then, like, tomorrow, you could call, and then we could talk on the *phone*, okay?"

"Lou."

"Come in if you want—I'll call you a cab."

Willie steps off the path to let Joe get by, stares at the ground, then walks off angrily with the wastepaper baskets, to the garbage bin.

Louise walks directly to the back room to call a cab. She is dialing when Joe steps in, tentative, shy, just a lonesome cowpoke, wearing faded jeans, a pullover sweater she gave him last Christmas, with no shirt beneath it, or at least not one that shows. He stands in the doorwayof the cafe as if trying to decide whether or not to stay.

Georgia stares at him as if he is standing there naked. "Hi, Georgia," he says out of the corner of his mouth. "Hi, Jessie," he says loudly.

Jessie looks up from her book. "Oh, hello," she says. Then she smiles and looks back down at her book. Louise says thank you, hangs up the phone, and stands watching him warily. He walks towards her. Jessie slowly turns to look over her shoulder with her mouth and eyes wide open.

He stands four or five feet away from Louise, takes off his cap, and begins twisting it. Eva is looking over at him. Louise looks down at her feet.

"I'm sorry," he says softly. She nods. "I'll call you in the morning?" She nods. "You look really good, Louise." She shakes her head, still can't look at him. "You *do*. You've lost weight."

"I've *gained* weight."

He doesn't miss a beat. "It looks good on you."

She smiles at the floor.

"It's pretty quiet tonight."

She nods. Jessie is staring at Joe's back as if there is a knife handle sticking out of it.

"Come here," says Louise, stepping past him. "I want you to meet my friend." Eva looks at her in confusion, and Louise nods that it's all right, that we might as well get this over with, and Joe walks behind her, and his scent is warm in her nostrils, his smell like bread.

"Eva? This is Joe Jones. And Joe, this is our friend Eva Deane."

"Hello," he says gently.

"Hello," she says. He extends his right hand, and, as she's reaching for it, he sees the tiny sores around her nails, the rash on her wrist, and Louise sees him see this.

"Eva teaches science," she says.

Joe nods. Eva covers her mouth with her left hand.

"Lou? Should I wait outside? So Willie can come in?"

"Yeah, maybe so."

"Nice to meet you, Eva." He's very sweet, he really is, even though he's also a louse. Eva nods, smiling shyly, and reaches to hold down the stem of her wineglass as if it might be about to take flight.

The parentheses that frame Jessie's mouth are deeper than ever. "Why didn't you *tell* me it was you?"

He looks at her, full of longing and shame, and shrugs.

Willie peers around the corner and then pulls back out of sight.

"Willie?" Joe calls. Silence. "Willie? Just poke your head out for a second." After a moment, Willie looks out at him, impassive. "I'm sorry," Joe says.

Willie scowls. One side of his mouth turns down. He nods.

Louise goes into the back room after Joe leaves. Willie is staring at the dishes in the sink. "God, I'm glad he's gone," he says. Louise exhales loudly. "Arrogant *cock*sucker."

"Shhhhhh," she soothes.

On the porch Louise inhales the clean night air. It smells of grass and the sea. She sits on the top step and watches the four-second buoy flash green. Then she bends forward so that her face is on her knees and cries for a while.

TEN

JOE CALLS THE CAFE on the first day of summer from a pay phone near the Colonel Sanders on Lombard. Willie answers and is civil if not exactly friendly.

"Lou there?"

"Yeah, I'll get her, just a sec."

Joe and Louise have established telephone détente, although she hasn't wanted him to come by since he blundered in that evening two weeks before. Today he gives her the phone number of his new motel, and she takes it down appreciatively although she knows she isn't going to call.

"Why did you move?"

"Oh, never mind," he says, "you'll just think I'm nuts."

"I already do, Joe," and he stammers out that it was because he'd noticed that this entire East Indian family were covered with strange moles, and it was giving him the willies. She laughs, in an affectionate way, so that he can laugh at himself, which he does. Slyly then, he asks her if he might pop by today, and she says no, not today.

"When, then?"

"I don't know. We'll see. Hey, we're doing *good*."

It is the "we'll see" that makes him exhale noisily. His mother's favorite trick. His head is filled with longings and dread, with a vast hazy existential confusion. He stands staring at the phone after he's hung up, then bends so he can study his image in the pay phone's mirror.

"I hate men," says Willie. "I really do." He is in the back doorway, bent over with the crown of his head against the door frame, rubbing it like a young deer with itching antlers. "Really, I do, Louise. If I hated *women* I'd probably be straight."

Louise smiles.

"Do you mean Joe?"

"No, I mean *Dav*id. That whole—oper*a*tic dream stuff is a crock, man. I mean, if you want that kind of toxic rush, you should just take a bunch of drugs."

"Oh, Willie."

"They wear *off* faster." He stops rubbing his head on the frame of the door and scowls. "You know what I want to do? I want to just *trash* the guy, get him all strung out over me, and then break his stupid heart."

"It's not in your best interests," she says, but he's waving at her, as if he's waving away smoke.

"No, no. No. Don't Lulu me now, okay? Why can't you just let me be all fucked up about this? Why you have to go around putting *Band*-Aids on everybody?" She flushes and has to look away. He nailed her right where she lives and he sees it. "Oh, boy," he says, "I'm sorry, Lou." She shakes it off and tries to smile. "Oh, boy, I'm sorry." But she just shrugs and says don't worry and shuffles off towards the grill.

A minute or so later he comes crawling out of the back room on his hands and knees, crawls over to her at the grill, and she smiles.

Later he artfully cons her into giving him advice that he doesn't want and probably won't follow: See, it's all *right*. It's perfectly human to have the basest instincts, the vilest fantasies, but if you act on them, you probably won't feel very good about yourself.

Then he says, "Give me the Walk Tall pep talk," and she flushes again, bashful and kind of annoyed. "You're making *fun* of me. I know I'm ridiculous, Willie. So just don't make fun of me."

He hangs his head in contrition, but she can see he is smiling. "Willie's being bad," he says.

Jessie arrives at noon by cab, and Georgia not long after. Jessie looks beautiful and is wearing porcelain Easter lily earrings that Willie gave her last Christmas, but she's muzzy today. Even though she's got her hearing aid in, it is clear when Louise stands talking to her that she hasn't caught much of what's been said, but, God knows, she's polite and even encouraging about the whole thing.

Early in the afternoon she seems to doze while sitting up, and, when Louise shakes her gently, she blinks, confused.

"Is it still today?" she asks, and Louise nods. "Well," she says. "I suppose it always is."

"Grandma? Maybe we should give your doctor a call, just to be on the safe side."

"Oh, *bosh*! Don't you dare!"

Sam and Boone arrive with crayons and paper that Sam takes to a table.

"Give your nutty Aunt Lou a kiss," says Louise, and bends down. He kisses her, then tears towards the back room to find Willie. He digs into his front pocket with his tongue hanging out and then, absolutely awestruck, hands Willie a dead, crumpled butterfly.

"Wow!" says Willie. "I *love* it, Boone." Willie bends down and

lifts him in a hug, and then Boone dashes back to his father, crying, "Daddy, Daddy."

The men who work on the docks arrive in their Rauschenberg
blue jeans at one. The Rednecks come in for burgers and beer.
Fay stops by briefly to drop whine bombs about the fog. A few
sea scouts in mufti come in, and one even stops to admire the
picture Boone is making with crayons. And Central Casting
throws in a few real lulus today: for instance, there's the most
adamantly cordial and reserved English couple this side of
Monty Python; the man, in fact, might be from the Ministry of
Silly Walks. The woman explains cheerfully to Willie that they
are "lying doggo" in America, each recently separated from a
long-time spouse. And then there's a friendly fat woman of sixty-
five or so, with a Barbara Cartland novel, who orders tuna on a
sourdough roll. When Willie brings her plate to her, he asks her
where she's from, and she says from Sackwamentoe—she wooks
in a rihwee big wybrehhwy—and he nods at her almost tenderly,
and she lifts off the top piece of bread and tiles the tuna fish with
corn chips.

Jessie seems to have more energy after she and Georgia finish
lunches of minestrone. Georgia stares with a mischievous expression out at mudhens who swim near the shore, black, duckish
birds with white beaks. Jessie is entertained by Boone's enthusi-
asm; he's dashing back and forth between Willie and his daddy,
hides from time to time under his father's table, where he holds
intense chattery conversations with himself.

Jessie beams at Sam. Sam beams back at Jessie.

"We were so little once, Sam." She stares off into space for a
moment. Something is coming back. "If my memory serves me,"
she says. "If my memory serves me, Sam, they used to call us the
little *min*nows," and it seems as though she's talking about Sam
and herself. "At the general store . . . we would go in for penny

candy and the woman behind the counter would say, "'Here come the little *min*nows.'"

Eva comes in at dinnertime with *The Oxford Book of Death.*

Just in the last few days, she has grown even more stooped and emaciated. There are dark bluish-black half-moons under her bright amber eyes. She looks like something that has been spit out.

For the last few nights she has sat alone, after exchanging pleasantries with Jessie and Georgia. "I have too much reading to do," she says. "And I'm feeling under the wire."

Sometimes she drinks herbal tea, some nights she drinks wine.

Tonight Willie bounds over to the table where she sits alone, and he asks, full of hope, "Want some tea?"

She smiles and shakes her head.

"You want wine, don't you?"

"Yes, please."

It is a quiet night. Jessie and Georgia are eating cassoulet, and an Italian family of five who come in from time to time are eating chicken curry, and an elderly black couple have just been served bowls of Willie's raspberry Bavarian.

"Can *I* sit with you now?" Willie asks, sometime later. Eva bobs her head, and he sits in the chair beside her. "So. Did you bring the drugs?"

She covers her mouth as if she's just remembered that she was supposed to have brought the drugs.

"You for*got*?"

She nods solemnly.

"Oh, well." She smiles and reaches for her wineglass. "Have you ever taken drugs in your life?"

"Oh, sure. Didn't we all."

"Yeah, I guess, even the old philosopher queen," he says, jerking his thumb towards the grill.

"I am *not* the philosopher queen."

"Even the *Princess* used to do a lot of dope. What sort of drugs did you like?"

"I did a bunch of cocaine for a while." Willie shakes his head slowly in disbelief. "Yes!" Her eyes grow wide. "Really!"

"I can't imagine. I guess it's the *snorting* part that throws me. Snorting isn't even something I could associate with you."

"I just—*loved* it," she said. "It made me feel . . . It made me feel like I would have if I hadn't had such shitty parents." Willie nods.

"I'm not like a heavy *coke* aficionado," he says.

"Hey," calls Louise, "Why don't you talk—"

"Oh, dear," Willie says to Eva. "I *believe* that the Harvard Drug Series lectures are about to begin." Louise smiles at herself and scatters some cilantro over the pot of steaming black beans.

"Speed, now, man, I love that stuff. It's like *air*plane-chasing time, but like with *coke*, I don't know, man. *B*asically I don't approve of drugs which you crave as you're doing them. You know what I mean?" She nods and laughs and takes a sip of wine, then, when she sets it down, she burps, softly, and covers her mouth.

"*Well!*" says Willie, drawing back. "There goes the *r*omance. I mean, there goes the corsage."

Louise sends the two old women home by cab early that night. "You gotta go get some good *sleeps*," she implores, buttoning up Jessie's car coat. "Couple good sleeps and you'll be back to your old self."

"My un*for*tunately old self," Jessie says. Willie smiles.

"See?" Willie says, after they've put the women in the cab. "She's still got it."

Louise sits down at Eva's table for a minute and stares out the window at a sky full of white stars. Eva takes a sip of wine and follows Louise's gaze as if something specific is happening in the night. Seeing nothing, she returns to her book.

It. There's a crane operator in your head who gets the unconscious command: Rub your nose, blink, reach for your cigarettes. In Jessie's case the crane operator is eighty, stiff, somewhat foggy, and hard of hearing. But there is also another inhabitant in your head who doesn't age. This one is like the being in the sonagram Eva brought in that day, who also looked like Casper the Friendly Ghost. Louise can see this young child in Jessie's face. She stares at the stars.

Is Duncan up there somewhere with her parents? No, probably not. Heaven is a state of grace, not a place. But looking at the night sky she imagines the dead people in her family mingling with other souls—Joe's father Edwin, Willie's folks—as if it is a big cocktail party.

Eva has a small episode that night, is sitting quietly reading her book one minute, crying the next time Louise looks over.

Louise and Willie exchange a look, like: Here we go again, but Louise goes over to soothe her.

"You're sad again."

"I'm afraid."

Louise nods and sits down.

"It's okay when I'm here, but then I have to go home, and it's *fucked*, Louise." She looks angry now, frail, weepy, and mad. "I go, Anybody here? Hmmmm, no, I guess not." Louise smiles. "You think I feel sorry for myself."

"I think you got some very heavy shit to work your way through." Louise points at the book. "I think you're playing guts-ball right now, and you gotta . . . play it alone, with us to keep you company sometimes. I mean, that's where the body's buried."

"Listen to this," says Eva after a minute of staring fiercely at Louise. Then she looks blearily down at her book. Her lip trembles. Louise prays, *Please, God, don't let me burst out laughing.* "Nietzsche," says Eva, "Nietzsche, Louise." Louise nods. "'One must part from life,'" she has to stop for a moment, "'one must part from life as Ulysses parted from Nausicaa, blessing it rather than in love with it.'"

Louise shakes her head in wonder. Blessing it rather than in love with it. Eva shakes her finger knowingly at Louise and says, "*That* is where the body's buried," then shakes her head. "You ignorant dropout." Louise's mouth drops open and she bursts out laughing. Eva grins.

The fog burns off around noon the next day, and it's crowded but peaceful at the restaurant. Boone is the only obstreperous element; not even Willie can get him to smile, and Sam takes him home not long after they arrive. Tourists drop by, as do kids who are now out of school. Sister Peter-Matthew eats three of Willie's crème brulées while reading Gerard Manley Hopkins. The nutty writer spends most of the day on the porch drinking beer and reading one of the *Paris Review* "Writers at Work" collections. Georgia in her white beaded turban stares off to sea all day, alternately morose and fascinated, chainsmoking. Jessie is still reading Emily Dickinson and nods as if in agreement each time Georgia makes the bazoo. Willie is in a wonderful mood, full of mischief and teases and kisses for Lou, and all day she thinks, you are enough proof for me.

Joe calls that night after dinner.

"I bought a Ranchero," he says. "For practically nothing; this baby's a steal at twice the price. I mean, if I don't get a job coaching, I could somehow make a living with this car. I could haul stuff or something. This car could be my ticket out of this hell-hole."

"You sound so happy."

"It was like, right place at the right time."

"Oh, that's just terrific."

"Hey—Lou . . . you want to see it?"

"No," says Willie. "You didn't say yes."

"Yes, I *did*. I got con*fused*."

"Fuckin' A, Lou," he says and stares up at the ceiling above Eva's table.

"It'll be all right. Just be nice to him."

Willie shakes his head.

"I just felt sorry for him, love. He just got a new car, and he doesn't have anyone to share it with."

Eva smiles. "You're kidding yourself, Louise."

"I beg your pardon." Louise, who is standing by Eva's table, puts her hands on her hips. "What was that again?"

Eva smiles enigmatically.

"You don't hardly even *know* the man," says Louise. "Why're you doing this to me?" Eva smiles all-knowingly. "What're you talking about?"

"I'm talking about hate. Sadomasochism."

Louise sighs deeply and turns to go. "You two just be nice."

Willie turns and gives Eva a perfect Herschel leer.

Willie is hiding in the back when Joe arrives half an hour later. Jessie claps her hands in delight. Louise waves from the grill and drops her eyes, then holds up a finger: one minute. She is making burgers for the Rednecks, who call to Joe as if he is their long-lost brother, and soup for a middle-aged couple who have been bickering quietly over steins of beer.

Joe's got this friendly shyness about him, like a big dopey dog.

He holds his head at a tilt, and his eyes crinkle up, and he bends down to kiss Jessie, who immediately begins peeping and cooing again for the first time in days. This fact is not lost on Willie in the back room. He starts pretending to make himself gag. Georgia acts demure for a minute, and then pulls a face, as if she is straining to see her eyebrows. Joe looks at Louise and smiles. Louise smiles and drops her eyes again.

"You're wearing my *sweater*," Jessie cries, and he nods sort of sadly. She gave it to him for his birthday last year. She pats the empty seat on her left, and Joe stands twisting up the baseball cap that he removed when he first stepped in. He salutes Eva, who is making a fan with her napkin.

"Where's Willie?" he enthuses. Louise jerks her thumb towards the back room, and Joe, ever the rogue and the gentleman, stands waiting for Willie to come out. "Hey, Willie," he calls.

Willie, unseen at the sink, rolls his eyes. "Hi, Joe."

"Now you sit down, Joe Jones," Jessie commands.

"I will in a second, Jessie." Louise dishes up the soup and carries it to the bickering couple herself so that Willie can keep hiding, and in the meantime, Joe has taken several steps towards Eva. He asks her what she's reading, and she grimaces before holding up the book. On the cover is a reproduction of *Charon Crossing the Styx*, by Patinir, and carved stone lettering that spells out the title, *The Oxford Book of Death*.

"That looks like big fun," he says.

Jessie's eyes dart towards the back room. "Willie," she cries, "Joe is here—where are your manners?" Willie takes a deep breath. Louise, who is back at the grill, flipping a hamburger patty, looks up, waiting. After a moment, Willie steps out into the main room.

Joe sighs, and you can see the boy, eager to please, earnest and shy, behind the mask, behind the lonesome cowboy face, and he's playing the car keys on his key chain as if they're castanets. Willie stares back at him with something like gruff affection.

"Hi, Willie."

"Hi, Joe."

"Oh, we missed you *so* much," Jessie cries.

"Yeah. It was just terrible," says Willie.

"He's so fucking *broth*erly," Willie complains in a whisper, when Louise finds him skulking around the back room. "It really pisses me off. Don't start fucking him again."

"I'm not going to."

"He's so fucking brotherly." Then Willie steps around Louise and shakes his finger at Joe, who is sitting next to Jessie now, eating a bowl of stew, drinking a beer. Joe looks up, shy, sly, arrogant, and Willie scowls. "You better—behave yourself, Joe Jones."

"That right, dude?"

"That's right, dude."

Everything is all going to be okay. Louise feels like there's been a thin shell, like the candy crust of an M&M, around her heart for the longest time, and now it's been broken and she can breathe again.

Joe tells Jessie and Georgia all about his car, about the man he bought it from, about the bus ride out to buy it, while mopping up gravy with a piece of white bread. Jessie hangs on his every word, but Georgia gets frozen in the earlier position of trying to see her own eyebrows. Willie grumbles over to clear Joe's place, and Joe begins rubbing a fleck of meat into the table. Willie's eyes blaze. "Joe! You're makin' a meatwood *bump*." Joe freezes and then throws back his head and laughs.

Jessie improves visibly day by day. Her color is good and her hearing is better, and she just seems stronger in every way. She waits for Joe each night as if he's her gentleman caller. She watches

Willie tease him—Willie is trying to cling to his grudge but it isn't going very well—and she looks like her family has been reunited after the war. Joe helps the two old women to their cab every night, and he helps Willie with the dishes when things get busy, and he comes behind the counter to watch what Louise is doing at the grill, and he tries to get Eva to eat more, and he's everybody's brother.

He feels as if he's been reborn.

He feels, for the first time in ages, that he is a good man.

He sees how much these people adore Louise and it makes his heart feel buttery, makes him somewhat faint—just, for instance, to watch Louise help button Georgia's overcoat when the cab comes. He wonders if and when he and Louise will be lovers again, but over and over he reminds himself of Alfie and the nickel: Go for the dime and the game's over.

"So what does Eva have?" he asks Louise. "She's wasting away."

"We don't know for sure. She hasn't told us yet. Not cancer, but something as bad, she said."

"I mean is she, you know, dying?"

"I think so. She's getting worse by the week."

"I mean, but, in a—*soon* kind of way?" Louise shrugs. "Well, I mean, do we go ahead and renew her subscriptions?"

"Joe!"

He tugs on the brim of his baseball cap.

"Look, Lulu. I'm the guy who couldn't even cope with the moles on the people at my motel. How'm I supposed to cope with this? I mean, it gives me the willies, man."

"Meatwood *bump* gave you the willies. I saw it on your face, right before you laughed."

"It's a *ter*rible phrase, Louise. It's like something from *The Seventh Seal.*"

Louise shakes her head at him, smiling.

When Joe isn't looking, Willie makes the sign of the cross with his forefingers and holds it in front of his face, as if to repel a vampire.

Joe feels about Eva like everyone else does. She makes you want to hold her in your lap like a feverish child, but he treats her with courtly reserve. He does not want to make Louise or Willie jealous.

His days are spent in a state of frantic boredom. He takes to arriving at the cafe earlier and earlier, fairly bounds into the cafe now by midafternoon. Louise is kind, jocular, and cautious.

She wonders whom she will have on her hands when Rush Week ends.

One day Eva brings a National Geographic book on fish for Jessie and Georgia to look at. She places the book between the two women and sits down next to Georgia. Jessie turns the pages, peeping and cooing, while Eva supplies names and details. Georgia is spellbound.

Joe arrives with a big bag of the season's first peaches.

"Look at this wonderful book!" Jessie cries out to him. He peers at it over her shoulder.

"Wow," he says. "Is this your book, Eva?" She nods. "Fish, huh. Boy, you really get around."

"Look at this beautiful fellow," Jessie exclaims. She taps the photograph of a large, flat, tropical-looking fish.

"Oh, you know what this one does? This is sort of interesting. These live in the Amazon, Jessie. And when the baby fish are born, the mother secretes a nutrient through her scales, and for the first few days, the babies graze on her body."

Joe shakes his head in wonder. "That's really beautiful," he says, and stares at the fish as if he might burst out sobbing.

Sam and Boone arrive for dinner that evening. Boone tears off to find Willie.

"God, he got so big so fast."

"Yeah."

"I understood why Dana might want out of her marriage, but why would she leave Boone?"

"Why is not a useful question."

And that night after dinner Boone performs a small miracle while drawing with crayons: Sam watches him make swirls and squiggles, looking back and forth between the paper and the concentration on his son's face, when Boone makes a long straight line, and then raises his crayon to cross it.

"First time," Sam tells Louise proudly, showing her the drawing. Boone wiggles down off his chair, hitches up his blue jeans, and runs to the back room to walk to Willie.

Joe watches Boone and Sam intently, from Jessie's table. When Boone returns from his conference, Sam gets up from his chair and lifts him high above his head. Boone stares down into his face, smiling—an airplane—and then slowly turns his head up and around. He sees the lacy watermark on the ceiling, reaches for it, pointing, and Sam rises on his toes so that his boy can touch the ceiling.

"I get jealous," Willie tells Louise sheepishly. "I get afraid you'll go back with him, and I'll be a Lonely Guy again."

"Willie? You're like my—husband; I love you more than anything else in my life. He's like this sad, troubled brother of mine. And I don't feel like sleeping with him."

Willie hangs his head.

"So," says Joe, rather jovially one night, at the grill. "You want to go get a drink somewhere when you're done?"

"No. Not tonight. It's too *dangerous*."

"Don't you think we should try to *deal* with some of the—you know—stuff that happened between us?"

"No," she says.

Joe starts to have what Louise calls a little minibummer. He's been coming in now for a couple of weeks, and it's just like he and Louise were never in love at all. He gets a beer and sits out on the porch brooding.

Then he shuffles back in and over to the grill, where Louise is frying some hamburgers.

"Can I make myself something to eat?"

"Sure, what do you want? I'll make it."

"Maybe a quesadilla?"

"You got it. Grate up some cheese, and I'll do the rest."

He scrapes one of his knuckles rather deeply on the grater and he whinnies, grips the wounded hand, and watches himself start bleeding to death.

"Shit," he says.

"Ohhh." Louise grabs a paper towel and wraps it around his finger; blood seeps through. "You got an owwie." She applies pressure, and he tries to breathe through the pain. He watches it gravely, bravely, and she says, "You got a boo-boo." After a while the bleeding stops.

But half an hour later he is still walking around with his arm jutting stiffly out as if it's in a cast, and Willie keeps glancing over and rolling his eyes. Finally, he goes to the back room, finds a Band-Aid, and takes it over to Joe.

"Here," he says, "put it on."

"I think it's better for it to be exposed to air."

"No, I just can't *stand* watching you go around looking like it's a *bullet* hole."

Joe wakes up in his motel room from the worst dream he has ever had. It begins at the Lost Weekend, where he is trying to call Jessie's

Cafe, but he can't remember the number. He dials Information.

"I need the number for Jessie's Cafe."

"One moment, please.... That number is 232-1200."

"No, that can't be," says Joe. "The only prefixes it can be are 332 or 331. There are no 232 prefixes around here."

"I'm sorry, sir, but that is the number. 232-1200."

"It simply cannot be. He hangs up and calls information again. A man answers.

"I need the number for Jessie's Cafe."

"One moment, sir—Sir? That number is 232-1200."

It thoroughly freaks him out. It is as if someone in authority has just told him, beyond any shadow of a doubt, that his name is not Joe Jones. That it is in fact *Phil*.

It throws him off for the entire day. He has to do hourly Existence Checks. He calls the cafe at noon.

"Yo, Joe."

"Hi, Willie."

"What's wrong?"

"I don't know. Well, I had a nightmare this morning."

Willie laughs when Joe tells him the dream.

"I'm laughing with you, Joe," he says.

Joe frowns. "Let me talk to Louise."

"She's out on the porch, watering the plants."

"Well. Tell her I probably won't be in 'til dinnertime."

"Okey-doke."

Joe's frantic boredom reaches a new high.

He gets in his Ranchero and cruises aimlessly around San Francisco for a while, and then drives to Steinhardt Aquarium. He wants to see Butterball, the ancient manatee who hides shyly in a corner and looks like the inside of Joe's soul.

It turns out that Butterball died a month ago.

It breaks his heart. He sits in his Ranchero blinking back tears of frustration.

All day, everywhere he goes, it is 232 this and 232 that. He drives into North Beach to see his favorite bartenders, but Bobby doesn't work at Enrico's anymore, and Al is no longer at the Albatross, and by now Joe is so thoroughly unhinged that he goes to Market Street and watches a movie he has already seen many times, the most depressing movie in town, *The Rose Tattoo*.

Louise brings Jessie and Georgia plates of spinach linguine with pesto sauce that night for dinner. Jessie is sitting with one hand in her lap and one hand held stiffly at her side. Louise sets the plates before the two old women. Georgia is studying Jessie with angry alarm. Louise gets the chill.

"Does your arm hurt, my love?"

"It keeps going to sleep."

"*What?*"

"What a nuisance."

Louise sits down to her left and places an arm on Jessie's shoulder. "Are you okay, lovey?"

"*Lou!*" says Jessie.

"Jessie, what's happening, I'll get a doctor—*Willie!*"

Jessie is starting to look drunk. She stares down at the food in front of her and her head starts to droop, and Louise keeps calling to Willie, while trying to hold Jessie up by the shoulder. Willie steps out of the back and is, in a second, on the phone, wide-eyed and hyperventilating.

"I feel very queer," Jessie says slowly. Louise hears Willie ask for an ambulance in a shaking voice. He gives someone their address. She is immobilized—it all seems unreal. Jessie stares with a drunken look at her food. "I felt so—"

"Don't talk, don't talk."

"I felt so queer, Louise, but now I can see the trees. I can see the trees again."

Willie rushes into the room to his grandmother's side.

"We have to lay her down. Everybody out. You have to *go* now," he tells the roomful of gaping customers, and they all get up from half-eaten meals and tiptoe past the old woman. "Help me lay her down," he says from the very top of his throat, and they gently pull out the chair. Louise lifts her shoulders and Willie her legs. Her body is clammy and limp, but she is trying to look around.

Georgia is frozen, stock-still. Louise wipes Jessie's forehead with a napkin, and Willie is holding her hand and peering encouragingly into his grandmother's face. No one can swallow and no one can breathe. Then two ambulance attendants come in with a gurney and a resuscitator. They hook her up to the machine and lay her on the gurney. Willie is holding her hand and she's looking at him with absolute wonder.

Everyone but Georgia runs out the door. They won't let Willie ride in the back with her, and they close the door on Jessie. They get into the ambulance, turn on the siren and red flashing light, and drive away.

"What do I do, what do I do?" Now Willie starts crying. He's flying apart and Louise grabs him by the shoulders.

"Go!" she says. "I'll meet you in a second—"

"Come with me—"

"There's food on the grill, there's Georgia—"

"Help!"

"I'll get a cab for Georgia. Can you drive?"

"I don't know, Louise." Tears are streaming down his face and he's shaking badly.

"Go. Hurry. Be *careful*. Calm down—"

"Is it a heart attack—"

"I don't know; I think so."

"Hurry, Lou."

"I will, I will."

Georgia is still in shock, stares open-mouthed and then squints at Louise, and it seems that there is a superhuman intelligence in her black troubled eyes. Louise grips her by the shoulders. "I'm gonna get you a cab, don't worry, don't worry." It isn't until she tries to give the taxi dispatcher the address that she starts crying.

There are fries in the deep-fat fryer, burgers on the grill, and she dashes around on automatic pilot, praying, *Oh, please, please, please,* turning off everything she can think of. The cab finally comes and honks, and she helps Georgia on with her coat, and it seems like it takes twenty minutes to get her out to and into the cab. Louise helps the dazed old woman into the back seat, opens her purse, finds Georgia's checkbook, and reads off the address to the driver. There is a lot of money floating around in Georgia's purse, many bills, and she doesn't know if Georgia has the ability to pay the taxi driver, but she doesn't ask. She reaches in to kiss the old woman on the cheek and then runs for her own car.

There's a family of four in a white BMW leaving the parking lot when Joe pulls in half an hour later, but there are no other cars. His blood turns cold, and he can't swallow. He gets out and goes to the window outside the cutting-board counter, and he sees that there's no one inside. He imagines them all dead, slashed up in the bathroom. He runs around the side and up the path. He's thinking now he may get murdered, too, but he runs up the steps and into the cafe.

"Hello?" he says, fighting down the worst panic he's ever felt in his life. "Louise?"

Willie and Louise sit huddled together on a couch in the waiting room of the coronary care unit. Willie is still crying, in silence. Louise is in a trance. An hour ago, the doctor said that all he knew right now was that it had been a heart attack. They were doing everything they could. You may as well go home. She's stabilized. We don't know how bad it is. We'll call you the minute we know more.

"But what if she wakes up?"

"She's not going to, tonight."

"What are we going to do?" he asks Louise.

"Go to your house, I guess. And wait. She's gonna be okay."

"Can we just sit here another minute?"

"As long as you want."

Please, she prays, *please please please.*

Willie finally falls asleep in the living room around four that morning, with his head on Louise's lap. Most of the brandy is gone—there's an inch or so left in the bottle on the coffee table.

The cats are milling around suspiciously.

Out the window she can see the black sky, white stars, the yellow moon, branches. She studies the golden lights of the city, the golden lights of the Bay Bridge. She dozes finally, sitting up, and wakes to a red-black dawn. Tries to hail Mary. The bay stretches out before her, perfectly flat and black with just enough blue so you can see the houseboats huddling with their backs to you and behind them a million spidery masts in the harbor.

Joe called right after they got back, and she told him what little news they had, and he said he'd locked up the cafe—all you had to do was push a couple of buttons—and he asked if they wanted him to come over, and she said very gently, No, I don't think so. I'll call your motel as soon as we hear anything.

Now the sky is red and split miles above the water by a wavy band of blue. A canoe glides onto the scene, dark and noble and stealthy and for just a second you think it's an Indian manning the oar, and soon it is light enough so that when she looks down at Willie's shoulder, she can see a patch of blue T-shirt through a tear in the seam of his sweater.

ELEVEN

THE CATS STALK INTO THE LIVING ROOM at seven. Willie has gotten off the couch, shuffled into Jessie's room, and turned on the *Today Show*. All eight cats begin meowing at Louise. There are two imperious Siamese, three junkyard winos, a calico, a tabby, and a long-haired white cat. Louise thinks that if she had a gun she would open fire.

There is an aching so bad in the pit of her soul's stomach that it's turning her into a stone, a huge cold fearful stone. She is immobilized. She watches the cats as if they are auditioning. Finally, though, the meowing gets to her, and she goes off to the kitchen to feed them.

It is a sunny blue morning. After feeding the cats, she makes a pot of coffee and sits down at the kitchen table. She fiddles with her bangs and listens to the birds who sing from the oak trees outside the window.

She feels something that she has never before put her finger on, and it is something she now thinks she has felt all of her life. She feels defeated.

After a while she takes two cups of coffee to Jessie's room. Willie is stretched out on the bed. He glances away from the set for just a second. He has put on gray pajamas patterned with little red fish. Something has shut down behind his eyes. His hair is matted on one side, and he has closed all four white lacy curtains to keep out the morning sun. She puts one cup of coffee on the night table beside him.

"Can I lie down with you?"

He nods but doesn't look away from the set. There is room on the bed for Jessie and all of her cats, or for two people.

"I think visiting hours start at ten."

After a minute he looks at her, as if he's trying to remember where he's seen her before.

"What," she says.

"I don't want to see her on a bunch of fucking *machines.*" He scowls and drops his eyes.

They stare, exhausted, at the television set.

When she finishes her coffee, she gets up and returns to the kitchen, where the cats now sit cleaning their paws.

The nurse who picks up the phone in the coronary care unit is crisp and sympathetic. She says Jessie is holding her own. The doctor will be in to see her soon, and he will give them a call.

She calls Joe. He is so concerned and so eager to be of use that she sniffles the entire time they are on the line. She asks him if he will call Eva and Sam. They are both in the book, she thinks.

She pours herself another cup of coffee and lights a cigarette. There's someone else she ought to call. It will come to her in a minute. Everything feels gelatinous.

"Georgia? This is Louise." Louise clears her throat. "Look, uh, Jessie had a heart attack. We don't know for sure how bad it was. But, I just want you to know—that we'll keep you posted. And you can call us anytime you want. I mean, I know you're not, like, heavily into talking. . . ."

Louise rubs her forehead. She hears the rustle of a matchbook, hears the sulphury snap of a match being lit, a loud inhalation. "Okay, love. I'll call you when there's any news. You take good care of yourself."

She sits at the kitchen table for another half hour. The big eraser in the sky is going to come down and rub out Jessie. Her mind spins with sorrow for Willie. He is so young to have had so many amputations. Well, she thinks, at least he has me, at least we have each other. She'd almost forgotten that.

He sleepwalks into the kitchen and she gives him a smile that conveys both misery and encouragement. She tells him what the nurse said. He looks at her as if she is speaking a language he had studied for six months his freshman year in high school. She is about to suggest that she make them some breakfast, when he goes to the refrigerator and takes out eggs, butter, scallions, and cheese.

He works in silence. She doodles on the table with her finger. Soon the kitchen fills with the scent of melting butter. He cracks seven eggs into a clear glass bowl. Whisks them with a potato masher, minces scallions, grates cheese. He steers the eggs around the skillet with a wooden spoon, tosses in the scallions and cheese. Then he scrapes it all onto a plate, opens a drawer for a fork, and walks out of the room with his eggs.

She remains at the table for another twenty minutes and finds herself thinking about how much weight she will probably lose in the next few weeks.

Joe has the jim-jams bad. He paces around his motel room vibrating anxieties, then stops and bites himself on the wrist.

In the bathroom he stares at the dejected face in the mirror and pulls out a few gray hairs.

Finally he calls Information to get Sam's and Eva's numbers. He and Sam have a short manly talk: How is Willie? Sad.

Then he calls Eva. He sighs and tells her the news and she begins to cry. He listens to her sniffle and to the catch in her breath, and he looks to his glittery ceiling for help. This is not his specialty, crying women, but in fact he isn't sure what his specialty is. He tries to be a quiet warm presence over the phone and then finds himself saying, "Look, why don't I come get you and take you for a drive?"

On the Golden Gate Bridge it occurs to him that baby-sitting Eva is the solution to his problem of what to do while waiting. He can be of use—it fills him. The bay is a silver blue carpet held in place by Alcatraz and Angel Island.

Eva needs him and he would be lost right now if she didn't. The bay is crowded with sailboats, freighters, and birds. Once when he was talking to Louise during an existential crisis—what she would call one of his episodes—he said he doubted that even once in his entire life had he really done something for anyone else. That all of his acts of kindness, of comfort and giving, had been to make himself feel needed and less alone. And she said, I think your inner intention is good. Your inner intention wants to cheer or fill people up, but you don't trust yourself so you root around for a selfish motive. Try not to be so hard on yourself. He sees himself telling Louise that he took the grieving Eva for a drive, he sees her smile at him, lovingly.

He eases his Ranchero up to the curb in front of the address she has given him. Her house is small and old and next to a grammar school, in a middle-class neighborhood where kids would meet in the schoolyard on summer nights for kick the can, where Good Humor and doughnut truck men still come by. After a minute her front door opens and she peers out at him. He gets out of the car and takes off his 49ers cap and begins walking toward her. She steps outside and locks her front door.

Just before he hugs her he sees the shadows of her wet snaggly lashes high on her cheeks. She smells like shampoo.

"Want to go up on the mountain?" he asks—she looks off over his shoulder as if the mountain is there to consider, and, eventually, nods. He takes her by the hand. It's as small and frail as bird bones, and he walks her to the car, opens the door for her, and stands at attention while she gets inside.

The doctor calls at about the time Joe and Eva start up the winding mountain road. Louise takes the call in the kitchen.

"It is not as bad as we thought," he says in a voice that is somehow crisp and dull. "Only one of the three vessels is damaged. We won't know the full extent of the damage for a few more days, but the initial electrocardiograms are encouraging. I've removed the ventilator, she's breathing fine on her own, and the nurses will keep a full-time eye on her monitor. And now, well, we're just going to have to wait and see. I'd say if there are no complications, if she lives for the next three or four days, she has a very good chance...."

"Hot *damn*," she says, coming into Jessie's room. Willie is on the bed watching the *Andy Griffith Show*. She turns down the volume and tells him what the doctor says. He gives her a thin smile.

"It doesn't look so bad, dude."

He nods, but it is clear that he is waiting for her to move away from the set. She is blocking his view. She comes to sit by his side. He doesn't want to look at her. On the nightstand beside him is the plate flecked with curds of scrambled eggs, and two bowls where threads of Wheat Chex float on puddles of milk. He stares into one of these bowls as if he is reading tea leaves. Hope is what has shut down behind his dark gray eyes.

"Let's get dressed and go see her."

He shrugs. "You go. Maybe I'll go later."

"Honest? You don't want to go in now?" He shakes his head. Louise looks mildly annoyed.

She is on her way out the door when Willie appears in the hallway. "Wait," he says and glowers at his bare feet. "Let me go get my clothes on."

They talk to a tall horsey nurse in the coronary care unit, who is watching small TV screens of heart monitors at her station.

"Go on in," she says. "She woke up not long ago." Willie bites his bottom lip, nods, and glances skeptically at Louise.

They step into her room. Jessie's in the first bed, separated from the other by a curtain. The area looks like a space station, and her presence here seems as eerie as Neil Armstrong's on the moon. Beneath the white blanket is a figure the size of a small child. A bank of machines panels the wall above her feathery white head. Soundless blips of light describe several patterns across the screen of the heart monitor. Willie looks at Louise and licks his lips. Five IV tubes hang on a stand next to the bed. Several are plugged into each other, so three lines of tubing disappear into Jessie's arms. Willie tiptoes around to the far side of the bed and bends down to peer into the old woman's face. He solemnly signals Louise to join him.

She looks like a wizened male elf. Willie and Louise stand scrutinizing her for a long time.

They pull up chairs and sit side by side at the head of her bed. Louise begins to silently hail Mary. Jessie's going to die. It is so obvious to Louise that she fixates on Jessie's face to avoid seeing Willie's. She is about to get up and go have a smoke when Jessie's eyelids flutter. Willie opens his mouth and looks to Louise. Jessie opens her rheumy blue eyes.

"Grandma?" he whispers. She looks at Willie and runs her tongue around her gums.

"Hello," she says. He smiles. It's Jessie's voice. Then she closes her eyes and falls back to sleep.

Louise stops in the doorway on her way back from the waiting room where she had a cigarette. Willie doesn't see her. He is studying his grandmother through eyes downcast with pain, like the *mater dolorosa*.

But there's some shadowy light again in his eyes. He and Louise sit side by side in their chairs, watching her.

Nurses come in and out to check the levels in the IV, to take Jessie's temperature, to study the tracings on the monitor of the electrocardiogram. The nurses are sweet and competent. They make you wish you were a nurse.

"Her mouth seems dry," says Willie, and a nurse brings him foil-wrapped cotton swabs that are wet and lemony, and shows him how to run the swab over Jessie's gums and parched lips.

Every few minutes Louise hails Mary, and every few minutes Willie swabs his grandmother's lips.

Her eyes open again.

"*Hi*, Grandma."

She tries to focus her eyes.

"Are we still on the train?" Willie tilts his head birdlike at her. Her voice is soft but unmistakably Jessie's. He takes her hand. "I'm so tired," she says. "I feel like aging light."

They speak to her loudly. *Hello! hello! hello!*

"I'm so tired of being on the train," she says. "When can we go home?"

"As soon as you're a little stronger," says Louise.

"When can we go home?"

"As soon as—oh, she doesn't have her *hear*ing aid." Willie bends in close.

"How far are we from home?" Jessie asks.

He cranes his face to within six inches of hers.

"TWENTY MINUTES."

"Oh, she says, and falls back to sleep.

Louise goes out to the nursing station and arranges to have Jessie's hearing aid put in.

"Did you ever hear how Jessie got the cafe?" Joe asks.

Eva shakes her head apologetically. They are parked by the side of the road on top of the mountain looking out over the aquamarine Pacific Ocean and the foothills green with woods and grass. Eva is folding a Jack-in-the-Box napkin into a fan.

"Would you *like* to hear?"

She has been covering her mouth so often that Joe has been trying, ever since he picked her up, to catch a glimpse of her teeth. While he was driving them up the winding old fire road that leads to the spot where they now sit, it suddenly occurred to him that her teeth might be buck or stained or God knows what, and he keeps trying to make her laugh. But when he does, she covers her mouth. He watches her now with an almost paternal tenderness. She has unfolded the napkin and is using it to bandage her forefinger.

"Well, you see, she was born on a farm near New Orleans. Her uncle—her father's brother—and his wife were killed in a car wreck when Jessie was three. Their son, Jessie's cousin William, went to live with their grandmother, in her cottage, several miles away from Jessie's farm. Well, one day when William was six, his grandmother sent him off to pick cherries—she wanted to make a pie.

"So he took the basket and left, but on the way to the cherry trees, he ran into his friends. They were headed to the pond for a swim, and he ended up going with them. And he just sort of forgot about the cherries.

"He didn't go home for hours, and then without the basket, and his grandmother was on the porch waiting for him—she was very old at the time. She saw him coming, when he got close enough to hear she said, 'I can't raise you anymore. Ride to your uncle's house.' So he got on his bike with a small box of clothes and rode over to Jessie's house—her father was William's uncle—and they raised him as their son. Jessie always thought he was her brother. They just adored each other—he moved with them to New York when she was ten.

"William moved west after college, and ended up buying the cafe, and he ran it for like fifty years. In the meantime, Jessie's son—Willie's father and mother—were killed. Did you ever hear how? In a *plane* crash. Jessie moved out here with Willie, who was about six at the time, to be near William. She got a job as a saleswoman at Magnin's, bought a shitty little tract house in Corte Madera, and then, about seven years ago, William died, and he left everything to Jessie, and everything was the restaurant."

Willie and Louise are in the waiting room. He paces. She starts to cry again.

"Lulu?"

"I'm just tired."

"You didn't get any *sleeps*," he says. She sniffles. "Did you eat anything today?" She shakes her head. "Well. Why don't you go out somewhere and get like a sandwich or something? I'll be okay here alone."

The parking lot of the restaurant is empty. She turns off the ignition, eyes the deserted cafe, and decides against going in. She walks instead down the path to the bay.

The tide is all the way out, and the rocks on shore are covered with moss. The pilings are covered with barnacles and white lichen. Logs and driftwood, tires, shore birds, ducks, and litter stick out of the mud flat and the beach. She sits on a boulder near the shore.

The biggest egret she's ever seen swoops down and lands on the beach not far from where she sits. He has his back to her but is close enough so that Louise can see his yellow star feet. Then she sees a flash of the brightest blue, looks up to see the underside of a six-foot wingspan, a great blue heron, out of nowhere, who swoops down on the egret as if in attack but then lands a good ten feet away. Louise blinks hard. The birds' backs are to each other, and they begin to pace off, as if one will whip around in a second and shoot the other. They stop when they're twenty feet apart and remain there in a brooding standoff. After a few minutes the heron jumps into the air, flies away, and disappears around a bend in the bay.

"Hi, Lou," Willie says when she returns. She comes up behind him, puts her arms around his neck, and lays the side of her face on top of his head, and they stare at the sleeping woman. "She's been talking a lot about the train. She told me she's been to Mt. Whitney twice. The first time was okay, but now she's tired and stiff. The doctor popped in for a minute."

"What did he say?"

"Said that she may be pretty spaced out for a while—that he was, what did he call it?—*guard*edly optimistic."

Louise lets go of Willie and sits down beside him, and watches the tracings on the monitor, as if she knows what to look for. She remains in the hypnotic trance of exhaustion until Jessie wakes up again.

Jessie squints into Willie's face. He bends close, smiling.

"What's her name again?"

"*Whose name?*"

"That very, very old woman."

Willie thinks for a minute—Does Jessie mean herself?
He scratches his head. "*Georgia?*"
"Yes," she says. "That's right." Her eyes flicker but remain open,
more or less. "I could never pronounce it," she says.

Willie tucks Louise into bed at eight that night. He puts the
phone on the nightstand next to his side of the bed, then goes to
the kitchen for a few minutes. He returns with two plates of cinnamon toast and two mugs of hot chocolate.

She looks at him blearily.

He turns on the television and crawls into bed beside her.

She drinks the cocoa and falls asleep with the plate of toast on
her chest.

She wakes up in the middle of the night. Willie's breath is soft
and he is radiating heat. He must have opened the curtains at
some point. By the smoky moonlight in the room she can see his
face in repose. Patches of his hair are matted, other patches spiky.
She sighs. Jessie said, not long before, *Our Willie is saucered and
blowed.* When she was young, you poured your steaming tea into
the saucer, blew on it until it was cool enough to drink.

*Suffer her not in the last hour any pain or fear of death but let
Thine arms . . .*

Louise gets out of bed and goes to the window. There are a
hundred thousand white stars fixed in the blue night, but where
is God? *What if I just made Him up?* She swallows hard, studies
the stars. *Bear with me,* she prays.

She squints at the gleaming white moon until it looks like a
hole in a cask, a hole in the bowl of earth's sky, as if on the other
side of the dome there's a sky that is brilliant white fiery light.
Then she walks back to the bed and crawls in beside Willie.

Joe lurches out of a dream late the next morning and bolts to a
sitting position in his bed at the motel. He was flying over the

Pacific, soaring. He has a vague impression he was hang-gliding, but maybe not, and as always in his flying dreams, he panics—even before he starts to fall—he gasps: *The wax will melt.*

He stares at the ceiling, at the cottage-cheesy ceiling with its gold glitter, reaches for the phone, and calls Louise.

She is feeding the cats when he calls, wearing only her underpants, a sweatshirt, and Jessie's furry pink flip-flops. Willie is still asleep. The kitchen is sunny and smells of fresh-ground coffee.

"I feel like Lazarus," she tells him.

"I called you last night, but Willie said you were asleep. It was like about eight thirty. So, you feel better?"

"Yeah, I do. How are you? How did Eva take the news?"

"Well, I told Willie but I guess—"

"He's still asleep."

"Well, she was real sad at first, sort of freaked out or something, so I told her I'd take her for a drive. We went up on the mountain." Louise's stomach feels jumpy. "And we just, you know, talked about stuff. She told me about her flat tire. And about her old Hewlett Packard. And she was just sort of very shy and squirmy. But you know, she's got those wonderful stories. And theories. I don't know. We thought maybe we could come see Jessie today?"

"Well," she says, "listen. I think you guys ought to wait until tomorrow. They only let the family in. I'm like—they sort of understand that I'm like—a relative. I mean, you are, too, but it would just sort of complicate things today. Tomorrow we'll say you're her grandson, in from New York or something."

"Oh. Okay."

"Don't be mad at me."

"I'm not mad at you."

"Good, okay." They listen to each other breathe. "She's got like a real fighting chance, I think. She wakes up, she talks. . . ." Louise trails off.

Joe doesn't say anything. It is irrational but his feelings are hurt.

They are both quiet for a minute and then they're saying, Look, I'll talk to you later, keep me posted, yeah, I will, goodbye, and after Louise hangs up, she goes to the stove, stares at the pot of coffee, and wraps her arms around herself, gripping her shoulder blades, as if her gray sweatshirt were a straitjacket.

"Morning, Eva. It's Joe. How are you?"

There's a soft sharp intake of air. "Oh, I'm all right. How is Jessie? How are Willie and Louise?"

"Everyone's better." He tells her what the doctor said, he tells her that Willie was funny last night on the phone, he tells her that Louise finally got some sleep, and he tells her it would be better if they waited till tomorrow to see Jessie.

"Okay," she says.

He finds himself to be hesitant, tongue-tied. "Do you have, uh, plans for the day?"

"I have to go to the doctor at one." He rubs his eyes with a thumb and finger.

"Want me to take you?" he asks.

"Oh, that's so nice of you. But it will be so dull."

"That's okay," he says. "I don't mind dull."

"Willie?" They are sitting out in the sunshine on the front step, shoulder-to-shoulder, drinking coffee. "I was thinking. I should post a sign at the cafe, and call off deliveries, go through the fridge, chuck anything that might go bad."

He nods, shrugs. "Do it."

"And also—I was thinking maybe Jessie would like to see Georgia. Maybe that's why she asked what her name was." Willie shrugs again. His lips are still pouty from sleep, and he's been wearing the same fraying blue T-shirt for days. "Maybe—do you think if I called her and had her take a cab to the hospital, you could meet her in the lobby and take her up?" Willie grimaces. "I know, but at least if she took a cab there and back it'd save us a couple hours, and it might do Jessie good."

"Yeah, I guess. Sure."

Then he strains to hear something, not the songbirds or the breeze. "Listen," he says. He crooks his head and they see at the same time something crawling out from the hedges. They get up to investigate. A cat is crawling towards them on his belly, dragging a crooked back leg behind him, wailing.

"It's a sick *pussy*," says Willie. He's stricken. It is an orange junkyard cat who has lost most of his hair, all of one ear, and the other is in tatters, but still it snarls at them as they approach, baring its teeth and crying like a siren. "It's not one of ours," says Willie. He looks at Louise with alarm, and then says, matter-of-factly, "I just can't deal with this."

Twenty minutes later he is watching the yard from behind the living room window. A man from the Humane Society, an old guy with fluffy white hair and black spectacles, is catching the screaming cat with a net that is on the end of a pole. Three of Jessie's cats—Little Cat, Nora, and Thor—have appeared but are keeping their distance. Louise is standing on the step with her back to Willie.

The man eases the cat into a small cage he has brought and then goes to his van for a minute. He brings Louise a clipboard and a pen. The cage is twenty feet away. The sick cat keens. Little Cat, Nora, and Thor tiptoe over and peer in at him through the chickenwire cage, like a team of doctors. Then they post themselves on either side of the sick cat, until the kindly old man comes to take him away.

"That was the fuckin' weirdest thing I ever saw, man—the way Grandma's kitties sort of were like, commiserating with it or guarding it. I could hear it crying all the way inside." They are both really troubled. They are picking at the plates of scrambled eggs Louise made. "Do you think it's like some creepy omen?"

"No," she says, although she does, and smiles in what she hopes is a reassuring way. The day Jessie died, she will say—and this is a true story—a dying cat appeared in our yard. This is a true story, you say, in the face of coincidence and synchronicity. This is a true story: Ten years ago she and her Uncle Duncan were keeping a vigil at her father's hospital bed, where he lay dying of a stroke. She was flipping through tattered *New Yorker*s she had snagged from the waiting room. She turned to an Edward Koren cartoon in which a chipper talk-show host is addressing the four seated guests. Off to one side, approaching from the wings, is the hooded figure of Death with his long-handled sickle, and the talk-show host cheerfully tells his guests, "Well, it looks like our time is just about up."

Louise had passed the magazine to Duncan, pointing at the cartoon, and right then, exactly as he was reading it, her father died.

Willie gets up from the table. "Guess I'll get going," he says.

Sunshine streams in through the windows of the cafe. She stands in the open doorway looking in. The sound of the absence of people makes her insides crawl, like she's the sole survivor of the neutron bomb. Half of the tables are covered with plates of food that is beginning to rot. She steps inside and opens all the windows. Then she puts an old Dixieland tape on the stereo, *Bunk and Lu*, Bunk Johnson and Lu Waters, and, pushing back her shirt sleeves, begins to carry the plates out to the back room.

She breathes through her mouth while scraping the food off the dishes and takes the garbage out to the dumpster. Then she fills one of the sinks with steaming soapy water, puts on the yellow rubber gloves, and for the next three hours or so feels a frenzied kind of relief. When the dishes are done, she calls Willie via the nurse in the coronary unit. He sounds tired but cheerful. Jessie has awakened several times to tell him and Georgia about the train ride. The doctor came in and said that this was to be expected, these dreamy delusions, and he thinks she is doing just fine. And Georgia's being good, Willie says. She sits beside him, watching Jessie. "She hasn't made the farting noise once."

"I need another good hour or so," says Louise. "Gotta water the plants on the porch, then clean out the refrigerators." Willie says he's sorry she got stuck with all the mess, and she says, "Willie? It is a godsend for me, just what the doctor ordered. You take care. Love to Georgia. Love to you. See you soon."

She chants while she cleans out the refrigerators, *Agnus dei qui tollis peccata mundi...dona nobis pacem*. She works and is feeling better.

Joe gives Eva a peck on the cheek when he says goodbye to her, outside of her doctor's office. Then he ambles down the street. It is tree-lined and largely residential. He is wearing his 49ers cap and has his hands in his pockets as he whistles a Willie Nelson song. He passes a convalescent home. Through the windows old faces gaze out blandly as if at a rainy day. Dogs and children play in gardens behind fences, teenagers conspire in front of a 7-Eleven, couples—the men in suits—pass by in newish cars.

He has got to find a place to live pretty soon. His money is running out. Maybe his mother is good for another thousand. He ought to call her tonight, but probably won't. He would probably love her more, in a wistful, amused, sentimental way, if she were dead. She would be more real to him then. He would be able to feel she was really his *mother*.

He shakes his head at himself as he walks along.

Joe had felt, and believed, she was really his *mother* until around fourth grade. That was the year Mary's periods began and the house grew whispery and sinister. He stopped calling his mother Mommy. Before Mary's periods he was Huckleberry Finn. Afterwards, inside, he was a cross between King Lear and the hunchback in *Candy*.

He snorts softly, smiling. He read *Candy* for the first time in eighth grade. Boys were passing around a tattered copy in a book cover made from a brown paper bag, which had *The Rise and Fall of the Roman Empire* handwritten on it. What a wild book— Candy angelically making love with the bitter hunchback, whose head is full of thoughts of steel wool, bathtubs filled with living and broken toys, excrement, and pig masks....

God! Jessie's in the hospital, remember?

Joe Jones frowns and marches on. His brow is furrowed and there is a lopsided set to his mouth, as if he is ventriloquizing.

On the way back to Eva's doctor's office, he stops at a gas station and steps inside the phone booth.

He asks the nurse in coronary care if Louise is in with Jessie. She says no, but that Willie is here with his aunt. Joe tilts his head and after a minute asks if he might speak with Willie.

"Aunt *Georgia's* here," Willie announces cheerfully, and a bug-eyed lizard in Joe's reptile brain flicks its tongue, like when you say hello in passing to someone and they don't say hello back. He can't believe that Georgia gets to visit, and he doesn't. He half listens to Willie's progress report. Jessie's apparently better, but there's sick disbelief on Joe's face and in his heart, then chagrin, then anger at Louise, then sorrow, and then, after the next blink, a steely resolve. Fuck me? Uh-uh, baby, *fuck you*.

He is in the waiting room when Eva tiptoes out. He rises out of his chair, flips the new *Sports Illustrated* back onto the coffee table, puts his cap on his head, and they give each other small reassuring smiles. Then he takes her arm with grim dignity and leads her out the door.

They both watch her feet as they walk along to his car.

Eva looks up into his face and then looks back down. "She thinks my eyes are better," she says. "She thinks the things on my retina are smaller."

He smiles paternally and opens the car door for her, waits until she's gotten in, and then closes it. When he's behind the wheel, she tilts her head at him and says, "She thinks my cuticles are not so bad," then balls her hands up and drops them into her lap. She gives the passenger window a meek shrug. He is smiling at her when she looks back over.

"You want to go get an ice cream or something?" he asks.

"Do you really want one? Or are you just having a nice idea?" He watches her squirm. "You are so sweet," he says.

"I'd just sort of like to cruise," she volunteers, and so he says, "We're off to the Mighty Petaluma, Father of All Waters."

The car is warm and full of sun, and it encloses them like cell membrane. By the time they start passing meadows and hills instead of buildings, she is hardly squirming at all. They pass fields, green fields full of cows, yellow hills of grain.

She begins to bandage her finger again.

They drive past the river and out to Bodega Bay. There they stop for a glass of wine at a restaurant on the water. They stare out the window at the fishermen and fishing boats, gulls circling overhead, the pier, a tugboat, the bay. "What's the matter?" she asks.

He shrugs, looks wistfully at some pelicans, sighs.

"Someone lied to me this morning. Someone who I really trust. It's just really sort of throwing me a bit. I feel foolish."

"Oh." She takes a small sip of red wine. "People can't help lying. It's the nature of the beast."

He looks at her sadly.

"You see," she says, looking up and down from her lap to his eyes as she speaks: "When you were a little tiny animal, you were shown a game trail down to the river. Some of the time, if you behaved in certain ways, if you were being good, you got down to the river, and found food, water, and love. The things you needed for strength. But sometimes you would go down that same game trail, and the bear would jump out of a bush and bite you, bad. Because our parents were inconsistent. They were not the gods we made them out to be. They were all fucked up, like we are. So one day, you're 'good,' and your god smiles down at you in the crib. You see love and approval and it gives you strength. But the next day you look up into the face of your god—and he or she is unhappy about work or the marriage or money or health—so you're looking into these cold, flat, reptilian eyes.

"You feel a cellular recoiling, of shame, betrayal, confusion. You live in fear of the bear. And you've got to get down to the river, so you find another trail—lies, guile, whatever. You learn to stay on the alert. You learn not to trust. It makes you terribly paranoid and full of bad conscience. Alone.

"But you see your god lie. Your mommy lies, your daddy lies, and it just becomes second nature for you to lie. And then you really have to stay on the alert for the bear. The whole game goes from being alive and full of trust and gaining strength, to learning how to seize power. If we didn't get down to the river, we would die. It's like, we couldn't even help it. It was survival, but, *boy*, being rejected by that first god of yours makes you want revenge."

Joe looks into Eva's intent, impassioned face, looking hard, like he's trying to remember the words to a childhood song. After a moment, he asks, "Do you have time for another glass of wine?"

"Joe just called from Bodega Bay," Willie tells Louise at the nurses' station. Only one of them can go back into Jessie's room. There is a two-visitor rule. Louise has just arrived.

"He was like totally *speed*ing or something. He said, like, he suddenly understands pretty much everything there is to know about people."

"Eva can really throw on the lights."

"Yeah, and he said, he *loves* you, and he loves *me*, and he loves *Jess*ie, and he *likes* Georgia." Louise smiles again. "And he'll call you at our house tonight."

"Now you go get some lunch," she says.

She kisses him goodbye and walks down the hall to Jessie's room, where she finds Georgia sitting next to the bed, adjusting her red velvet crown.

"Hello, my love." Louise smiles tenderly at the old woman. Georgia's dark, almost-black eyes are covered with the milky veils of old age, and she holds her gnarled spotted hands in her lap, they look like dried leaves against her yellow pantsuit. Louise goes to kiss her. Georgia looks at her imploringly.

Louise takes the empty seat beside her and they watch Jessie sleep. Georgia turns to study the foot of the bed, where Jessie's feet just barely raise the blanket, then swivels back to look at Jessie's face, then back to Jessie's feet, and back to Jessie's face. She might be watching a tennis match.

"What is it, my love?"

Georgia squints at Jessie's face, then bends forward and shakes Jessie's shoulder. Jessie opens her eyes and gazes blankly at the old empress.

"Hello," she says, and falls back to sleep. Georgia turns and leers at Louise.

Louise automatically begins watching the five blips, which cross to the right of the screen and then reappear at the left.

After a while she sighs and turns with an inquiring look to Georgia.

"Shall we go have a smoke? In the waiting room? And if you want I can call you a cab from there. You've been here all day."

Georgia doesn't appear to hear, but a few minutes later she reaches down to the floor beside her chair, and lifts up a gold lamé clutch purse, which has a clasp and a short snaky gold strap. Louise gets to her feet, extends a hand, and pulls the old woman up. She takes Georgia's free arm, which is as firm and weightless as balsa wood, and drapes it gently, as if it were broken, over her own arm. Then she begins moving the empress towards the door. Georgia clutches the purse by its strap, with her arm straight down at her side. Its weight makes her left shoulder droop so low that if you didn't see the flash of gold lamé, you might think she was lugging a suitcase.

Jessie doesn't wake up again until after Willie returns. He is watching her tenderly when her eyes flutter open.

"Hi, Grandma," he says loudly. "Are you having nice sleeps?"

She makes a crotchety face. "Louise made me go for a walk," she says. Willie looks with mock horror at Louise.

"Are you *sure*?"

"Yes."

"How far did she make you go?"

Jessie runs her tongue around her gums, and then says, quite grimly, "Five miles."

Louise smiles. Willie is bent in close to his grandmother, enunciating carefully.

"Where did she take you on this walk?"

Jessie doesn't respond for a minute, but then states firmly, with some indignation, "On the freeway."

She wakes up one more time early that evening, licks her gums, and addresses the space between Willie's and Louise's heads.

"Are we all alone on this boat?"

It is perfectly quiet in the room until Willie clears his throat. He shakes his head. "We're not exactly alone," he says. "There's other people on the boat. But we have our own room."

Joe calls that night while Louise and Willie are watching an old movie on Channel 44, *The Red Slippers*. Louise is ever so slightly distant as she tells him how Jessie is doing, and then Joe says, "Boy, Eva tells me this thing today, and it totally blows my mind." He tells her about the game trail.

"And I'm walking around the city tonight, by myself, and everything's sort of falling into place. Like I got really hurt when you said I shouldn't come in today? And then I was like, furious when it turned out Georgia was there? And while we were driving up to Petaluma, I was sort of thinking up ways to get *back* at you, like I thought I could make you really jealous, and I'm just so fucking crazy, Louise. But, I mean, I really think Eva's *on* to something, and I'm just really sorry, and..."

Louise interrupts to say that she *was* jealous, and how sorry she is, and she shouldn't have interrupted, and he says, "No, go ahead," and she says, "No, you go," and they do this Alphonse and Gaston for a while.

"I'll call you in the morning," she says. "Willie and me'll meet you at the hospital. And Eva, too, if she can come."

"Yeah, bring Eva," Willie says to Louise.

"We'll take turns being visitors, two at a time."

"I send my love to both of you," says Joe.

"We send our love to you."

Jessie dies in the middle of the night.

Willie takes the call. He and Louise bolt from sleep into sitting positions on the bed. He grabs the receiver. By the faint mist of moonlight that streams through the window, she sees how violently his arm and hand are shaking, how wide his eyes have become.

"Okay," he says into the receiver and hangs up. Louise doesn't breathe. The bed is shaking. He lies down with his back to Louise and pulls the covers up over his head.

When Louise whispers, "Is she gone?" Willie begins to cry.

TWELVE

WILLIE HAS OPENED THE DOOR to Joe and Eva as if they have tracked him down. He is wearing his gray pajamas with the tiny red fish, and his hair is matted. He holds a snifter of brandy in a disheartened and proprietary way, as if this glass is what they have come to collect. He puts it down on the floor and then reaches up to put his arms around Joe's neck. Joe holds him. He feels Willie's wet lashes on his neck. It is nearly five o'clock on Friday morning. Behind Joe, Eva is standing as pale and pinched as a porcelain gypsy doll. The night is black, yellow black, and there are many white stars and a fine misty drizzle.

Willie and Eva are hugging when Louise shuffles in from the kitchen. When Joe hugs her she smells of campfire, brandy, and Ivory soap. Holding her, he nuzzles her soft hair with his nose, like a mother horse.

The living room is lit by soft low light from lamps with fringed shades, they all settle in with brandies. Willie takes one of the sedatives Eva's brought with her, and huddles up against Joe on the couch. Louise sits in the Shaker rocking chair to the left of the couch, and Eva sits in a faded yellow easy chair, tracing the sworls of lace on one of the antimacassars.

Outside, it's becoming day.

There are cats everywhere you look. Two of the junkyard cats lie side-by-side on the braided rag rug. A Siamese lolls on the marble-topped chest of drawers. On the wall above it are glass cabinets that hold what Jessie called her funny little things: Buddhas, ivory elephants, jade roses, tiny dolls from foreign countries, porcelain thimbles with painted shamrocks and windmills and cats, blown-glass figurines, the lumpy clay horses and people Willie made as a child.

Out the window, lights of the houseboat village pulse like candle flame on the black-green bay. A solitary gull flies by. An egret appears. Soon more and more gulls arrive, and a hooded woman in a yellow slicker rows out to sea in a canoe. Men in black raincoats walk purposefully down the dock, hunched against the drizzle.

Willie can hardly keep his eyes open, but he glances at Louise from time to time as if worried she's no longer there. "It's like that dream you told me over the phone," he says to Joe. "Yesterday. No, the day before. 'Cause I know she's just in the kitchen soaking her Grape Nuts or feeding the cats. I take that for granted. She'll be out any minute."

"What dream did I tell you?"

"Don't you remember? 232."

Willie falls asleep on his side with the crown of his head lodged against Joe's thigh. Louise covers him with the afghan that had been draped over the arm of the couch, then they all watch him sleep. He moos but does not wake up, and Joe strokes his shoulder like he's a cat. Eva looks blankly out the window. A motorized skiff chugs by with a huskie standing at the helm keeping watch. Willie thrashes around and then quiets himself, brings his right leg out from under the blanket and wiggles his bare toes.

"That's called rafting," Eva says. She points to Willie's leg. "It's what seals do . . . ?" She looks at Louise, who gives her a look that says, Go on. ". . . to cool off, when they've been swimming too hard or too long."

Eva reaches for a Kleenex, folds it in half lengthwise and in half again, and they watch spellbound. "You see," she tells the Kleenex, "the blood vessels in their flippers are closest to the surface. So when they're hot, they lie on top of the water with their flippers out in the cool air."

Joe and Louise are smiling at her with genuine interest but she cannot see this because she has covered her eyes with her palm. She shakes her head. "Jeez," she says. "Eva's *Fascinating Facts*."

"I wonder," Joe says sometime later, "I wonder where it all goes."

"Where what, the time?"

"No. Like, Jessie's spirit. You think it survives, don't you, Lou."

She studies the oily wash that the brandy has left in her glass. "Yeah, I guess I sort of believe it survives. Whether or not her soul rose when she died, like steam, well, I'm just not sure about that."

It plagued him when his father died. *Where had it all gone?* He was with him at the hospital, there by his father, who lay in bed wasting away. And he listened to his father's breath go in and out, in and out, and *it* was all still there, stored in his father's mind: the kindergarten picnic, the taste of ants, his first long pants, and how the thin wool felt on his shins. His first car, first dance, the day he met his wife, the birth of his daughter Mary and his son Joe, a big crazy movie, his life. Billions of moments, scenes and scents. Even if many of those memories were intractable, it was all still in there. And then he breathed in, and then he breathed out, and then he just didn't breathe in again. He was dead. *But so where did all that stuff go? The taste of ants, the feel of wool on his shins?*

They sit in silence, watching Willie sleep.

Joe glances over at Louise from time to time. Her head is bowed, she is hugging herself.

Louise has said that since energy cannot be created or destroyed, the souls of the dead must go somewhere. But now he wonders: If you have a lamp on at night, and the room is filled with its light, when you turn off the switch has the light *gone* somewhere?

"I don't know, lovey. I really don't."

"You're not afraid of dying, are you, Lou."

"Not very often." She gets up and begins to pace. "I just gave up one day. Around the time the news about toxic shock syndrome came out. I thought, *Fuck me, man,* I give up. Come and get me. You know where I am. Now I'm more afraid of disgracing myself. Of it turning out that, way down deep, I'm not a good woman." She stops, looks over her shoulder at Eva, and lifts one corner of her mouth wistfully. "Sometimes I'm scared. Like on this one night I woke up in the middle of the night, and it was so still, so quiet and black, that I was sure there'd been nuclear bombs. And I thought I'd have to band up with a bunch of desperado survivors, and I thought, you know, I'd be the one in the Shelly Winters role—in this shrill panic, pushing and shoving and clawing my way to the food." Joe smiles. She shakes her head at him.

"How can you say that, Louise? You'd be going up to these people who had horrible radiation burns, and you'd scrinch up your face and go, 'Ohhhh. Ohhhn.'" Louise sits back down in the rocking chair and closes her eyes.

Eva is on the end of the couch when Willie wakes up a couple of hours later. He sits up, pouty with sleep, and rubs his eyes.

"Do you want some coffee?" she asks. He shakes his head. She slides over and slips her arm through his, and they huddle together like a starving old married couple on a park bench in a chilly wind.

"Where did they go, Joe and Louise?"

"They went to the hospital to sign some papers."

He looks away, as if she has hurt his feelings.

"Do you feel all right, Willie?"

"A little rocky."

"Shall I make you something to eat?" No, he shakes his head and gets up to pour an inch of brandy into one of the empty snifters. She stares out at the gray sky. He sits down beside her again.

"So you got stuck *baby*-sitting me."

"I wanted to be with you."

He scowls at his lap, and then at hers, where her hands lie idle for once. "Your hands are better, aren't they?" he says, and she balls them up. "Let me see again." She holds out her fists as if there is a coin in only one of them, and he taps the left one. She turns it over, palm up, and uncurls her fingers. He takes her hand and turns it over so he can study the cuticles. The lesions have all but disappeared.

"Better," he says.

Louise and Joe are in the Ranchero and halfway to the hospital when it suddenly occurs to Louise that a relative probably has to sign the release forms. "What about Auntie Georgia?" Joe suggests.

"That, my love, is the old Y.I. The old Yankee Ingenuity," she tells him. He's come to a stop at a red traffic light, he smiles. She nods. "The old Y.I.," she says, "as Duncan used to say. That's what won the war."

"This is the first time in awhile we've been alone," he says. She reaches into her purse for cigarettes then stares at the people going about their day in the village. She nods.

"Does it make you nervous?"

She shakes her head, No, then reaches back into her purse for gum. She unwraps a stick and leans over to fold it into Joe's slightly open mouth.

She talks at Georgia for the second time that day and arranges to pick her up in twenty minutes. Then she calls the house, expecting to hear Eva, but Willie answers. She can hear the television in the background.

"Hello, sweet person. You guys watching TV? I'm at a gas station. We gotta pick up Georgia because I think we need the signature of a relative at the hospital. Then I guess we'll bring her by the house for a drink, okay?"

"Okay."

"Now you sure you don't want to see Jessie again?"

"I'm sure."

"Okay. You guys need any supplies?"

"We're out of brandy now. And get something to eat."

"Like, what do you want?"

"Gee, I don't know. Like *Wheat* Chex or something."

Georgia is standing in her front doorway waiting when they arrive. She is wearing a black raincoat over black pants, black Japanese bedroom slippers embroidered with gold dragons, a black velvet *cloche* hat with bugle beads and braid, and black harlequin sunglasses.

After they help her into the car, she removes the glasses, hands them to Louise, and dabs her eyes with the back of her hand.

Louise rides between them to the hospital. Georgia stares forlornly out her window. Louise rests her head on Georgia's bony shoulder. Georgia smells like the oldest white woman in the world, she smells like old books, Phisohex, talcum powder, lavender, and age.

"Now here's what we're up to, my friend. Willie is too tired and sad to go to the hospital, and he doesn't want to see Jessie's body. But a relative has to sign a release form so that the mortuary can pick her up. So, you're going to be Jessie's sister, and all you have to do is sign your name. Me or Joe'll say you have bad arthritis and fill out everything else. *Can* you sign your name?" Georgia mulls this over, then closes her left eye.

They walk in marked time down the hospital corridor to the admitting office. Joe has begun to have a bad bout of Heart Awareness. Louise is cool to the women at the counter. She explains that Georgia is Jessie's sister and will sign for the body. Jessie's grandson William is listed as being the closest living relative, but he is at home, under sedation. They can call him if they need to, but they don't.

Joe looks supremely bored. He is whistling in the dark.

"She has arthritis," says Louise, "so I think it would be best if I filled out everything but the signature." The woman behind the counter agrees.

Georgia studies the proffered form on the clipboard, with a squinting pout that makes Louise start crying. Joe is praying to the God in Whom he does not believe: *Let us pull this off.*

"All right, darling," Louise says, sniffling. "Sign on this line."

Joe has begun in his mind to tell the story of their adventure to Eva.

Lou hands her the pen and it's like she doesn't quite know what to do with it. She holds her fingers and thumb poised, like you would describe half an inch, and Lou works the pen into position, the way you set someone up to use chopsticks for the first time.

Right away I begin to overheat rather badly, Joe thinks. I'm expecting sirens to go off.

Georgia bends so far forward to inspect the dotted line that, another inch, and she'd be resting her nose on the counter. Then she pushes back her sleeve and begins to write. The "G" takes a good two minutes, I swear to God, the "e" takes maybe one, and I'm starting to climb the walls. Lou is so patient and sweet, but I'm like totally decompensating, I'm feeling like we're body snatchers, you know, and any second the cops'll arrive.

Tears are streaming down Georgia's face. Louise is kind of mopping her up every few minutes. Louise is crying, too, and the signature is slowly, slowly forming, in this tiny cryptic hand, like when you wrote on an Etch-a-Sketch screen.

"Georgia" takes a good ten minutes, maybe more, but then she seems to get the hang of things. The "M-a-l" go by pretty fast, like maybe three minutes, but then she puts down the pen and fishes around in her purse for a smoke. And Louise very graciously says, Listen, my love, three more letters and we're done. Why don't you wait until then to smoke.

So she goes ahead and finishes. I'm thinking, Thank You, God, now we can make our getaway before the FBI arrives, but then the lady brings out the death certificate and a bag with Jessie's stuff inside—her jewelry, clothes, and so forth—and asks Georgia to sign her name again!

He sees Eva's bright amber eyes crinkle up at the corners. He stares off down the corridor with the Windsong look on his face.

"Is she in the morgue?" Louise asks the young woman, who nods. Louise looks at Joe, who seems to have been spiritually and emotionally broken by the forty minutes they have spent getting the two signatures. "I'd like to see her, Joe."

Joe sighs.

"You don't have to come if you don't want. Georgia? You want to see her?" The old woman peeks over at Joe. He looks like a man who has been too long at a showing of terrible art or a child trying desperately to stay awake for just ten more minutes.

"You guys can wait in the car if you want. But I want to see her one more time."

The man who works in the morgue is young, maybe thirty, with bright rosy cheeks and a long crooked nose. There are two drawers in the room, low to the ground, one on top of the other. When the man grasps the top handle, Joe feels a dreadful suspension, like when you're in the shower and you hear a catch in the pipes and you know that in a second the water will be either scalding or cold. The man pulls the drawer open.

There she is. Sound asleep. Louise reaches out and strokes her jutting cheekbone. It is a refrigerated drawer and Jessie is very cold. "Hello," Louise says in the inquiring tone one uses with a person who is just waking up, a person who has not yet quite remembered who or where she is. "Hello, my love . . . Jessie." She wants to ask, "Are you okay?" Jessie is wearing a hospital gown. Her eyes may flutter open in a minute. She could be alive if not for the fact that she isn't breathing.

Georgia cocks her head and peers at Jessie, as if she is straining to hear her. Then her face begins to list, and she hangs her head, closes her eyes, and starts to shiver. Louise puts an arm around her. Joe is barely breathing. What he sees is his father in the drawer. The emaciated dead look vaguely Egyptian, beautiful in an eerie way, like a warm wind in the middle of the night. He bows his head and begins to cry.

Lying on the bed watching TV, waiting for *Bugs Bunny* to begin, Willie watches Eva doze and sips coffee laced with rum. The fine silent drizzle continues. He glares when the phone beside him rings, and Eva wakes with a start. He picks it up and says hello.

She watches his face drop. His Adam's apple bobs. "Hi, Sam," he says. "Oh, gee. God, listen, wait." He hands the receiver to Eva. They both seem afraid.

"Hello?" She listens for a minute. Willie's swallows are audible. "Oh, well, you see, she passed away last night." Willie closes his eyes. "This is Eva Deane. Could I have Louise call you when she gets back? Or Joe? Okay? Goodbye."

Willie rocks slightly. Then he looks over at Eva and his face is gray with grief.

"I know," she says.

He swallows and starts to breathe asthmatically. After a minute he climbs off the bed and stalks around the room, as fair and wiry as an arctic fox, water-bright eyes searching for escape, prepared to chew off his leg to get out of the trap.

"It's not all just *sad*, Eva. It's worse than that. It's all just like fucking gro*tesque*. Everyone dying. You so sick. I don't know how to live with that."

He storms to the window, stands staring out with clenched fists, and then clasps his hands together on top of his head. "I have taken—too many blows." His arms come down and drop to his side. Then he winds up his right arm and pitches his fist through the window.

The glass shatters, tinkles, cleanly, and the rain comes in.

His shoulders droop and he looks down at his hand, as if to see what time it is. There isn't much blood, just spidery rivulets on his knuckles. He looks over his shoulder at Eva, but she is frozen, absorbed. He turns back to the window, peers through and down the ragged hole, with the suspended craning gaze of someone who is watching a rock fall from the cliff of a canyon to water below.

Finally she asks, "Are you hurt?" He smiles pleasantly at her, looks at his knuckles, licks off the blood, and shakes his head.

She stains his knuckles red with Mercurochrome and blows cool air on the stinging wounds. Soon they are back in front of the television. The rain is gentle, silent. Willie sips a rum, neat. Eva nurses a glass of water with a wedge of lemon in it.

"What should we do about the window?" she asks.

"Lou'll know what to do."

"Visqueen," says Louise. "Plastic sheeting." When she first walked into the room, Willie and Eva looked around, shy and mischievous, as if they were waiting for her to notice that they had put panties on the cats to amuse her.

She stares through the hole, at the deepest green velvety moss on the trunk of the aged oak, green as velvet from *Gone with the Wind*. She moves to the bed, slow and stately, picks up Willie's hand, studies it, and kisses the cuts. "You were lucky," she says, and sighs. "We've got Georgia with us now. Joe's fixing her a drink. You guys up to a little visit?" Then she lies down across the foot of the bed with her head near Eva's feet and appears to sleep.

Sam walks in an hour later cradling dozens of gladiolas—red, yellow, orange, white, pink, peach, and purple—and holding a scroll of Visqueen. Boone is behind him in faded Oshkosh overalls and his orange and black 49ers cap, clutching a staple gun and holding a flaming bird of paradise by the stalk. He gazes at its crooked waxy red neck and its tongues of orange and indigo, as if it is a lit sizzling sparkler at night.

Joe and Sam and Boone are in Jessie's room putting up the Visqueen. Georgia is on her third brandy and is beginning to look like Woody Allen overdosing on the Orb in *Sleeper*. She is sitting beside Eva on the couch and turns to her from time to time with a drunken smile. You can still smell Jessie in the room, over the smoke, brandy, cats, and gladiolas, which Eva has put into sundry vases. Louise is rocking in the Shaker chair, smoking one of Georgia's Pall Malls, listening to the Beatles. Willie is still in his pajamas and sits in the easy chair nursing another rum, staring out at the houseboats, at egrets on pilings, at flying gulls whose cries he can't hear.

"Lou? Know what I was just thinking? That she was always saying, 'I told *him* where the cow found the cabbage,' but I can't remember her telling us *where* the cabbage was." White sunlight glows now in a corner of the sky and casts slanting shadows on the furniture and walls.

Boone charges in and skids to a stop in front of Willie's chair. Willie tousles his hair and smiles. "Hey, dude. Want to sit on my lap?"

"No." He turns, bends down, and grabs a calico by the tail.

"Booney, be careful." The cat hisses, snarls and escapes.

"Make nice with the cats, Boone." Boone looks at Willie with wide-open eyes. "Look, man, I don't give a shit about the cats. I mean for all *I* care, you can smash their heads in with the *lamp*. But I don't want them to scratch you." Boone sticks out his tongue and stares down at it, then casts a surreptitious glance at Georgia, who is leering at Eva, who is doing origami with a Kleenex. Boone hunches his shoulders down and tiptoes toward Georgia as if towards the back of a dark scary cave. "Make nice with Georgia, too, sweetie." Boone advances. Georgia slowly turns towards him. He freezes, several feet away from her, frozen like he might be about to pounce on her. Her eyes widen. Then she raises her left hand, reaches towards him, brings together her thumb and finger tips, and opens and shuts them, again and again, as if to make the shadow dog bark.

Sam stretches out in a box of sunlight on the carpet and Boone curls up beside him. Joe ambles in from the kitchen with two Ballantine India Ales and gives one to Sam. Then he perches on the antimacassar on the armrest of the easy chair where Willie sits sipping rum. Joe picks up Willie's hand and gazes at it, as you might gaze into a crystal ball. Willie splays his fingers in a nellie way as if to let Joe admire his new engagement ring. Joe shakes his head. Willie pulls his hand away and sits on it.

Eva bows her head and starts to cry.

"You should put her down for a nap," Willie tells Louise. No, no, Eva is shaking her head and sniffling, pleading, a child who doesn't want to go to bed. She tries to compose herself.

"Yes, darling, listen," says Louise, getting to her feet. "You've been up nearly all night, and you've been sick. Why don't you try to sleep for a bit and then we'll have some dinner."

"You should make her a cup of tea," says Willie.

"It would keep me awake," Eva says.

"Not peppermint," Louise says.

Louise straightens the covers on Jessie's bed while Eva changes in the bathroom. Ain't much left of *any* of us but buttons and hair right now, Louise thinks. She plumps up the pillows and hails Mary, full of grace. Voices from the living room filter in low and clear.

Eva appears in the doorway, wearing a pair of Willie's pajamas. She looks like a Vietnamese boatperson.

Louise tucks her in. She stares up into Louise's broad sweet face.

"We're like some odd daycare center here," Eva says.

Louise nods.

"Please don't close the door. I want to hear your voices."

"All right," says Louise. "I'll go see if the water is boiling."

"Do you think Willie will be okay?"

"Of course he will, if nothing else goes wrong, which of course it will."

Eva lies studying the ceiling as if the word for it is slowly coming back to her.

Louise moves slow and stately around the kitchen finding the right mug and a bag of peppermint tea. How could you say, "If nothing else goes wrong"? Eva's going to *die*. She begins to chastise herself but over the din of judgement, she hears her Uncle Duncan: Eva. May you live until tomorrow. May tomorrow have no end. Old Ibo proverb:

> ndu-ibi
> echi-echi
> ada aqwu-aqwu.

Duncan sent it to her on a postcard. I love you, he wrote in his cramped Presbyterian script, and miss you, and only worry about you in a way that a girl likes. *Ndu-ibi, echi-echi, ada aqwu-áqwu.* "May you live until tomorrow. May tomorrow have no end."

Joe takes the tea in to Eva and sits on the bed beside her. She blows waves across the surface of the tea. They listen to Sam telling Willie something about the Bubble Boy. When Eva finishes her tea, he puts his arms around her and helps her slide down under the covers. The pajama top she wears is drab green with baby blue pinstripes. She asks him to leave the door open.

"Lou?" Willie asks.

"Yeah?"

"Will you live here with me for a while?"

"Yes, of course. I was planning on it."

"Sam left his staple gun," says Joe. Louise looks over suddenly.

"Joe? You know what? You might as well stay at *my* place tonight."

"That would be terrific."

Alone and awake in the dark, Eva stares at the ceiling.

"Let me get you a brandy, Lou."

"Okay. A small one."

"Throw me those cigarettes," Willie asks.

"Willie, you don't smoke."

"Maybe I want to start."

"No fuckin' way."

"How you gonna stop me, Joe? You *god*forsaken moron."

Eva hears Joe laugh softly. "Hack yer head off with a machete."

"Oh yeah?" Willie snorts.

"Hack it off and watch that pineapple *roll.*"

Eva turns over on her side and dozes off.

When she wakes up, night is falling in swashes of dark pearly blues and grays and roses above the city. White streamers, filigree. The waning moon has appeared in one corner of the sky. She listens to Joe talk. After a minute she gets out of bed and pads off towards the living room. They all look up at her and smile. She sits on the floor near the couch and hugs her knees to her chest.

"Did you get some sleep?" Louise asks. Eva nods. "Shall I fix you something to eat?"

"No, thank you."

Willie closes his eyes and starts to cry again. "God," he mutters. Joe brings him the box of Kleenex and sits beside him on the couch. Willie blows his nose, snuffles for a moment, and looks over at Louise with anger.

"Lulu?" he says. "Right before I had the little altercation with the window, I just started feeling sick. Thinking about how gro*tesque* it all is. I don't know how you can possibly believe in

God. To me He just seems like some *ass*hole." He glowers up at
the ceiling. "I don't even know how you can *cope.* I mean, it just
all seems like this ghoulish struggle."

Louise yawns and lets her head drop onto her chest. Everyone
is watching her. She seems to have fallen asleep.

"Lou?"

"Huh."

"Maybe you should go take a nap."

"I'm just thinking."

Willie tilts his head towards her. "What are you thinking?"

"I was thinking about Duncan."

"Tell me what and then you gotta go and take a nap."

Louise yawns again and rubs her eyes. "Do you remember how
insanely sad I was when he died? And for months afterwards I
had those terrible nightmares. Remember, Joe? Duncan would
be in this trap. I guess because he'd been sick for so long. In a
berth somewhere on the bay, docked next to sailboats. The trap
was like a Vietnamese underwater bamboo cage. He was naked
and I would be keeping watch, making him sip tea with honey.
And I would just be in a state of torn-to-piecesness.

"And every night in this dream he'd reach these long bony
arms towards me, and all I could do was to pour tea between his
lips and try to soothe him when he cried. And then the *mooring*
would always break and he'd start to drift away, with his arms
out towards me, crying. And I'd stand there, sick with panic, sorrow. Impotence. And then I'd wake up screaming.

"And then I started like throwing myself into everyone at the
restaurant. Booney had just been born, and Willie, you were still
on kind of shaky drug ground. Joe was in the middle of another
midlife crisis, and everyone needed me. I tried to take care of
you all. I started getting kind of well again. And then one night
I dreamt that Duncan stopped by for a drink and brought me a
book he'd written. On the cover was a photograph of Angel

Island, and huge stone letters superimposed on the island said
KIND WATERS. And he told me he'd spent his life flailing, cursing the currents. Going under, getting water up his nose. But
that since he'd been gone he understood how kind the waters
really are."

All of them put her to bed. Willie, Joe, and Eva sit on the bed
drinking brandies. Louise begins to snore softly. They tiptoe into
the living room and finish their drinks. When Willie starts to
yawn, they hug and kiss him goodnight. He walks around the
house like a man in a labyrinth.

In Jessie's room he turns on the television and crawls into bed
beside Louise.

Eva's eyes are bright with brandy or tears in the car. They drive
along in silence. Joe tries to imagine how he will feel when he
walks into Louise's empty house, the house where he used to live
with her. It will be empty. He will be empty. He looks over at Eva
and sees her alone at her house, wringing her hands, dejected.
He sees himself embrace her. He stares at the road and sees Jessie
in the drawer. Sorrow and loneliness wash through him, and he
can hardly swallow. He turns and sees that Eva is watching him.
She looks away and puts the insides of her wrists together so that
she looks handcuffed, and she still has them like that when they
pull up to the curb in front of her house. He turns off the engine
and clears his throat, sick with desire, love and fear, lust and self-
loathing and need.

They look down into their laps.

Fearful of dark longings and rejection, he shades his eyes from
the light of the streetlamp. He bites his bottom lip, and looks up,
rubs his brow, and signs. Then he takes a deep breath and tells
his window. "I want to stay with you tonight." She is straining to
see him far off in the distance. "I don't want to be alone."

"Louise and Willie would hate me." Neither says anything for awhile. "But I want you to stay, too."

He takes her hand as they walk slowly to her front door. It is the most beautiful night, black, silver, like mother-of-pearl in a mussel shell.

She is shy and squirmy and frail, at first, and so they make very gentle love. They lie in the dark, tired and warm.

He strokes her hair. It is soft and fine and smells of shampoo and it reminds him of her voice.

"I know this is wrong," she says. "But it's so wonderful. I didn't know if I'd—have this again, one more time." He listens, stroking her shoulder blades.

When he first wakes up she is curled up against him with her bottom against his belly, and it is still night. He falls back to sleep clutching her hipbone. When he opens his eyes sometime later, he sees a band of yellow resting on the city skyline. Then it is day and the sky is red with sun, and when he absently traces her ribcage, he remembers the feel of being a boy, walking beside picket fences, tracking the slats with his fingers.

THIRTEEN

WILLIE SPENDS THE NEXT FEW DAYS watching television. He has discovered the soaps. "I still love you as much as ever," he tells Louise during a commercial. "It's just that I don't *need* you anymore." He smiles rather blithely and turns his attention back to the TV screen. He tells Eva the same thing when she calls, tells Joe, when he drops by to visit, as he does several times a day.

When Jessie's lawyer comes by to discuss the will and probate, Willie turns the volume down and conducts this business in his pajamas on the bed, half listening to each. Willie rarely mentions Jessie. He doesn't want to have a memorial service or a wake. They can scatter her ashes, which are now in a gold cardboard box on the floor of the hall closet, some other time. Maybe next month, he says, on Jessie's eightieth birthday.

Four nights after Jessie's death Louise crawls into bed beside him. He is watching *Jezebel*. She watches with him until the first commercial. "Lovey? What are we going to do about the restaurant?"

He shrugs. He owns it now.

"I don't know."

"Do you think you might want to start working again soon?"

He shrugs again. He doesn't need the money. Jessie had a little socked away. "I really just don't know."

"How long do you think you can do this?"

"Do what?"

"Do nothing."

"Years," he says.

Louise is desperate to get back to the cafe. She feels like she used to when she lived with Joe and he was depressed: thwarted and numb, like a snail going the wrong way into a shell that's a bit too small. And Joe has been staying at her house since Jessie's death, when Louise started staying with Willie. She has not said anything to Joe about him moving out of her house, so he has gone ahead and brought his things from the motel. He is doing everything he can for Willie and Louise—he arranged the cremation and then picked up the box of ashes. He helped Louise pack up Jessie's clothes, then hauled them to Goodwill in his Ranchero. He brought over a week's worth of cat food and the new *People* magazine. He brings Willie *TV Guide*, milk and Wheat Chex. And then every night he goes to Eva's.

Mano a mano she flourishes in his company. She squirms less, talks more. They hold each other late into the night and talk in the dark. She feels like skin and bones; her skin is as soft as a baby's.

In the mornings they sit outside in her small backyard, reading the paper and drinking coffee. Joe feels like there is warm butter in his heart. He traces the planes of her face with the back of his fingers and she hangs her head, sad and ashamed and loved. Birds are everywhere these days. Kestrels hover in the sky. Mourning doves rest on telephone wires. Sparrows sing unseen in the oleander bushes, and Eva cries about Louise.

Joe says, "I don't know how this is all going to shake down. But I swear to you, she doesn't want me anymore."

Eva shakes her head in wonder.

"I just blew it with her," he explains. "I went out a few times with other women when Lou was working late. I don't even know why. It was like that old joke, you know, '*I* didn't want to go to Las Vegas, *he* wanted to go to Las Vegas,'" pointing to his crotch.

"But also, I wanted children, and she never had any luck having babies. She miscarried twice in her twenties and she had a little baby who had a hole in his heart. Who died. She probably told you that."

Eva nods, hangs her head.

"So, of course, I felt terribly guilty going out with other women, but I really thought I wanted a bunch of children." He shakes his head. "But she found out one night. I mean, I didn't rub her nose in it or anything. Well, I guess I actually did. I got in late one night, and I'd only washed my crotch. It wasn't like her being like a bloodhound or anything, but it smelled like soap. It was way too *clean* . . . and that's how she found out. So that was the end."

On the fifth day after Jessie's death, Louise feeds the cats, then throws them into the yard, reads the *Chronicle* twice, stares at the ceiling in the kitchen for the longest time, and then pads off to Jessie's room. Willie has a bowl of Wheat Chex on his chest and is watching *Wheel of Fortune*.

"Willie," she beseeches. He looks over to the doorway where she stands.

"Yeah."

"I have to go to the cafe."

"Well, then," he says, and shrugs, "go to the cafe."

She hangs her head for a moment. "It would be the best therapy in the world for us to work again."

"Speak for yourself, Princess."

"Willie, I mean it: We gotta get back on that horse and *ride*."

He shrugs. He's lost weight and has not taken a shower in days. She comes over and sits on the foot of the bed. He drops his eyes and grimaces.

"Part of me wants to, Lou. Most of me isn't ready."

"I know."

"Her chair's gonna be empty."

"I know."

"One of these days I'll just sneak up behind myself, and wrestle the straitjacket on. But not today, okay?"

"Willie? I love you more than I've ever loved anyone else in my life. I think I'll go in for a while, just putter around a bit."

The potted flowers on the porch are wilted, desperate, needing water. Louise puts the key in the lock but does not turn it right away. Then she opens the door to the cafe and steps inside. *Hello,* she says mournfully, *empty cafe.*

Everything here is so old, the tables and chairs and prints on the wall. Everything is dry, covered with dust, not really *here* anymore, like Jessie in the drawer in her hospital gown.

She opens all the windows, and the sun shines in like a breeze. She turns on the oldies station and fills the cafe with the Everly Brothers, stocks the refrigerators behind the bar with warm bottles of beer from the back, empties and scours the deep-fat fryer.

Jessie's old *Joy of Cooking* sits on the sill above the counter. Louise picks it up and thumbs through it as if it were a photograph album, smiling at the spots of dried sauces, frostings and batter: osso bucco, raspberry glaze, corn fritters. It's turned into a scratch-and-sniff cookbook, she thinks.

She waters the plants on the porch, and then goes back inside to phone Willie.

"Hello, sweet person. What are you watching?"

"*Guiding Light.* It's a *great* show."

"Yeah?"

"A *great, great* show."

"Lovey, listen," she says. "Can I call our delivery people, and have them bring us supplies?"

There is a pause. "Sure. But don't count on *me*, Louise."

"I won't, I just—Willie, my broccoli's saying, loud and clear, I need for this place to be open again."

"So? Do it. Just don't count on me."

She calls the various people who deliver to the cafe, tells them to bring her meat and cheese and milk and butter, produce, candy, wine, and beer. Jessie died, she tells them, but we're opening tomorrow.

Then she sweeps the floors, the main room, the back room, the bathroom, the cooking area, mops them with Pinesol and water, and goes outside to wait for them to dry.

It's low tide, a young snowy egret stands in the green water a foot away from shore. He cranes his downy head just above the water, suddenly strikes, quick as a shutter, and catches a fish. He shakes it in his beak for a few seconds, tosses his head back, and swallows it whole. Gulps, blinks, and then in that graceful jutting way of egrets walks forward through the water looking for more.

"I went and saw Willie today," Eva tells Joe that evening. "Just for a while. And he seemed less dead."

"What did you talk about?"

"Not much. We watched his soaps."

She is wearing a green shawl over a long flannel bathrobe, and she's staring out her bedroom window, listening to the night birds. He watches her from the bed.

"I'm so afraid they'll find out."

"Come here, Eva." She shakes her head.

"They saved my life," she says.

She turns to face him, framed by the window, before a backdrop of blue-black sky. "I was so afraid before I met them. Now I feel like Lou says: Fine, fuck you. Come and get me. Hit me with your best shot."

"Shall I get us a drink?"

"Maybe. In a minute." She comes over to the bed, sits down with her back to Joe, and stares out the window again.

"I was the World's Oldest Toddler when I first met Lou and Willie. That's what she called me once. I had no idea what my life had been about, and here it was about to end.

"And she sort of *goad*ed me into, what she called, cramming for my finals. Reading what the poets thought, poets and philosophers. About death and the old H.P. And they just loved me so much. And made me laugh, you know. And I sort of got that Huxley sense of God she talks about, the rich round feeling in the pit of your stomach. And little by little there was a vague sort of clarity." She turns to him.

"The more I read and watched and thought, which she sort of tricked me into doing, I could almost, honest to God, believe that having to face my death so soon was part of some higher design. I'm no longer full of terror all the time. Just sad. And it's largely because of Louise. You and Willie and Jessie. Even Georgia. And the only reason I fell into your lives was what I would have thought was pure coincidence before. My tire went flat, and at the same time, Louise knocked over her coffee cup and drenched her cigarettes.

"And like she would say, it's almost enough proof for me.

"So, of course, I'm confused," she says. "Because, it's also like a miracle to have you to love and be with. I never imagined something like this—like you—could happen for me one more time. For the road."

She closes her eyes. He stares at the ceiling.

She begins to cry in the middle of the night. He holds her in the dark silence. Then he says gently, "Tell me."

"I feel sad," she says, and he nods. "I'm going to have to go away pretty soon."

"No."

"Yes. And right now I feel sick that, the movie will go on, but I won't be here to see it."

"Don't go, then," he says.

"That's not what I mean."

Louise goes into town that morning, buys a bag of produce, and is putting it in the refrigerator when the man who delivers meat arrives. He flirts with her and she remembers what it felt like to have fun, and so, sometime later, she cradles a white package of rump roast and addresses it, hunter to stag. "I'm sorry. Thank you. My family needs you to live."

We're going to make pot roast, she tells it, and puts it on the counter. Then she puts on a reggae tape and begins to cut up carrots, swaying in time to the music and hailing Mary. God, to have Jesus, that would take the edge off good, but that's almost cheating. It's an unfair, unhealthy advantage, like being bulimic. But Mary—her serenity, her downcast eyes—is what love looks like, she thinks, as she quarters onions.

Joe is lying on Louise's bed, waiting for the aspirin to take effect. His brain tumor is acting up again. He calls Willie to see if he feels like company, and Willie says, Sure, *Days of Our Lives* is just beginning. "I'm too antsy for TV," says Joe, "maybe I'll go to a movie. Where's Louise?"

"At the cafe."

"Maybe I'll go to the city and look for a job. I'm a good bartender."

"Go see a movie."

"All right."

High Noon is showing on Market, and all the way over the bridge "Do Not Forsake Me, O My Darling" wafts around his head. But, seated in the old theatre, behind a sleeping wheeze-bag, he notices a round bump on the wall beside the stage. It is an old clock, he sees, wallpapered over. The discovery gives him the heebie-jeebies, he has to leave in the middle of the "Road Runner" cartoon.

He studies the reflection in the pay phone for a while, then calls the cafe and tells Louise about the clock.

He can tell she is smiling. "I know it's stupid, but it was total meatwood bump time."

"Oh, lovey. You're just off your feed today."

"But I'm starving for a movie, Lou. Maybe I'll try *Fanny and Alexander*. It's right down the street. Or maybe I'll go get a beer."

"Your head gets like a roomful of *Swedes* sometimes, Joe Jones. I mean, when you're not thinking about getting drunk or killing yourself, you want to go off and see some *film* by Ingmar Bergman."

"Do you think I need a psychiatrist?"

"No, we're too far gone, you and me both. I mean, face facts: *All* the king's horses and all the king's men?"

He tugs at the bill of his cap. "Come here and hang out if you want. I'm making a pot roast, Joe, I wanna get the *show* back on the road. I might call—hey wait, you want to make yourself useful? Call whoever you can think of: Eva, Sam, Georgia—they're all in the book—call Fay, too, Joe. Hey, this is a great idea.... Tell 'em, pot roast on the house at six. What's that Redneck Woody guy's last name? Is it Stewart? I'll call him. And we will all baby-sit each other. I just don't think we're well enough to have a lot of free time on our hands."

"Hey, Noreen," Woody Stewart calls to someone, while Louise holds the phone to her ear. "Guess what. Jessie passed."

Joe stops off at Perry's on Union before heading back across the bridge. It is a stupid mistake. He feels Ratzo Rizzo among the up-wardly mobile. He leaves halfway through the meal and walks with a slight limp to another pay phone. Eva isn't home. He hangs up. He has an uneasy feeling that he can't put his finger on.

Soap? he thinks. This has something to do with wanting Louise to suspect that he and Eva are lovers, but why? Well, maybe just for the attention, he thinks. He doesn't even want to, exactly, doesn't want to plant a kernel of suspicion in her ear. It's just that he might, he realizes. Don't let me do it, Joe prays, praying to the God in Whom he does not believe.

He calls Willie, not knowing what he will say.

"Hey, dude. What are you doing?"

"Watching TV. But there's a commercial on. What are *you* doing?"

"I just had a little episode at Perry's."

"You in the city?"

"Yeah."

"What a stupid idea."

"Willie! I feel like such a failure."

"You're not a failure. You're still alive, man, and you haven't killed anybody yet."

Joe smiles his wistful smile. "I know, but I'm poor."

"How can you *say* that? I mean you've got a Ran*chero*. Look, Joe, quite frankly, I'm not in the mood for a bunch of mewling and puking, so try to pull yourself together."

Joe smiles again. "See you later."

"Hello, sweetie. What are you doing?"

"Twenty guesses, Lou."

"Which one is it?"

"*One Life to Live.*"

"Is it a good show?"

"It's a *great* show."

"Willie, I made a pot roast. And I did something sort of behind your back. I invited a bunch of people to dinner. Here."

Willie doesn't say anything.

"Are you angry with me, love?"

"Of course not."

"Is there any chance you...?"

"No. I just, you know, hope it goes well."

"Do you think you'll ever leave the house again?"

"No, I really don't think so, Louise."

Joe and Louise push four of the smaller tables together into a four-leafed clover and cover them all with white tablecloths. We should have bought flowers, she thinks, but then Woody the Redneck arrives with his girlfriend Noreen and they both carry bunches of blue daisies. Sam brings irises, indigo licked with white and yellow. Boone, who has learned to bark and snarl, brings yellow narcissus. Fay brings black red roses—this is the darkest red that could ever be, a red so dark it looks medieval.

No one sits down right away. Rather, they mill about like a group of people gathered together for a surprise party for someone no one knows very well.

"We must drink *immédiatement,*" says Louise, and opens several bottles of the finest red she has in stock. Noreen puts the flowers in vases, arranges them on the table. Woody opens two bottles of beer and puts Waylon on the stereo. Georgia arrives by cab wearing the black cloche hat with the black braid and bugle beads. Joe goes outside to help her in.

They sit together drinking toasts, all except Boone, who runs around barking. "Go call Eva again," Louise tells Joe, but he shakes his head. "She'll be here," he says, and Louise raises her glass again and holds it out to Woody. "Remember when she punched you?"

"Shit, man—sorry, ma'am," he says to Georgia.

"'Cause you said the word 'nigger,'" says Louise.

"*I* didn't say it. What I mean is, I said it but I was only *repeating* it. I was taking that course at the jaycee. And we read this story in the class by Flannery O'Conner and someone in the story says it—'Jesus was a trick on niggers'—and I'm only *repeating* it when she comes over and slugs me."

Georgia and Boone are playing, in a manner of speaking. Georgia does the shadow dog barking with her gnarled spotted hand, and Boone barks at it.

Sam says, "When Booney was born—right after Dana and I took him home—Jessie used to come and do the street vendor calls for him. He's like six days old and she's holding him, mournfully crying 'IIIIIIII've got algator pears,' and then she'd peer at him, and say 'Avocados, you see, that's what they call avocados.' Remember that, Louise, in the last few months, she'd be talking to me like we'd been in school together? She'd say, 'Sam? Remember how they called us the little minnows when we went to buy penny candy? They'd watch us come in the door and say, *Here come the little minnows.*'"

So they sit talking, laughing, drinking until finally Eva arrives wearing a black silk dress. The conversation stops as all look up somewhat apologetically while she hovers in the doorway. Louise has the most fleeting evil thought: Maybe her shyness is something else. See how she uses it to control the room?

And it's just in this second that Louise is looking at her with this thought in her head, that Joe looks at Louise, sees her thinking bad thoughts. His heart stops—I'll deny everything, he thinks.

Eva sits down next to Sam and says hello to him shyly, and to Louise and Georgia, Fay, and the Rednecks. "Hello," she says to Joe across the table.

"Hey, Eva," he says. "We're telling Jessie stories." Then he turns to Louise. "Remember that look she'd get during football season? She'd stand near the bar when a game was on, and sneer, 'Push, push, push.' Then Willie pointed out Joe Montana—who never pushed anyone. Then she got such a schoolgirl crush on him that Willie got jealous."

Louise smiles at Joe. "Willie started calling him Jo-Jo," Louise says. "Jo-Jo, the Dog-Faced Boy."

"She said this beautiful thing one time," says Sam. "She said that when the cafe was full, it was just like a tidepool village. Hermit crabs and seaweed, barnacles and teeny tiny fish."

Louise bends forward hugging herself. She listens to Boone chatter to himself underneath the table.

"Stop that, Boone," Fay says.

"What's he doing?"

"He's touching my toes."

"Boone, darling," says Louise, peering under the tablecloth, "don't touch Fay's toes. You know how she gets." When Louise sits back up, Fay has her arms crossed and she seems embarrassed. Louise winks. "Your turn, Fay. Tell us a Jessie story."

"I don't have any. I never got to know her very well."

"You saw her nearly every day."

"But I sit and read my paper. My books. I never really talk with people. Only you, a little." Louise looks into the plain, prim, aging face, middle-aged Fay, the World's Most Negative Person. Louise smiles at her, anyway.

"Don't you have *one single story*?"

"I'm not an interesting person, Louise. I don't tell stories, and I don't mingle well and the only story I remember is? Never mind, I won't do it justice."

"Please try, darling."

"She told me one time, 'My daddy died on Armistice Day.' Must have been World War I." Louise nods. "And she told me that he was from England. Manchester, England. Working class. And the first night of his enlistment, he put his boots outside the door. To be shined. And the colonel said, something like, any man who showed that much brass ought to *be* brass. And he made him a captain."

There is a long silence. Georgia and Joe close their eyes. Georgia bows her head, pouting. Louise can't breathe.

"I wish Willie were here," she says, sometime later.

"I'll give him a call," says Joe.

"It won't do any good."

"I think the pot roast is burning."

"Oh, fuck the pot roast. You think that bottle's breathed enough?"

"I'll give it CPR."

"I'm getting drunk," Louise says. "Good and wasted."

"Maybe we ought to have some kind of service," says Joe.

"We should have given Jessie a Viking funeral. Put her in a rowboat. Set it on fire. Pushed it out to sea."

Joe smiles. Louise wipes her eyes.

"I know a chant we could sing," Louise says. "Duncan sang it at my father's wake. Wait. Let me get some candles first."

She finds four silver candlesticks and long white candles and arranges them on the table with the flowers. "Shall I go ahead and light them, or should we take turns?"

"You do it, Lou," says Joe.

"All right," she says when the candles are lit, "this is how it goes." She sings:

O, go in beauty,
Peace be with you
Till we meet in our hearts
In the light.

"Okay? Now everybody sing."

O, go in beauty,
Peace be with you
Till we meet in our hearts
In the light

O, go in beauty,
Peace be with you
Till we meet in our hearts
In the light.

Willie appears like a wraith in the open doorway of the cafe, and the singing stops. After a few seconds Joe winks and Willie nods solemnly, like he's here to size up the damage. Louise, at the grill, turns and smiles at him. Boone wakes up, emerges barking from underneath the table, and rushes Willie at the door. Willie scoops him up and kisses him, winks at Eva, who is crying, but bypasses the arms that reach for him, feinting, shaking his head. His face is all but frozen in a numb vague smile, and the shaking of his head is constant, like a tremor. With Boone in his arms, Willie makes his way to Louise.

Eva helps Louise dish up plates of perfectly stringy wet pot roast. Willie is huddled next to Joe wearing Joe's Giants cap, swilling down red wine and refusing to eat.

"But you won't be able to keep drinking if you don't eat," Joe tells him.

"Yes, I will," he says.

"I'm pretty sure he's speeding," Louise tells Joe in the back room after dinner. He is scraping leftover pot roast into a roasting pan to give to Jessie's cats. She is filling one of the sinks with soapy water. "I can't believe he came." She peers around the corner to look at the main room through the doorway. Willie is jabbering at a transfixed Eva. "Definitely speeding," she says. "Still, you know, whatever gets you through the night."

"Yeah, I know. Patch, patch, patch."

Sam volunteers to drop Georgia off on his way home.

"Oh, don't go," Willie pleads, "the night *is young!*" But Boone is getting cranky.

"I should get going, too," says Fay.

"Oh, fine," says Willie. "Everybody leave at once."

"I don't want to go home," Willie complains, when only he, Louise, Eva, and Joe are left. "Can we go somewhere and have a nightcap? *Please?*"

The night sky is a cathedral—white moon, white stars. They are standing outside a nightclub, squaring their shoulders. Louise takes Eva's clammy hand and leads her inside.

The club is half full—a quartet of black musicians is playing jazz.

They sit at a table right in front. Small red and blue lights pulse in a circle surrounding the stage. The last time Joe was here, six or seven months before, he was with a young woman named Dixie. They'd had several hits off a powerful joint that had Joe thinking a spaceship was lowering itself down from the rafters directly onto him.

Willie and Joe order Guinnesses, Eva orders red wine, Louise orders a Scotch and soda. The band begins to play "Paper Moon." Willie hangs his head, and Louise puts her arm around him and kisses the back of his neck.

"Have a sip of beer, Willie, love."

He nods, sniffling, still hanging his head.

"Right now," says Louise. "*Immédiatement.*" He scowls.

"Mee-ja-mow," he says wearily. "Mee-ja-mow."

Eva gets up to go to the bathroom half an hour later.

"One more wine and she might have a episode," Willie says.

"What do you mean?" Joe asks.

"She used to get like *slightly crazy* when she'd have too much to drink." He is whispering.

The band is playing "Brown-Eyed Girl" when Eva returns, but she doesn't come to the table. She stops instead by a post near the stage and leans with her back against it, watching. Even from fifteen feet away, they can see the jut of her hipbone.

"What do you think she weighs, Louise?"

"I don't know, sixty-five?"

"No, really."

"I don't know, maybe ninety?"

"She's got black circles again. Underneath her eyes."

"She probably isn't sleeping well."

Joe sighs.

Then an aging hippie with a kind face and a long black pony-tail approaches Eva and says something. She covers her mouth. She squirms and shakes her head. He cocks his and nods, and she shrugs and dips her head. You might think he has just tried to tickle underneath her chin with a feather. Then he takes her by the hand and pulls her gently away from the post.

Joe sits up straight with a look of panic on his face, but Louise grabs his shoulder and tells him to relax.

"What's going on?" he asks.

"They're going to dance," says Louise.

Eva closes her eyes and begins swaying, undulating her hips and her shoulders, only somewhat stiffly. The hippie smiles at her and does the two-step stomp, and Joe, doing an Existence Check, has to dig his thumbnail into one of his knuckles.

Her movements are sultry and possessed. Lights blink on her face and body and she writhes. She and the hippie are only a foot or so apart. Willie and Louise stare in wonder. Joe is beginning to overheat.

Joe is sick to his stomach with jealousy and confusion, and prays to the God in Whom he does not believe that the song will end, but it goes on and on and on and Eva dances with abandon. Joe cracks all of his knuckles. Eva writhes and jerks with her eyes still closed.

Willie shakes his head, leans toward Louise, "Curiouser and curiouser," he says. "Will wonders never cease?"

Finally the song ends and the hippie bows to Eva. She shakes her head and squirms, and points over to the table where her friends sit feigning nonchalance. She walks to them with her head down. Joe gets up and pulls out her chair, trying to look kind, but he feels dirty and jealous. Willie applauds. Eva smiles down at her lap.

"You were so sick and *stiff* a month ago," says Louise. "I mean, I guess we're going to go ahead and cancel the organist."

"Joe was going crazy," Willie says in bed that night. "I think he thought she was making a fool of herself."

Louise nods. They are lying in the dark. She is thinking of something Salvador Dali said, years and years before, during the disco days. He was asked, Why do young people dance the way they do? He said, They dance in jerky motions because they are trying to shake off their genitals so that they can become angels.

"I *have* to go away," Eva tells Joe in bed that night. She is under the covers. He is standing fully clothed at the window.

"It's the wine talking."

"No."

"Why do you think you *have* to go away?" He comes over and sits on the bed next to her, and he rubs her belly through the blanket.

"Because it *is* like a tidepool there. Jessie was right. Like a little village of sea anenomes and crabs. Keyhole limpets, algae."

"So?"

"So, I don't want to be the thing that pollutes it. And anyway, I want to see my brother and his kids again."

She closes her eyes and is asleep almost at once. She seems now by the moonlight a perfect stranger. He stays beside her on the bed for a while, daydreaming about Louise. He feels terribly afraid all of a sudden, afraid he may be dying. His heart races. After a while he swings his legs off the bed and reaches down to unlace his tennis shoes. After he kicks them off, he walks softly down the hall to the bathroom. He stares at his reflection for a while. He has a dozen gray hairs. Then he steps on the bathroom scale; he's fat as a pig. Next he opens her medicine chest, studies the rows of prescription drugs, and locates a bottle of Valium. He shakes one blue pill into his hand, swallows it with a gulp from a glass of tap water. The prescription bottle is still half full. He shakes another five pills onto his moist palm and tucks them into the watchpocket of his Levi's.

Willie's first few days back at the cafe are wracking. Sun pours onto the table where Georgia sits alone watching the ducks and egrets, and the empty chair where Jessie used to sit is a presence, complete and incomplete, like the riderless horse at Kennedy's funeral.

But word has spread through the community and along the waterfront that the restaurant has reopened, so there is always something for Willie to do. He often hides in the back room, hyperventilating, and then steps into the main room like a spiny blenny—a tiny fish who lives in caves, who pokes its head out nervously, scoping the water for predators, dashes around looking for food, vibrating with nerves.

"What can I get you, sir?"

"Water to start with, please."

"Hot or cold?" Willie asks.

Louise stirs a pot of black turtle beans. He's doing pretty well, she thinks, all things considered. Getting around on what stumps he has left. Every so often he clutches, and his head tilts at a forty-five-degree angle, as if a puppeteer has just pulled on the string attached to his left ear, and he is pulled sideways, scuttling, out of the room to the bathroom.

Over and over Louise goes off to find him. He never locks the door, and he's usually just staring up, deciphering clouds on the ceiling, sometimes teary, sometimes not.

"This isn't going to work," he tells her calmly in the bathroom, over and over. She just watches him until he's ready to go back out, from the wings back on to the stage.

"I'm going away soon," Eva whispers to Louise at the grill.

"No, no," says Louise. "

"I have to."

Louise puts down her wooden fork and studies Eva's face. "How come?"

"I just do. I want to go see my brother. And—there are places I want to see again."

Eva's words knock the wind out of Louise. "When will you be back?"

Eva shrugs, then sighs.

"When are you leaving?"

"Soon." She looks stricken. "Don't tell Willie yet."

Louise bows her head.

"Eva says she's going to go away," Louise whispers to Joe later.

"I know. She told me the same thing."

Willie is watching them from the doorway of the back room. She looks over at him. He sticks his nose in the air and closes his eyes. "If you have something to *say*," he says primly, "you might tell the *whole class*."

A few minutes later she goes back to the sink where he stands washing dishes. He ignores her.

"Kisses!"

"No."

"How come?"

"Because Princess bein' bad; Princess be whisperin' with Joe."

"You can't just *leave* like this," Joe whines at Eva in bed.

"I really have to, Joe," she says.

"When are you going to go?"

"I don't know."

"Soon?"

"Uh-huh."

"Are you going to tell Willie?"

"Of course."

"Tell him you'll come back." He feels her head nod on his chest. "Tell him tomorrow, okay?" He feels her nod again. "I really don't understand any of this. Why don't—oh, never mind."

He lies in the dark wishing she were already gone, remembers wishing after the heart attack that his father would go ahead and die. Get it over with, let a boy get on with his life.

He doesn't sleep at all that night, but doesn't want to take another Valium.

There is a mosquito in the room—he keeps turning on the lights to stalk it. Eva doesn't stir, even when he smashes his fist against the wall, missing the mosquito, which bites him on the webbing between his fingers when he doses off.

When he doesn't get enough sleep, he faces the day grimly, with a sort of death about the eyes that a stranger might interpret as a migraine. In the morning, he is almost too tired to shower and shave.

It is a cold, foggy morning, and Willie trudges around the cafe, bored and fidgety, like a child who's been dragged along to department stores all day. "I called Eva this morning. She's going to tell him today," Joe whispers to Louise at the grill.

Louise's eyes hood over, like a clown's. She takes a deep breath, and looks around absently, as if she is not quite paying attention. She seems to be profoundly depressed but trying not to let that *get her down.*

Georgia arrives by cab and Willie trudges out to help her in. Louise and Joe watch through the window. Willie waves half-heartedly to Georgia as he approaches.

They step inside the cafe ten minutes later. He pulls out Georgia's chair for her, but she's having a hard and swaying time of it today, and he has to keep moving the chair for her, to this side and that, forward and back, like he's a fire department rescue net aiming to catch a falling woman. Finally, the chair and her bottom connect, and he umphs her forward.

Louise brings Georgia a cup of tea and sits down in Jessie's chair after shooting Willie a knowing glance. Joe shuffles outside and sinks wearily onto the top step, waiting for Eva to come. Willie calls Sam and demands that he come in, but Boone has a cold, says Sam. Sister Peter-Matthew comes in and sits with Georgia and Louise. Willie makes her a sundae. Fay comes in and sits by herself reading the paper. Willie kisses her on the back of the neck. She tries to smile but leaves soon after. He sits back down with Louise, Georgia, and the nun, and stares at Joe's hunched back through the window.

Later Willie sits down on the step beside Joe and stares at the bay. "Do you think Fay is a replicant?"

"Do you?"

"I'm con*vinced* of it. First of all, her ears don't quite match." Joe smiles. "And she's *so* negative. Did you hear what she said when she left? She folds up the *Chron* and then she looks at her watch like she's in this terrible hurry, she's like all *morbidly* businesslike. And she says, 'I'm expecting war.'"

Joe bumps his shoulder against Willie, who blithely chatters on. "I swear, she was *assem*bled somewhere. Like even her *name* is a replicant name. Fay *Mus*berger? Are you kidding me, man? I mean, I was not born yesterday. That's a Martian committee name if I ever heard one. Really, it's like, 'Okay, we need a name for W212, she leaves for Earth tomorrow. What about *Fay*? Fay...*Mus*berger, that sounds good to me. What do *you* think, Fleaklig?'"

"Eva *Deane*," Willie exclaims at three. She is in the doorway, shuffling. He and Joe are sitting at Georgia's table, playing gin, while Georgia keeps a directorial eye on the ducks swimming about near the shore. Louise's heart sinks. She is at the grill stirring sherry into jambalaya and she sees Eva look at Willie with apologetic expectation, and she sees Joe look at Eva with something akin to boredom.

"Sit down with us," Willie commands. "Lulu? Bring my girl a cup of tea." He pulls out the empty chair to his left and pats it. "Sit sit sit sit sit." Eva walks to the table. She sits down heavily for such a weightless person.

Louise arrives with the duck cup. "Here you go, darling." Eva nods. Georgia refuses to look at Eva. She tilts her head so she can study the Surgeon General's warning on her pack of Pall Malls.

"What's so sad?" Willie asks Eva.

Joe cringes. Eva bandages her forefinger.

"I'm going away for a while, soon," she says.

"Go on."

"That's all."

"Okay. Let me see if I can get this straight. You're going away for a while, right?" She nods. He tugs at his cowlick, mulling this over. "Go in peace, my child. But if you're not back in two weeks, it's her ass," he says and jerks his thumb at Louise. "I'll hold Lou hostage. I am prepared to kill her. I have nothing left to lose."

Eva doesn't respond for a moment. "It will be longer than that."

Willie looks at Joe. Joe is grazing on the hair of his forearm. Louise too nonchalantly reaches for Georgia's Pall Malls. Willie clears his throat and drops his eyes.

"Excuse me a moment," he says, and his head begins the tilt as he stands. They watch him scuttle off to the bathroom.

Someone has written on the bathroom wall next to the paper towel dispenser: "Where was Chinatown when dinosaurs ruled the Earth?" Willie continues reading it five minutes after Louise comes in and sits on the toilet seat.

"Don't Lulu me," he says quietly.

"I won't."

"I feel like every time I turn around, someone slips me the banana. It's *just* like the soaps, man. It's like what I said about David, you know, that the fucking you get is not worth the *fucking* you get. And that's what I don't know how to fucking *live with*."

FOURTEEN

THERE IS A WHITE CRESCENT MOON behind ghostly clouds on the evening of Eva's leaving, white on white that appears yellowed against icy blue, like a white cat in the snow.

A retired longshoreman and his recently widowed brother, visiting from Stockton, sit at the bar with Redneck Woody. They are watching a baseball game on the silent TV. At the far end of the bar the sad nervous writer is reading *The Art of Fiction*, drinking burgundy. The English couple who are lying doggo in the States sit bickering over plates of meatloaf and mashed potatoes. At Jessie's table, Joe, Willie, Georgia, Louise, and Eva pick at plates of jambalaya studded with condiments: coconut, scallions, Spanish peanuts, and Jessie's pear chutney.

Why don't you let me drive you to the airport, Joe had pleaded with her at dawn. He wants a scene. He wants them to hold each other and cry like in the movies. It would mean it had all really happened.

He watches Louise try to wheedle a sullen Willie into being a better sport about Eva's departure. He glances at Eva, who appears to be deep in prayer. Then he looks back at Louise and swallows hard—God, she would *die* if she knew. The icy hand of jealousy and betrayal would squeeze her heart to death.

"So," he says to Eva, "Seattle."

She clears her throat, but takes a moment to speak.

"Yeah. Seattle. Mt. Ranier. Orca's Island."

"This is such a stupid plan," says Willie. "It's like something from one of my soap operas."

Joe kicks him underneath the table. Willie glares.

"Stop kicking me, you asshole."

"*Light*en up, Francis," says Louise. Willie hangs his head. Then he peers over at Georgia who has not yet taken a bite of jambalaya. She is still at work accessorizing it, first applying the strands of coconut with grim efficiency.

"Georgia, eat it," Willie whines. She turns up her nose. Now she is inserting scallion wheels one by one. Willie looks like he may rise up and scream at her.

"It's not a *crib*bage board, Georgia," he says.

"Lovey, get off her case."

"Well, she's just *bury*ing it in condiments."

"Pffft."

Eva's face is pinched with earnestness. Louise reaches over, strokes her cheek with the back of her fingers, then looks up at the ceiling, rocking slightly. Willie scowls.

"Darling?"

"Don't Lulu me, man, all right? It's easier for you. You believe in *mag*ic. You think God sent Eva to us, and us to her."

"Yeah, I do."

"What, so she's like the fucking Man from Glad? On *assign*ment?" Eva shreds her napkin. He looks at her with irritation. "And why does it have to be so my*steri*ous? I mean, you act like you're some space man, drop in on our planet for a few months, and then it's like, la-dee-da, you're a rambling guy." He crosses his arms and stares at Georgia's plate. The old woman reaches for a single peanut, places it in the center of her jambalaya, and reaches for another. Willie glowers and throws up his hands.

"Georgia!" he yells. "You're killing me!"

"Pffft."

Joe cannot think of anything to say. He feels as if he is viewing this all through a hangover.

I know we'll never see you again, Louise thinks to Eva. They both look about to cry but don't. There are a million birds where you are going.

Willie looks like he has been on a sailboat in the biting fog for too long.

He is the first to sense that the car that pulls into the lot at nine on the nose is the cab—his face goes blank when it begins to honk. He looks up at the ceiling and then into his lap and bends forward to push himself up from the table. He stops behind Eva's chair, dazed, puts his arms around her neck, lays his head on top of hers, and stares absently out the window. Louise pushes herself away from the table. Eva's eyes are closed and her jaw is clenched and then Willie lets his arms drop, and his head begins to tilt, and when it is nearly perpendicular to his shoulders, he is pulled by an invisible wire off toward the bathroom.

The car honks again and they get to their feet, all except for Georgia.

Eva says "Georgia?" and the dowager empress looks around slowly to locate the sound. Eva bends down somewhat stiffly and peers into the ancient face. "Goodbye. You take good care."

Georgia broods, apparently indifferent to them all. Eva pats her shoulder. Georgia pouts. Joe looks at Louise, points to the parking lot, nods, and all but tiptoes out the door.

The cab driver gets out of the car, an old man, a Charles Addams cabbie, and he opens the trunk while Joe goes to his Ranchero for Eva's two suitcases.

He waits by the cab, swallowing the lump in his throat, listening to the night birds, owls and crows. Eva has come out onto the porch. He can hear the knocking of her heels on the wood.

Louise follows her out, holding a letter and a box wrapped in a page from the Sunday comics. Eva has stopped walking and stands staring out at the moonlight and buoys on the bay.

Louise takes her hand as they walk in silence to the cab— it's trembling and as light as a child's. Joe toes the dirt and listens to their footsteps grow louder, listens to them crying. He licks his lips. While the women are hugging goodbye, he looks up to see Willie's face in the window. Joe beckons him, but Willie shakes his head, and then tucks it down against his shoulder, as if to protect his face from further blows, then steps out of sight.

When Louise releases Eva, they all three for a moment stare at her pigeon-toed feet in navy blue high heels. Then, without looking up, Eva moves against Joe for a hug. It is liking hugging Willie, she's so frail.

"What was in that box?" Willie asks in bed, glumly. They are watching Johnny Carson and drinking beer.

"The bronze dinosaur paperweight Duncan gave me."

"That is like, so stupid, Lou," Willie says. "What will she need a paperweight for?" Louise shrugs. "Well, what kind of dinosaur was it?"

"Brontosaurus."

"Oh. Well, that's a little different. What did the letter say? Did you Lulu her?"

"Of course." Both are silent then.

"Can you live here with me a while longer?"

"Yes, of course."

"You think she's coming back?" he asks.

"No."

"Me either, but I'm going to pretend I do." They're silent.

"Oh, *fuck her*, man. There are like so many other fish in the sea," Willie says.

Joe is in the bathroom at Louise's house studying his face in the mirror. His jeans and sweaters and shirts lie in a tangle on the floor.

"Isn't there some way you can stay?" he'd asked Eva that morning at dawn. "We could stop sleeping together."

"But we wouldn't," she said. "If I stay, we will sleep together."

"But maybe she won't find out?"

"Do you know how many times since 1900 couples have had secret affairs that *no*body ever found out about?" He shakes his head. She looks around her bedroom, pulls in her bottom lip, and then announces. "Seven."

He smiles. *You are so sweet, Eva Deane*, he's thinking.

He looks at his face in Louise's bathroom mirror for a while before he opens the medicine chest, where he locates and swallows one of the Valiums he's stolen from Eva.

He leaves the bathroom. Lying on Louise's bed, he sees himself call her at Willie's, whispering in someone else's voice that Joe and Eva have been lovers, then closes his eyes.

Three days after, they get a postcard from Seattle at the cafe. There is a photograph of a mallard drake on one side, her tiny printing on the other: "There are a million ducks up here. Georgia would be in heaven. I am with my brother and nieces, with a view of Mt. Rainier and the lake. I loved your letter, Louise, and I love all of you." Joe reads and rereads the postcard, looking for a coded message.

Joe watches Louise season ox-tail soup. Willie is hiding in the back room washing dishes. It has been a quiet day. He sees himself telling Louise: There's something I've got to tell you. He hangs his head.

"What is that all about?" he asked Eva their last night in bed. "My wanting Louise to know."

"Well, we're both—sadomasochists," she said gently. "We're paranoid-schizophrenic, manic-depressive, addictive-compulsive sadomasochists." She said this with enormous tenderness.

"Does this tie in with your game-trail theory?" She nods. "Is it like, for me, put them all together, they spell Mother?" She nods again, smiling.

"Yours was inconsistent," she says. "My daddy was, too. It's the worst horror of childhood. No wonder we're ambivalent."

"So what do you do about it?"

"You end the neurotic cycles."

"I don't know, Eva. I don't think I'm both. Sado *and* maso. Chistic."

"It's one word for a reason. The masochist *al*ways gets revenge, always does something that's passively sadistic, then he has to be punished. Then he has to get revenge for that punishment. If you tell Louise we were sleeping together, it would hurt her terribly. She'll push you away and then she'll have guilt and confusion— after all, I'm very sick and she already broke up with you a long time ago. But you will have punished her in the meanwhile for pulling away, and she will be hurt, and she will get revenge somehow, then you will be hurt, and on and on and on."

This is exactly how it has always been with him and Louise. He closes his eyes. This is a revelation. Absolutely everything makes sense right now. It feels like light coming in through the shades, and this is the estate Eva has left to him.

Willie cries out in the middle of the night. Louise bolts into a sitting position and turns on the lamp. He wakes up and starts crying. After a while, he says, "I miss her."

"I know."

"Grandma."

"I know."

"I just fucking miss her, man."

Louise nods and sits up with him until he falls back to sleep. Lying back down in the dark, she prays: *Send him someone to love. Shoot someone in over the transom.*

Willie brings an old black couple bowls of minestrone and smiles at them with tears running down his face. Louise watches him from the grill. He stops by the table of Sea Scouts and—listless and bitter—watches them eat cheeseburgers for a minute, then turns to stare at the empty chair where Jessie used to sit. Georgia is at the table shelling peas for Louise. She has been shelling one pound of peas for nearly three hours. She is almost done.

Willie turns around to look at Louise.

"Come here, love," she calls. He shuffles over to the grill.

"Shall I make us both a cup of tea?"

"I don't know. Don't worry," he says. "I'm all right."

"I wish I could cheer you up." He rubs his ear with his shoulder.

"I'm really all right," he says. "Maybe I should do some *ba*king or something."

"Willie?"

"Yeah?"

"You want to get married?"

"No, thanks."

"Why not?"

"Lou! I'm a *fag*got, remember?"

"I didn't mean that we would, you know, be lovers or anything."

Willie shakes his head.

"We're the most devoted friends who could ever be, my love.

Please, Willie? Think it over." He shakes his head, but she can see that he is amused. He smiles at the floor and nods solemnly.

"All right," he says. "I'll marry you."

After having decided that it is a perfect day for banana bread, he goes into the back room to assemble the ingredients. He is mashing bananas when Louise appears.

"Sam and Boone just pulled in," she announces.

"Yeah?"

"I'd like Boone to be in the wedding. Maybe he could be my spear carrier or something."

"Well. See if Sam's agreeable." Then he rolls his eyes again.

"I just *love* being engaged," she says. She really means it.

Willie lifts a squealing, wriggling Boone into the air over his head for the first time since Jessie died. "Lulu and I are engaged," he says. Sam cocks his head at Louise, and gives her a thumbs-up.

"Honeybunch? Darling? Will you get the phone?"

"Yes, dear."

Willie goes into the back room and picks up the phone. It is Joe, at a pay phone in the Marina.

"Did you find a job?"

"Not yet."

"How many bars did you try?"

"About ten."

"You want to talk to Louise?"

"Yes, please."

"She and I are engaged."

"I beg your pardon?"

"We're engaged. She is my betrothed now. I love her very, very much."

Joe laughs softly. "Let me talk to her."

"What's going on?" he asks Louise.

"I guess you heard the big news."

"Are you serious?"

"Of course not."

"Oh."

Louise smiles. "It's just, you know—patch patch patch."

"Yeah."

"You okay, doll? You sound low."

"I haven't found a job yet."

"Oh, for Christ's sake, it's your first day out. You gotta be patient. You gotta do like Jessie said. Develop the patience that isn't *waiting*."

"Lou?"

"Yeah."

"I'm homesick."

"Oh, Joe, we all are."

The next day the mailman delivers another postcard from Eva, this one from Vancouver. "Hello, my friends. I'm moving north tomorrow. I want to see Alaska. Yesterday I was stiff when I woke up and you will never believe this, but I went to a hot tub place. I actually took off my clothes and got into a large hot pool with friends of my brother. Who would have ever thought...? Best love, Eva."

"Good Lord, Willie. This is a woman who has anxiety entering a room full of fully *clothed* strangers."

"Fully clothed *friends*."

Joe calls from the city in the afternoon. He is bored and frustrated and has had to do Existence Checks all day, biting his thumb, tearing out strands of hair, and studying himself in bath-

room mirrors at the bars where he has gone looking for work.
Willie reads him the postcard, and Joe says numbly, "That's
nice."

"Having an episode, Joe?"

"Sort of."

"Having a really 232 kind of day?"

"I don't think I'll ever find a job."

"Let me go fetch my squaw. This is her department."

Louise takes the phone. "Still no luck, love?"

"Nope."

"Be patient."

Joe sighs. "I just don't even know what my life is about."

"I'll tell you what your life is all about. It is about paying attention to the movie, so as to glean small wonders and lines with
which to amuse, and edify, the drowsy princess—me. That is
your assignment. That is the meaning of your life. Okay?"

"Okay."

"Now, go get 'em, Harry."

He feels a little better after talking to Louise. He trudges down
the street towards his Ranchero. A blind man and a Seeing-Eye
dog are coming in his direction.

Want to know something funny, Louise? When I was a kid, I
wanted to be blind. My mom read me this story where this kid
and his friends light a firecracker in the lot where they're playing baseball. And it blows up in his face, and he goes blind and
gets to go to a special school and have a guide dog. So what I'd
do was, close my bedroom door, close my eyes, and feel my way
around the room, falteringly, bumping my head on bookshelves.
But I'd take it, man, you know, noble with suffering, under the
admiring sympathetic gaze of rich strangers. God, I was crazy.
I also wanted to break my leg so I could have a cast that everyone could sign, and get to use crutches. And for a long time I

wanted *braces*, Louise, on my teeth. Me and Stevie Gronewald used to mold Firestix up against our palates and pretend we had retainers.

"You are so crazy, Joe Jones," Willie says when he tells them that night about the blindness and crutches and braces.

"My thing was," says Louise, "I wanted to have to be in the hospital for a long time, in traction, with a body cast on."

"You two are both so fucking crazy."

"Well, what did *you* want, Willie?"

He thinks about this for a moment. "Parents," he says, and smiles. "*And* an older brother. I mean, is that the *wack*iest thing you evcr heard or *what*?"

Jessie slowly, like the approach of a new season, comes back to the cafe. Louise finds herself talking to her again, teasing her, hears her do Yellow Bananas. She keeps expecting her to return from the bathroom, peeping and cooing, to join Georgia at the table by the window, and Louise's eyes narrow frequently with memories. She can feel the old woman watching her, watching Willie, sometimes from within, sometimes from outside and above, and for this reason only, Louise is kind to the cats.

No one ever mentions the living arrangements. Louise sort of likes living with Willie, sleeping together like an old married couple who no longer have sex. She does not think she will ever make love again. She remembers crying in bed with Joe in the early days of their romance because she felt fat and unattractive and afraid that he would leave her for the first slender young woman who caught his fancy. He said, "Oh, Louise, you are so perfect for me. You are so sweet. Being in bed with you is like lolling around with Mrs. Claus after she's had a couple glasses of Madeira. It's just so lovely."

Sometimes, when Willie stays out late playing pool at Smitty's or stays all night, Louise fantasizes about sneaking over to her house and crawling into bed with Joe. She smiles then and shakes her head.

"I met a real dreamboat last night," Willie announces one morning in the kitchen, where Louise is feeding the cats.

She studies him—he seems calm. "You didn't do speed."

"There wasn't any."

"Oh."

"This guy is really funny."

"How old?"

"About thirty. Kind of a Dennis Weaver type. He even has a limp. I mean, I *like* that in a guy."

Louise laughs. She prays all the time that Willie will find a boyfriend and Joe will find a job.

"Is he queer?"

"I think so. Only one way to find out."

On his fifth day out on the streets, Joe is offered a job by a man named John at Benno's in the Marina. They shake.

By the time he gets to the pay phone out on the street, he is almost sure he made the whole scene up, but he dials the cafe.

"Drinks on the house," he tells Willie. "I got a job."

"*Bar*tending?"

"Yeah."

"All *right*. Where?"

"Benno's. In the Marina."

"How many days a week?"

"Four right now, eleven to seven. You guys gotta see the joint. Is Louise busy?"

"No, I'll go get her." Joe hears him put the receiver down, then hears him call out, "Joe got a job, everybody." He hears Louise go, "Yaaaaay," and then he hears what sounds like a lot of people applauding, and he feels as good right then as he's ever felt in his life.

"The guy's queer," Willie announces the next morning.

Joe doesn't start work for a couple of days. He is at the cafe when the mailman brings another postcard from Eva. It is a snowy mountain behind a great icy green lake. "I am on a train to Alaska now. It is unbelievably beautiful outside my window. I saw a bald eagle this morning. I am fine—because of you. I send all of my love. E."

"The writing looks funny to me," says Willie.

"Maybe her hands were cold. Or the train ride was bumpy."

Louise has a wormy feeling in the pit of her stomach.

Later in the afternoon Louise walks into the back room where Willie is carefully pouring hot cream into beaten eggs for a crème brulée, whisking it as he pours. He does not look up.

"Hello, my dearest darling," she croons.

"Hello, dear."

Joe, at the table with Georgia, cocks his head to listen.

"Are you crying, love?"

"No."

"Why are your cheeks all wet?"

Nothing. Dead air. Then: "What do you think she's doing?"

"Who?"

"Eva. Who do you think I mean?"

"Well, you don't have to get sore."

"Sorry."

"I think she's in Alaska by now, sitting outside a lot, all bundled up. Wringing her hands and staring at the mountains, at the rivers, at the glaciers. Sometimes I bet she takes bags of old onion rolls down to the water and throws them to the ducks."

"What if she's all frail and wasted again, like all trembly and stiff, drinking too much wine? Getting all bassett-deathy."

"I don't think we're ever gonna know, my love. So we might as well think whatever makes us feel better."

Joe watches the smoke waft away from Georgia's cigarette. She is oblivious to his presence.

Poor little guy, he thinks, looking over his shoulder towards the back room. A wave of avuncular concern brushes his heart and after a minute he gets up.

"I was thinking," he says to Louise although this is intended for Willie. She cocks her head. Willie is pouring his mixture into small, clear-glass bowls. "I was thinking, you know, that at most weddings, you put the groom's family on one side, the bride's on the other, right? Well, in our case, that doesn't work so well. I mean, who gets Boone? Who gets Fay?"

"I get Boone," says Willie.

Joe smiles. "Yes, you see, I think you do, because what I was thinking was, we put smokers on one side, nonsmokers on the other. You know, smoking and nonsmoking sections."

Louise watches Willie's eyes narrow, his face darken, then he looks at Joe and softly snorts.

Benno's bar is broken-in, broken-down, dark and musty, covered wall-to-wall with the kitsch of liquor distributors. It has a horse-shoe-shaped bar and four Formica tables. There is a jukebox with a great selection of rhythm and blues, rock-and-roll, Frank Sinatra, Mel Torme, the Supremes. An hour before he begins work, Benno's son John shows Joe the ropes, shows him the bottles, the glasses, lemons, icemaker, dishwashing soap, the peanuts and napkins, and so on.

"Think you can do it?"

"Piece of cake," Joe says, but he is shaky, wired to the gills with the prospect of failure, of being *found out.*

Serve people, make them laugh, remember lines with which to amuse the drowsy princess. He Lulus himself as he pours people drinks: an old Italian man in a beret, two cocky young sailors, unhappy couples, and men like himself. He smiles, he listens, he nods, and time passes quickly. Then business slackens and there's nothing to do and his legs begin aching and he wishes desperately that it was already tomorrow morning. The lemons are cut for twists and the coolers are stacked and the glasses are clean and the only person at the bar is a broken-down drunk who is going to be rejected by every cabbie he tries to hail when he leaves.

He uses the phone that is underneath the bar to call Willie.

"I'm cracking," he announces.

"You've been there for two fucking hours, you Godforsaken *mor*on. Let me go get Louise."

Louise is sweet until he complains that his legs ache, and she says, with some irritation, "Now listen here, Joe. It is impossible to get sympathy from a person who has been working for *six*ty hours a week, year after year after year, in the food industry, when you've been on your feet for all of two hours."

He sighs. He wishes Eva were still around. She would look at him sympathetically with those amber eyes, eyes the color of tea.

"Postcard come today?"

"Nope. Bills, bills, bills."

Maybe tomorrow a postcard will come. He wishes it was tomorrow. He has always wished it was tomorrow.

Joe limps into the cafe at seven-thirty and sits down with Sam, who is cradling a sleeping Boone in his lap, eating meatloaf slathered with catsup with his free hand. Georgia does not look up at him when he enters. She is watching a gull repeatedly drop a mussel onto the rocks just beyond the porch. She watches it drop the shell, pick it up, and drop it again, until it is able to wrestle out the meat. For the fear and excitement on her pleated face, she might be watching a mongoose and a cobra.

Joe salutes Louise at the grill. Willie turns around from the bar, where he is sitting watching *Name That Tune* in silence with the Rednecks.

"Want a beer, dude?"

"Yeah."

"Sam, you want another?" Sam shakes his head.

Louise comes over to the table, ruffles Joe's hair, and sits down next to him. "So tell me," she says. "What was it like? How much'd you make in tips?"

"Not very much. About ten."

Willie brings him a bottle of Leopard stout.

"Any feeling at all in your feet?" he asks.

Joe hangs his head, smiling.

"Are they big hot stones?" Joe nods. Willie gives him the nelliest flick of his wrist. "Oh, I know *just* the thing. A big pot of hot water to soak them in, with Epsom salts."

"That's okay."

"Oh, but I *want* to," Willie pleads. Joe shrugs.

"Okay, thanks."

"I've got to get Boone to bed," Sam says apologetically. Willie looks crestfallen.

"Don't go," he begs. "Have some dessert." Joe sees that Louise is watching Willie with amused suspicion. Sam shakes his head, and Willie shrugs him off. "See if I care," he says.

"Willie's flying," Joe says when Willie goes off to prepare a pot of hot salty water. "Speed?" he mouths.

She shakes her head and mouths, "Tea." Then with concern on her face she says, "Will you stay for a minute, after we close? I know you're beat to shit but there's something we need to discuss."

His heart stops, but he shrugs casually. "Sure." He still plans to deny everything. Louise gets up from the table and goes over to sit with Georgia.

Willie comes in bearing a big copper pot, walking slowly so its contents don't spill. "Take off your shoes and socks," he commands, bending down and under to set the pot next to Joe's feet. While Joe removes his footgear, Willie stirs the mixture with his fingers so that the Epsom salts dissolve. "Now, put your feet in the pot." Joe bends to look under the table, then dips a toe into the water, withdraws it quickly.

"Too hot!"

"It *has* to be hot. Ease them in." Joe exhales noisily again and again as he lowers his feet into the nearly scalding water. Willie cups one of his hands and begins basting Joe's insteps. Joe closes his eyes but flinches and opens them when Willie begins massaging one of Joe's feet.

"Don't touch my feet."

"*What?*"

Joe throws his hands up. "I just don't like having my *feet* touched." Willie cocks his head at him, askance. Joe blushes. "Look," he apologizes, "I don't even like to touch my *own* feet."

Louise, sitting beside Georgia, drops her head, shakes it back and forth, laughing so quietly you can hardly hear her.

"All right," says Louise, two hours later, settling in beside Joe with a beer for each of them. They are now alone. "This isn't going to be easy."

You're imagining things, he is ready to say.

"But you see, Willie likes this guy at Smitty's. I mean, I think he likes him a lot." Joe nods. "And he's taking it slow and easy. I mean, he said to me, what if the guy fucks him over, what if Willie gets—Well, he's trying not to worry it to death, but he asks me, what if it turns out they're not even remotely right for each other? What if his heart gets broken again *now*? I mean, insofar as is possible for Willie, he's approaching life with his hands cupped protectively over his giblets."

Joe is flooded with relief.

"But," she continues, "if it works out, he's going to want to be able to bring him to the house for the night instead of just going to the guy's house all the time. And God knows, I don't want to be down the hall in his old room with *them* in Jessie's room *doing it*, you know?" She looks down into her lap, grimaces, and looks back up. He waits. "What I'm saying is that, sooner or later, I'm going to have to move back into my house. And you will have to have found a place of your own." Joe waits another moment and then nods.

"Is that all?" Now she nods and reaches for her beer.

"I don't think you have to start looking this week, but, you know, tuck it away. Maybe post a sign at Benno's?"

"Okay."

"It will be chapter two for Willie, alone in a good-sized house. Alone for the first time. And for you, too, Joe. You have a new *job*, a whole new batch of *regulars*. It'll be like we have a whole new batch of people to gossip about. You'll have to be our eyes and ears over there.

"And *also*," she says. "You'll have a *girl*friend eventually." Joe scowls, shaking his head. "Sure you will."

"Tsss."

"You will."

Joe takes a sip of his beer and sighs. "Well. *One* of us will find someone first...."

"It won't be me, Joe Jones."

He smiles and stares out the window. "You think we could cope?" She shrugs, thinks, shrugs again.

"If you were *se*rious about someone, but only then, you should tell me, and bring this *trick* of yours by." They're smiling—it's all right, it isn't happening yet. "And I'll, you know, make her a *lovely* cup of tea, and then, you know," she is toying with her bangs, "*gouge* her eyes out. . . ."

That night, alone in the dark, waiting in bed for Willie to come home, she daydreams. Jessie says, tell the truth and be kind, do the best work you can, and all the rest will follow. She had the peace of mind that came from loving a kindly god.

Eva left with something else. Not peace of mind, exactly, but wonder at the series of coincidences that brought her to the cafe, where seven years ago coincidence brought Jessie and Willie, where six years ago Louise walked in to get out of the rain, where five years ago Joe stopped by, out of the blue, on a moment's whim.

I just want to sleep now. I know I'm full of shit. *Hail, Mary, full of grace, the Lord is with thee.* Eva may have put herself to sleep by now, in a motel somewhere with a view of the mountains and glacial streams and Duncan's bronze dinosaur on her night table. *Hail, Mary,* let me sleep, *Hail, Mary, full of grace.* Please watch over Willie tonight. I *know* I'm using this instead of Sominex, just let me get some rest. *Agnus dei qui tollis peccata mundi . . . dona nobis pacem, grant us peace.*

Joe is lying in Louise's bed dunking Oreos in milk, gobbling them down, feverishly turning the pages of the new *Newsweek* and ripping out the inserts with what looks like fear.

The plates of the earth have shifted again, all at once. He wants to call Louise, and say, It doesn't seem like there are any *adults* around anymore. I mean, are we supposed to be the adults now?

He also wants to tell Louise that yesterday he drove past Eva's house and saw a "For Rent" sign on her gate. But he won't. He gets off the bed and puts his cookies and milk on the nightstand. He's stuffed to the gills and the sugar is making his heart race. The old ticker could pop tonight. He bows his head, wipes his forehead with the sleeve of his sweatshirt. He's so alone. The only reason he loves himself at all, and it isn't very much, is because of the people who love him, Louise and Willie. Willie's face appears in his mind—he's rolling his eyes at Joe, going, *Lighten up, Francis.*

Joe smiles at himself, then closes his eyes and inhales deeply.

We're all just a bunch of old junkyard dogs, he thinks. Shredded tattered ears, three teeth left, hungry and losing our hair, cold, bitten by fleas, but still snarling.

He sighs.

They scatter Jessie's ashes on the morning of her eightieth birthday down the path from the cafe, in a circle of salt marsh described by three young snowy egrets, two mallards, and a bevy of mud hens. The mud hens suddenly swim away from the shore. They move as if their feet are bound underwater. The marsh is silver blue, speared with browning stalks.

Georgia is wearing a huge mink cap for the occasion and has her fists jammed into a ratty black Persian lamb muff. She's tired from her walk down the path and looks like an ancient Mongolian chieftain with better things to do back in the yurt. Joe holds his cap in one hand and Willie's hand in the other. Louise has the gold cardboard box of ashes at her feet. Sister Peter-Matthew is wearing a white habit and holding a King James Bible.

Willie stares across the water at the village nestled in the fleecy green hills. Even from here you can see the golden blond feathery shoots of pampas grass at the base of these hills.

Read us something beautiful and cornball, Louise asked the nun, several days before. Sister Peter-Matthew clears her throat.

When I was a child, I spoke as a child, I understood as a child; but when I became a man, I put away childish things. For now we see through a glass darkly; but then face to face: now I know in part; but then, I shall know even as I am known. And now abideth faith, hope, charity; but the greatest of these is charity.

Joe thinks of Eva. He looks out at the water in a trance, and sees a dozen headless ruddy ducks forage for food on the bay, and he sees an egret skimming along the water towards them, barely skirting the water. He watches it lift to barrel-race over the ducks.

Louise takes a folded, yellowing page from her back pocket and reads them a poem, which ends:

I forget my own trees
at evening moving in the day's
last heat like the children
of the wind, I forget the hunger
for food, for belief, for love,
I forget the fear of death,
The fear of living forever,
I forget my brother, my name,
my own life. I have risen.
Somewhere I am a god.
Somewhere I am a holy
object. Somewhere I am.

She folds it up again carefully and slides it into the pocket of her jeans, then picks the gold box off the ground. They watch her open it and untie the wire twist on the cellophane bag. Then, with a certain awe, she reaches for a handful of the ashes and shards of bone, and tosses it into the water. The egrets leap into the air and fly off.

She holds the box out for Willie as if offering him some popcorn. He clears his throat and reaches in for a handful. He holds the ashes in his cupped hand for a moment, studying them. Then his face darkens and he flings them outward towards the water, as if they are burning his palm.

Back at Jessie's Cafe, Willie goes to hide in the bathroom for a while. When he returns, Joe is getting ready to leave for work. "Come and see me after work tonight at Benno's."

"Oh, I can't."

"How come?"

"'Cause I'm meeting my new Special Friend at Smitty's."

"Gonna do a heart?"

"Maybe."

"Oh, Willie," Joe says, staring at the ground, "I know it's a tough day, her birthday and all, but I just *worry*."

"Joe," says Willie, kindly. "You ought to leave the Harvard Drug Series lectures to the Princess." Louise, who is making lamb stew at the grill, looks up at the mention of her name.

"I'm just afraid you're going to end up in the toilet. Start shooting up or something."

"I'd never shoot up, man. I don't like needles. I mean, syringes are like the last frontier."

"Just try to pace it. I just don't want you to end up in some ward for the seriously brain-fried."

"I won't end up in some ward. First of all, I don't actually do it very often. And secondly, there's always Bolinas."

A few minutes later Joe walks out the door to his car. He has to be at work in half an hour. A sea breeze fans him as he walks across the parking lot to his truck, and he hears a tinny clattering beside him. He looks down to find an empty Mountain Dew can rolling along, parallel and just slightly behind him. A cylindrical pinwheel of red and green and silver, it keeps on rolling along for the longest time, following him like the Red Balloon.

Louise watches from the window with her hands cupped around a clear glass mug of hot tea.

She sees him look over his shoulder at the can as he walks to his Ranchero. He looks back at her and smiles sheepishly. She waves. She remains at the window after he drives away, staring out at the blacktop and then at the bay. It is deep pale blue, the pure color of a perfectly clear sky.